The THIRD KIND OF MAGIC

ELIZABETH FOREST

The Third Kind of Magic

Arbori Books

https://www.arboribooks.com

Print ISBN: 978-0-9996894-0-0
E-ISBN: 978-0-0006894-1-7
LCCN 2017918287

Cover illustration by Kelley McMorris

CONTENTS

1

THE BONFIRE

THERE WERE three kinds of magic in the village.

Suli knew the first kind, of course; every girl did. There was no harm, folk said, in teaching girls to See for protection. And everyone agreed that the second kind of magic, Healing, was useful. But those weren't enough for Suli. She wanted to learn the third kind, the dangerous magic taught only to wise women.

It was New Year's Eve, and all over Teveral the villages celebrated the turning of the year with a bonfire. Suli walked to the village square with her grandmother and her brother Eb, to join their neighbors in the cobblestoned square around the bonfire. The villagers would sing songs, tell jokes, and jump over the bonfire to make a wish. Suli was excited to be wearing a new blue dress, and about the wish she would make. She'd asked to apprentice as a wise woman when she turned twelve. The village Elders, and Hedith, the wise woman, were considering her request.

The fire burned furiously, the smoke drifting into the crowd as the wind changed. A group of girls waited their turn, whispering and laughing. They cast sidelong glances at Suli, but she ignored them. The men had already jumped. Now her brother joined the line of boys. Eb ran and jumped over the fire, yelling happily with his friends. He caught his sister's eye and grinned.

It was the elder women's turn. Suli waited to see if Grandmother would join them. Every year she said this would be the last time, and every year she still leapt over the fire like a woman half her age. Some said the flames erased the old year's bad luck as well as granting wishes, but Grandmother said that was just a story, and that everyone jumped because it was fun.

Hedith, the wise woman, strode forward to take her place at the head of the line, while behind her back, a man made the sign against witchcraft. Hedith ran at the fire, shouting words of good luck. Then came the elder women, her grandmother among them, hooting and laughing and making bawdy jokes. Then the mothers. Last came the girls.

It was time. Suli straightened her shoulders and joined the girls in line. One girl glanced at her and looked away.

"Have you heard about the Investigator?" another asked in a loud whisper. "My cousin said he's looking for witches in Riverford, and that's just a day's ride from here."

"If the Prime Minister had his way, they'd clean up all the villages, and a good thing, too," Janet said primly. She was the leader of the girls and they all nodded. Suli agreed, too, but said nothing.

One of them noticed her and stepped away. "Watch out, the witch-spawn is here."

Suli stared in front of her, stony-faced.

Janet said, "You don't belong here, witch-spawn. You aren't one of us. You're cursing our bonfire. Go away."

Suli took a deep breath. No matter what she or Eb did, the children always called them witch-spawn. It didn't matter to her —she was strong. But Eb was easier to hurt; he liked everyone and couldn't understand why they didn't like him. The children wouldn't let them forget their mother had left them on Grandmother's doorstep when she was five and Eb only four. The mother everyone said was a witch.

If the wise women granted her request, these girls would need her help some day. Once Suli was a wise woman, everyone would fear and respect her. No one would dare call Eb 'witch-spawn' ever again. Suli smiled nastily at Janet, who looked away.

Eb came to stand beside her, his face smeared with soot. He nodded at the girls and said, "Are you ready to jump?"

Janet called out, "Come to protect your sister from us? That won't help when the witch Investigator comes here, Eb Wing. Everyone here knows what your mother was. Everyone says Suli has the signs, too."

Eb stepped toward Janet, his fists clenched tightly by his side. "My sister is no witch. You're just jealous because she's better at Seeing than anyone else."

Janet narrowed her eyes. "Speaking to me? Orphans from a no-good family should mind their place. You need to be taught a lesson." She darted to the bonfire and dragged a burning branch from it. She held it gingerly in front of her, walking slowly toward Eb. The other girls scattered.

The branch was too heavy for Janet to control. It swung awkwardly, too close to Eb's face. The flames leapt toward him. Eb swore and stepped back.

"Not so bold now, are you witch-spawn?" Janet mocked.

The blood pounded in Suli's head. Everyone seemed to be moving slowly. She ran toward Janet shouting, "Put that down *now*! Idiot! You could burn him! Drop it!" She lunged for the branch, smoke stinging her eyes.

But the branch wasn't there. White-faced and shaking, Janet had dropped it. She stared at Suli with a dazed expression, her mouth hanging open.

Two mothers rushed over and grabbed their daughters, their voices shrill with panic. Then Grandmother was there, leading her away. She looked back once. The girls stared at her with pale stunned faces while their mothers fussed and scolded.

❦

On the morning of her twelfth birthday, Suli entered the kitchen to find Eb and Grandmother waiting for her, her gifts beside her bowl. She could tell one was from Eb by the drawings of birds and animals on the wrapping paper. "Happy Birthday," Grandmother and Eb said together. She smiled and sat down to unwrap Eb's gift, careful not to tear the paper. Inside were two corncob dolls with painted faces, one wrapped in red cloth, the other in blue.

Suli walked over to kiss Eb. "They're beautiful. Thank you."

He smiled. "What will you call them?"

"This one," she pointed to the doll in blue, "is Princess Fig. The other is Princess Scarlet Runner Bean."

"Both princesses, eh? I wonder how that will work out. You'd better tell me their story," he said.

"No," said Grandmother. "Suli is twelve today, ready for her apprenticeship. She's too old to play with dolls. Sit down, Suli, I have something to say to you."

Stomach churning, Suli returned to her chair. Grandmother had said that what happened at the bonfire meant she must be apprenticed as soon as possible. She waited, holding her breath.

"You've been accepted for training to become a wise woman."

Yes! Her wish had been granted. She glanced at Eb. He scowled at his bowl.

Grandmother said, "Don't be too pleased. There are conditions. You must study with the right teacher. And Hedith has doubts; she worries your motives are dangerous, that you want folk afraid of you. You're going to have to prove that you understand a wise woman's magic is to help, not harm. But they had no choice. Everyone heard you use the Voice."

That was confusing. Could Hedith change her mind? Suli *did* want to be feared, but only by witches, or mean people like Janet. When she had power, she'd use it to protect innocent people who were attacked for no reason. Like Eb.

"I've found a teacher for you," Grandmother continued, pouring porridge into her bowl. "You'll study with my niece, Tala Wing, at her home in Weatherstone."

"Weatherstone? Why can't I study with Hedith?"

"That's at least a day's journey," Eb said, "why so far? There are other wise women nearby."

"Because the decision is up to me, and that's what I've decided. Suli needs what Tala can teach her."

Eb shook his head. "Bad enough she'll learn things that look like witchcraft, but you're sending her away where she doesn't know anyone."

Grandmother returned the pot to the stove and sat down. "There's no better teacher for Suli than Tala. And this is women's business and none of your concern. If you want to worry about something, worry about your own apprenticeship."

Eb made a face. Suli caught his eye and shook her head. She wanted to go, but she felt sick to her stomach.

Grandmother said to her, "I know you wanted this, but understand you no longer have a choice. You either accept the training or you'll be exiled from the village. *Do* you understand?"

Suli's mouth was dry. "Not really, Grandmother."

Grandmother leaned back and sighed. "Everyone heard you use the Voice at the bonfire. There's no doubt you can use the third kind of magic. Without training, such magic is dangerous."

"So this is because of me!" Eb said. "Because of a little teasing you're sending her away and forcing her to study magic? I won't let you!"

Grandmother shook her head. "No, Eb, it's not because of you, and it's not about teasing. The Elders are right. If Suli doesn't learn to control her power, we'll be waiting for the next thing to happen. Better she learns to control it now, while she's young and hasn't done anything irrevocable."

Eb looked confused, and Suli guessed he didn't know what "irrevocable" meant. "You can't send her away," he said miserably.

Grandmother rose and wrapped her arms around Eb from behind. She kissed the top of his head. "Silly boy. You won't be alone: I'm here. Suli would be apprenticed this year anyway—so why the fuss? You'll be off to your apprenticeship next year yourself. Calm down and try to help your sister. You don't want her hung as a witch, do you?"

Eb made a choking sound. "Why would she be?"

"Because if she doesn't learn to control the third kind of magic, that's exactly what she'll be."

2

THE JOURNEY

SULI STOOD on the doorstep with Eb, her possessions in the sack over her shoulder. Her grandmother kissed her on both cheeks, and tears rose in Suli's eyes. She'd never been away from Grandmother before. What if something happened and she never saw her again?

"Go with the Sisters' blessing and mine," Grandmother said, stepping back. "Suli, practice your Seeing exercises. Eb, stay with your sister. Thanks to the Outsiders, even a girl traveling alone isn't welcome these days. Be careful on the road coming back."

They set out in the cold grey light. Thick scarves of white mist floated over the fields. Suli and Eb walked quickly to get warm. By midday they were halfway across the still and dusty plains. At noon, they sat down to rest and eat beneath one of the elms that lined the road. Suli drank cool water from the jug she carried, then handed it to her brother; he handed her half of the bread and onion. After they'd eaten, they set off down the blazing white road again, the dust swirling and settling on their bare feet and legs.

They'd walked an hour in the heat of the afternoon, and Eb's fair hair was dark with sweat, when he broke the silence. "I'll miss having you around," he said gruffly, not looking at Suli. "If this cousin doesn't treat you right, come home."

Suli glanced at his profile and smiled. Strangers couldn't tell the fair boy and dark girl were brother and sister, but they read each other's thoughts easily. "Don't you trust Grandmother? She wouldn't send me to live with Tala if she wasn't..." She broke off, unable to finish the thought. What would someone who knew advanced magic be like? Like her grandmother, stern but basically kind? Arrogant and haughty? She felt a prickle of fear. She'd never seen this village, nor met the stranger who would order her life for years to come. Would she ever see Eb and Grandmother again? Her stomach knotted.

"I'll miss you, too, but don't worry. Once I know advanced magic, I'll be able to protect you, and Grandmother, and everyone." *And I'll finally learn real magic.*

Eb looked at her doubtfully. But he always worried about her. He was afraid she'd disappear one day, like their mother. She thought he was the one who needed protection the most. He trusted too easily, and was too openhearted. He was traveling with her to protect her from the villagers' fear of strange women, even girls, traveling alone, but it was up to her to protect them both from anyone who meant them harm. That's what her Seeing was for.

The flat horizon, seen across hedged fields, gradually became a range of mountains in the distance. Suli thought they should've seen Weatherstone by now, but by late afternoon there was still no sign of a tall blue mountain with a village nestled at its foot. A cool breeze came. She closed her eyes and breathed deeply, lifting her arms at the sheer pleasure of it. *If only I had wings,* she thought, *I could fly to Tala's house, instead of plodding along like this.* As if in answer to her thoughts, two geese lifted into the air, flying beside the road ahead. They flew a short distance and sank down behind the hedges that bordered the fields.

They walked on, thirsty and hot. There was only a little water left in the jug, and they didn't know how far there was to go.

Rolling green hills, dotted with trees, surrounded them. In the valleys between the hills, farms lay snug and orderly, alternating squares of green and yellow. They decided to stop and ask for water and directions. A lane ran from the road to three houses surrounded by neat fields. Suli whistled to the songbirds in the trees as they passed. They took a path leading to a trellised gate and knocked on the door of the closest house.

A woman answered, drying her hands on a cloth. Her face was deeply tanned and she wore a red kerchief over her dark hair. She smiled at first, then frowned at something behind them. She shouted, as though speaking to someone far away, "What do you want here?"

Eb stared in surprise. "Please, Mistress, we just want to know how far it is to Weatherstone. And we're thirsty; may we have some water from your well?"

"We don't welcome strangers here!" the woman called loudly, then under her breath she hissed, "You'd best not stay here. There's a witch Investigator, one of the Outsiders, in the next valley. Everyone's afraid to be seen talking to strangers."

"But why?" Eb asked. "Most folk aren't witches. How will you sell your goods at market if you don't speak to strangers?"

"Be on your way!" she yelled angrily, then whispered, "You should arrive in Weatherstone by sunset if you don't dawdle. Drink your fill at the well there, but do it quickly. I have nosy neighbors."

Suli looked over her shoulder. A woman in the garden of the house across the lane was watching them, a scowl on her face.

"If you don't go," the first woman called loudly for her neighbor to hear, "I'll set the dogs on you!"

"Thank you, Mistress," Suli whispered back. "We'll drink and be on our way." They drank their fill quickly, then Eb filled the jug while Suli kept her eye on the scowling neighbor.

"Why are folk so suspicious?" Eb asked once they'd returned to the road.

"I don't know. The Investigator, I suppose."

They were used to walking now, and kept a good pace. Two more geese, or the same ones, flew just ahead of them, but before they could catch up, the birds floated down into the trees by the road and were lost to view.

Late in the afternoon, when the sun was a finger's width above the horizon, they saw a tall, forested mountain with a village at its foot. From a distance, the stone houses looked gloomy and strange. Grandmother's house was painted yellow and roofed with golden thatch, but the houses of Weatherstone were built of dark blue stone quarried from the peak above. In the fading light, the dark houses had a gloomy look.

They passed through the gate in the town wall. Once inside they stopped, uncertain where to go. Villagers passed, ignoring them, intent on their evening meal. Some stared at them with suspicion. They had never seen so many strangers before. Suli concentrated on using her Seeing.

A middle-aged woman passed them in the lane, avid eyes sunk in a puffy face. She stared at the children with a hungry expression. Suli examined her and recoiled. She nodded brusquely to the woman and grabbed her brother's hand, pulling him along. "C'mon, Eb." He followed, looking back at the woman.

A woman with a calm, comfortable face stood behind her gate, looking down the lane. She wore a plain homespun dress with a clean, white apron over it and she smiled when she saw the children. Suli studied her face, and then focused her gaze on a spot behind the woman. Suli nodded and went over to her. "Excuse me, Mistress. My brother and I are strangers here. We're looking for Tala Wing's house. Do you know where she lives?"

The woman smiled and gave directions, pointing to the lane that would end at the foot of Blue Mountain. Suli thanked her, and she and Eb walked up the lane.

"Are you certain she wasn't misleading you?" Eb asked.

"Yes. She has a kind heart," Suli said.

Eb shifted his sack. "Good. I don't want to meet a witch at nightfall in a strange village. There must be a lot of witches here, or folk wouldn't be so scared."

Suli privately thought people seemed more afraid of being accused of witchcraft than of being a victim of it. She'd seen no sign of it on the journey. The first woman they'd passed in Weatherstone had a cold and greedy heart, and would have stolen from them if she could, but that didn't make her a witch.

The village street climbed upward, passing fallow fields, to end near the foot of the mountain. Night had fallen and the stars were out when the street ended at a wooden gate. Beyond it, a path climbed upwards until it was out of sight.

Eb groaned when he saw the steep path. "My poor feet! This better be the right place. Why is it so far from the other houses?" They closed the gate behind them. Suli didn't reply. She was out of breath, forcing her legs up the steep path, her sack heavy. The path entered a thick copse of trees and the moon disappeared. Suli stopped to catch her breath as Eb walked on ahead. The trees rustled, although there was no wind. She thought she heard a voice whisper, "Suli, Suli, over here. This way. Come this way, dearie."

"Is someone there?" Suli called softly. "Eb, wait." She stared into the darkness but could see nothing.

"What's wrong?" Eb asked, returning to her side.

"I thought I heard something. Let's keep going." They emerged from the trees, and water glimmered to their left. Suli could smell the spicy scent of bulrushes and mud.

At the top of the path they saw the dark outline of a house. No light greeted them, and the only sound was the singing of crickets, loud and shrill in the grass. The dark windows seemed to stare.

Suli knocked on the door. "Cousin Tala!" There was no answer.

"What if she's not home?" Eb said from the bottom step.

"Maybe she's feeding her animals."

"It's awfully late. I don't like this," Eb said.

Without warning, a loud flapping sound passed over their heads, a gust of wind ruffling their hair. Looking up, Suli saw the silhouettes of two large birds against the stars. One of the birds turned its head to look at her as it flew over the house.

Suli pounded on the door. "Mistress Wing! Your cousins Suli and Eb are here! Are you home?" There were sounds of movement inside.

The door opened without warning and a woman stood on the threshold, an oil lamp in her hand. She was a thin, dark-haired woman, with cheekbones like the outstretched wings of a bird, the bones of her wrists sharp with nothing extra anywhere about her. Only the streaks of white hair at her temples betrayed her age.

"Welcome, Cousins! Let me look at you," Tala said, holding the lamp high. She examined them for a moment. "Suli, you look like your father. Come inside. I've been expecting you all day."

They stepped across the threshold, and Tala led them through a dark parlor into the kitchen. A stone hearth covered the far end of the room. At the other end, an iron stove radiated warmth, the banked embers glowing red through the latticework pattern on the doors. The pattern resembled a face, and Suli felt it watching her. She looked over her shoulder as she passed, certain she'd seen it move.

"Do you want supper?" Tala asked.

"Yes, please, Cousin," said Eb.

"Put your things down. I'll show you where to wash.

Tala lit a lantern and led them outside to the pump in the yard.

"Wash while I'll warm up your food," she said, and leaving lantern on a bench, she went back inside the house.

When she was gone, Eb said, "Did you see those birds?"

Suli shrugged as though she didn't care, but she thought they were the same geese she'd seen on the journey. She couldn't tell Eb that, and anyway, maybe it didn't mean anything. She was more worried about Tala. When she'd used her Seeing, Tala appeared to be two people.

She couldn't tell Eb *that*. He'd be wary and suspicious, and might say something that would put them in danger. It was up to her to understand what it meant.

They walked slowly back to the house, Eb carrying the lantern. A huddle of goats stared at them with golden eyes, their chins resting on the half-door of their shed.

Tala stood in front of the kitchen steps, bent over two geese. They're just ordinary geese after all, Suli thought with relief.

"They've arrived safely, thank you," Tala said. She straightened and came toward the children, smiling. "They wanted to see the new apprentice."

Is she joking? "Your geese wanted to see me?" Suli asked.

"They're curious," Tala said. The geese peered around Tala's skirt.

"This is Suli," Tala said to the geese, "and her brother, Eb. They're Dafyd's children."

Not knowing what else to do, Suli said, "Hello."

Eb looked from his sister to the geese, his brow furrowed.

"That's enough for tonight," Tala said to the geese, "let the travelers eat and sleep. You should roost, too." The geese dipped their heads and disappeared into the darkness.

"Come inside, your food will be warm now," Tala said.

They followed her up the steps. They both ate quickly, tired and ready for sleep. Tala led them to the bedroom that would become Suli's and handed her the candlestick. "I'm just down the hall if you need anything. Goodnight, Cousins. We rise soon after cockcrow here."

Alone in the bedroom, Suli and Eb sat on the bed's bright quilt.

"Tala talks to geese as though they were people," Eb whispered. "Do you think she's a witch?"

"Hush. That's ridiculous," Suli said. "Lots of people talk to their animals. It doesn't mean anything. She probably doesn't see people very often, and it's become a habit." But she wasn't thinking about the geese. She realized she'd forgotten to mention the voice in the trees to Tala. Would her new teacher believe her? She was sure she'd heard it.

Eb shook his head. "This doesn't feel right."

"You can't say anything. If Tala thinks we suspect her of witchcraft, she'll be angry. That's not how I want to begin my apprenticeship." And if she *was* a witch, all the more reason not to say so. Besides, Suli wanted to know more about those geese.

Eb folded his arms. "I'll wait until morning to decide," he said, with the stubborn expression she knew so well. "I'm not sure you should stay here."

"No," she said, careful to keep her voice level, "You're making too much of this because you're tired. They're just geese, Eb. I used my Seeing; Tala doesn't mean us any harm. In the morning, you'll see everything's fine, and that's what you'll tell Grandmother."

"Are you sure?"

"Yes." She smiled with a confidence she didn't feel. She crawled beneath the quilt and lay down. She hadn't told him the geese seemed to have two identities, too. Long after Eb fell asleep, she lay awake wondering how Tala could be two people. And who had whispered to her from the trees?

3

THE GEESE

THE NEXT DAY dawned bright and clear and after eating a bowl of curds, Eb set off for home. He hugged his sister and told her to send word if she needed him. "You never know," Eb said softly, "Tala may not feed you enough." He laughed, but his eyes were serious.

Suli whispered, "Grandmother knows what she's doing!" She knew he wasn't worried about food; he was worried that Tala might be a witch. "Once I learn everything I can, I'll be safe, don't worry." She said loudly, "Safe journey home!"

They kissed each other on both cheeks. Suli stood at the gate, her long brown hair lifting in the wind, watching her brother until he was out of sight. Her eyes stung with tears; she'd never been away from Grandmother and Eb before. She was alone with a stranger who could be a witch, but she wanted to learn magic, and witch or no, she would.

Tala came briskly through the door, a basket over her arm. "Your brother is off, then? Tender partings? Then let's get to work. Summer is a busy time, and I'm glad of your help."

Suli wondered if she would be set to work weeding the garden that surrounded the house. It certainly needed it. Instead of orderly rows, all sorts of things grew together, higgledy-piggledy, with no clear path between them.

"What will I learn first, Cousin?" Suli asked.

"Come and meet the geese."

Suli followed Tala down the path to the circle of birch trees beside the pond. The air was cool and damp in the shade. "Here are their roosts. They like a warm place to stay in winter, but in summer they prefer to sleep under the trees. I'll introduce you. You must learn their names, so you can address them properly."

Her cousin sat down in an old wooden chair set in the shade, and called their names. Suli thought it sounded like a poem—or a song.

"Lamisa, Orion, Tessa, Wilo, Flax, Mara, Kriton—come meet the new apprentice."

Suli heard a flapping sound, and shadows passed over her face as the geese landed. Some were russet brown; some had dark backs and white faces. A few were pure white except for brown bars upon their heads. Two were white with pale pink feet and grey tips on their wings. They walked slowly and with dignity to form a line.

"How are you all this fine morning? Have you eaten?" Tala asked.

The first goose, white with a brown bar on her head honked loudly and flapped its wings.

"That's Lamisa," Tala said. "She's the leader; she enforces the rules. You must always show her the proper respect. Please come forward and introduce yourself."

This is ridiculous, Suli thought. But she curtsied and said, "Pleased to meet you, Lamisa, I'm Suli."

"Very good," said Tala, nodding. Lamisa dipped her neck in a bow, and gave a short honk. The next goose stepped forward. He was brown, with white feathers on his head and wings. "This is Orion. He's the head male in our group."

Suli curtsied. "Hello, Orion." *I'm talking to geese and they're talking to me.* She was pleased in spite of the strangeness.

Orion bowed and eyed her with curiosity.

She was introduced to each in turn, until the last goose bowed to her. They all had personalities, just like people. Orion was a cheerful sort, with a mischievous gleam in his eye. Wilo had honked softly, a wise old grandmother.

"Well, you've met the geese now," said Tala, "what do you think of them?"

"Do they really understand everything you say?"

"Of course. They're Sigur's geese, from Blue Mountain."

"I've never heard of them."

Tala raised an eyebrow. "Your Grandmother didn't tell you? Hmph. Well, explanations can wait until we know more about each other."

Suli wanted to ask about the two geese she'd seen flying over the house the night before, but Tala clearly expected her to understand more than she did. She didn't like feeling ignorant, so she kept quiet. "But *how* do they understand what we say?"

"All in good time, apprentice. Some things you must learn for yourself."

Suli bit back her anger. A teacher who wouldn't answer questions was of no use to her. "I just want to understand," she said. She noticed the geese were watching her. Their gaze made her feel uncomfortable.

"You will," her cousin said in a softer voice. "That's why you're here. The geese will teach you. Now come help in the garden." Tala started back up the path.

Suli followed her to the garden in front of the house. Tala explained that the plants she'd thought were weeds were actually the vegetables, herbs, and flowers of her cousin's garden.

"Why are they all mixed together?" They stood in front of a mound of dirt where corn, beans, squash, and flowers were growing together.

"Oh, your village grows them in rows, do they? That won't last," said Tala.

"Why not?" Suli asked.

"Because the plants need each other and like to grow together," Tala said.

"But how can you weed or pick them without rows? How can you see what needs doing?"

"You pay attention. I'll teach you. That's why you're here. I'll start you off, and then I must help the people waiting for me," Tala said.

Suli followed her gaze to where a mother and baby waited by the kitchen door.

Tala kneeled beside her and began to explain how the plants were of benefit to each other: some helped others grow, others kept the insects and snails away. Suli was to sit and just observe carefully, not pulling any plants yet, even if she thought she knew which were weeds. Then Tala left her to attend her patients.

Suli observed the plants, but it was hard to concentrate and she wasn't sure she was doing it correctly. She grew irritated and hot. Finally, when the sun was overhead, Tala called her inside for the noon meal. On the table was a pitcher of lemon tea, icy cold from being left in the stream, and a bowl of cool nettle soup with turnips that tasted of green things and the earth. Tala made a salad of beets and dandelion greens. The food was the best thing at Tala's house so far.

"Now we'll lie down for a while, until it's cooler," said Tala, "then you can return to the garden." Suli's bedroom was cool and dark behind the closed shutters. She drifted off to sleep, dreaming of plants that grew until they covered the house.

She woke to the bleating of goats and the sound of bells clanking. She flung herself out of bed and splashed her face in the basin before going outside. Late afternoon sunlight flowed in bars of gold across the yard.

A herd of fifteen goats had gathered by the water trough in

their enclosure. They stood in line, waiting to take a drink, calling with insistent voices. Suli stared at them in disbelief. The goats at home would never stand in line. How did Tala make them?

Tala was laying out piles of grain on the ground for each one to eat. "Suli," she called, "please watch what I do. I would like this to become your task once you've learned it."

Suli nodded. When the goats finished drinking from the trough, they lined up, each at its own pile, but did not bend their bearded faces to eat. They didn't push or run, but waited patiently for everyone to finish drinking.

"Why don't they all rush at the grain?" Suli asked. "At home the goats eat everything, and go where they are not wanted!"

"It's difficult to train goats, but not impossible," Tala said, with a brief smile. "And these goats have a peculiar history; they're special."

Tala's smile made her uneasy. Was she hinting at witchcraft? Or was there some other magic that caused geese to understand humans and goats to acquire manners?

"Once they know you'll take care of them and that you're serious about the rules, they aren't so unruly. But," she said and her teeth flashed in a real smile, "they're still very rude. Even waiting patiently, they're insulting each other. All animals have their own natures; you have to allow for that. Goats are rebellious, but they're curious, too. They like being here because they learn new things."

Suli decided she was right to be wary of her cousin. If Tala could make goats obey her, what else could she do? And how did she know what they were saying? Suli was about to ask about that when Tala turned to the goats and bowed. They bent their heads to their portions of grain and ate greedily.

Tala showed her how to do the evening chores. Besides feeding the goats and the geese, she was to make sure the chickens were cooped up for the night. When everything was done, Suli washed at the pump in the yard. As the water splashed over her hands and feet she wondered where Eb was, and whether he'd made it home safely. She went inside and set two places on the bright woven tablecloth.

While they ate, Tala explained which chores would be hers in the morning and evening. "The rest of the time, you'll learn what an apprentice your age should know."

Suli was silent, wondering if her grandmother had been fooled. Tala spoke to animals and they understood her; to Suli that looked like witchcraft. Maybe the goats were people Tala had turned into animals. There was a story about a witch who turned a little boy into a rabbit, and he'd been torn to pieces by his own dog. If Tala used magic to force her to obey, she'd know for sure Tala was a witch. But her Seeing revealed that Tala wanted to teach her, not harm her. Talking to animals was odd, but was it witchcraft?

She bit her lip. If Tala *was* a witch, she could be accused of being one, too, just by living with her. And she still hadn't learned any magic.

"Cousin," Suli said, once her plate was empty, "you said the geese will teach me. What did you mean?"

Tala stared at the tablecloth as though making up her mind. "I need to find out what you already understand, first. Your grandmother said you can be a little—willful, I believe, was the word she used." She smiled to take the sting from her words. "Your father was the same way."

Suli frowned. It was true she didn't let people tell her what to do unless she thought they knew more than she did. But she was here to learn. Why had her grandmother mentioned it to Tala?

"Your grandmother wrote and explained that you used the Voice accidentally." Tala was watching her. "Your village is afraid you'll become a witch. But your Grandmother also says you've boasted you'd be the first to report a witch to the Outsiders if you found one. Is that true?"

She blinked. Was Tala afraid she'd report her? "Yes," she said, wondering if her new teacher mistrusted her.

"Why do you want to learn magic? You wanted to be a wise woman before you used the Voice, didn't you?"

Suli nodded, and stumbled over her words. "Once I'm a wise woman, people will have to respect me and listen to what I say. And I'll be able to protect Eb, and Grandmother—everyone— from witches. Then no one would ever call me a witch."

"Let me understand," Tala said, frowning. "You want to learn advanced magic because you're afraid you'll be accused of being a witch? But you'll learn the same magic witches use. Did you realize that?"

Suli scowled back. Why didn't Tala understand? "With magic I can *prove* which side I'm on. People will need me. They say my mother was a witch and I'll turn out just like her. They say my Seeing is a threat, just because I'm good at it." The words came out even though she tried to stop them.

Tala rose and pushed her chair under the table. "Hmph. You probably upset people by pointing out when they were lying." She smiled grimly. "That never endears us to others. But why boast about denouncing witches?"

She didn't understand the question. If you knew of a witch, you had to turn them in so they could be stopped. "I wasn't boasting. I just said what I'd do."

"I see." Tala sighed. "Well, you're here to learn. Wash the dishes. I'll see to the other chores." She paused at the kitchen door. "I knew your mother, Suli. She wasn't a witch, just very sad, too sad to take care of you and your brother when your father died." She stepped outside.

Suli stared at the empty doorway. Her mother had been sad? That didn't explain why she abandoned her children. Was that the only reason people called her a witch? Grandmother simply refused to talk about her parents when she'd brought it up.

She took a deep breath and poured water into the stone sink and washed the dishes, lost in thought.

Lying in bed that night, Suli stared at the shadows dancing on the ceiling as the candle moved in the breeze from the window. Her memories of her parents were vague, slipping away when she tried to hold onto them. She felt lonely in the strange house and wanted to talk to Eb. For the first time, she doubted her Seeing was enough to protect her. She wished she could trust Tala, but her questions about why Suli would denounce a witch worried her. Still, Tala could talk to animals. It would be worth the risk to learn to do that.

She blew out the candle and lay down. Tala said the geese would help her learn. Maybe she would learn to talk to them first.

4

THE SECOND KIND OF MAGIC

THE NEXT DAY Tala taught Suli magic, but it wasn't what she expected. It was a lot more work, for one thing. After she scattered grain for the chickens and left them to scratch in the yard, she took the goats to a sloping field above the house for them to graze. Then she climbed down the hill to the stream below with two watering cans hanging from a yoke she carried across her shoulders. The first time, the water was too heavy and she staggered up the hill, slopping half the water. Tala waited for her in the garden.

"Next time," Tala said, "don't fill them so full. I don't expect you to carry as much as I can. Make more trips until you're used to the weight."

They finished the watering, and then her cousin showed her why certain plants had been planted together and how to recognize the weeds. "It's up to the plants to help each other and keep the harmful insects and plants away, but they need our help, too. And they repay us by letting us take their seeds and flowers to eat and enjoy."

"Is this magic?" Suli asked. "It seems quite ordinary. Common sense."

Tala nodded. "It's both. You understand the nature of a plant or animal, to See what it needs. Then you know what to do, although learning what the right thing to do *is* takes time. This is Healing, the second kind of magic."

Tala demonstrated how she looked at the plants sideways, not straight on. "If you look at living things from the corner of your eye, you'll see them differently," she explained.

It took some getting used to, but once she'd practiced, Suli saw things she'd never seen before.

"Once you See what a plant or animal needs, you'll feel an itch that tells you what to do. Seeing is only the first step," Tala said.

Suli wasn't sure she understood until she saw a group of sweet peas with white spots on their leaves. She touched one and used her side-Seeing. Maybe she could fix it. She closed her eyes and concentrated. She imagined the spots burning away, leaving the plant whole. She felt something changing and opened her eyes. All trace of the mildew was gone; the plant felt happier, too. She grinned. She'd known what to do! She glanced around, but Tala was busy with her own plants. The beans had aphids. Suli reached among the leaves of the first tall plant.

At noon, Tala called her inside to eat. The day had grown hot, but the house, made of stones from the mountain, was cool and dark with the shutters closed to keep out the heat. The dim coolness, and the cold soup and salad, felt wonderful after the heat of the garden.

They lay down to rest. Although she was tired, Suli kept drifting in and out of sleep, her mind refusing to settle. She thought she heard squirrels chattering outside her shuttered window. She got up and opened a shutter to look.

Tala was bent over two squirrels. Suli rubbed her eyes and looked again. Tala applied ointment from a jar to a squirrel's leg, making chattering sounds as she worked.

This was what she wanted to learn. Suli ran outside and found them.

Tala saw her and straightened. "Yes?" she said sharply. The two squirrels watched her warily, but didn't run away.

"Cousin, may I watch? I'd like to learn." For a moment, Suli could've sworn Tala looked pleased.

"Yes," was all she said.

After explaining how she healed the squirrel, Tala sent Suli back to finish her nap. It was mid-afternoon when she woke again. She splashed her face and returned to the garden. Shafts of late afternoon sunlight slanted across it, painting the rows of beans and hops with golden light. A cool breeze flowed down the flanks of Blue Mountain while heat rose from the ground, the black dirt pleasantly warm beneath her bare feet. Insects hummed in the grass; the garden was waking up.

Tala was nowhere to be seen. Suli found the place she'd stopped weeding. She knelt beside the marigolds, basil, and tomatoes and tried to See which shoots were weeds. She felt pleased with herself. She knew how to help plants, and she thought she could heal animals too, with some experience. Healing felt natural, like something she'd always known, and she liked doing it. It was magic that made a difference.

A soft honk sounded in her ear. Startled, Suli rose to her feet and backed away. A large grey goose behind her was watching her with an intelligent expression.

"Hello," Suli said faintly, her voice trembling. "Did you want something?" To her chagrin, she didn't recognize the goose. It had distinctive white markings on each side of its head, and black bars on its grey wings. Either it was a stranger, or one of the geese had been absent when she had greeted them the day before. With a sharp intake of breath, Suli realized there was third possibility: The white markings on the goose's head resembled the white streaks in Tala's hair.

The goose nodded once and walked off, turning her head on her long neck to see if Suli would follow. The goose walked down the hill to the pond, where the geese and ducks were enjoying the last warmth of the day. When it reached the thick clusters of reeds, it pushed through and swam out into open water. Suli sat on the bank to watch.

The goose turned its dark eye on her. Suli was certain it had brought her there for a reason. *Or I'm a ninny to think an animal is asking anything of me.* But all Suli had seen at her cousin's house warned her to treat the animals with the same courtesy she would give a human. So she sat on the bank and waited to see what would happen.

She heard the sound of wings flapping, like sheets on a clothesline, and the cries of geese coming toward her. A flock of wild geese, with dark heads and bars upon their grey wings, blocked the sunlight before settling noisily on the pond. The ducks, swimming placidly moments before, protested loudly and flew away. The white and brown geese continued to swim undisturbed. The large grey goose looked at Suli as if to say, *Watch closely now.*

One wild goose swam over to the grey goose and dipped his neck, honking once. He's greeting his hostess, she thought. They swam away together, side by side, calling softly. The wild flock swam away to give them room. In a few minutes, wings flapped and the flock was airborne once more, the grey goose flying with them, on the right flank of the formation. Suli watched them until they were tiny silhouettes, black against the light of the sinking sun.

With a start, she realized she could hear the goats bleating complaints, their bells ringing. She hurried back to the house and brought the sack of grain to where Tala had fed them the day before. When she finished making the piles (a little larger than Tala's to make amends for making the goats wait), she bowed. The goats bent their heads to eat.

She rushed off to coop up the chickens in the hen house. She feared Tala would be angry with her for idling by the pond when she should've been working. After washing her hands and feet at the pump, she lit the oil lamp and set the table for the evening meal. But Tala wasn't in the house. Suli knocked on her bedroom door, but there was no answer. The door was locked.

Her stomach was in a knot. She'd never spent a night alone before. She carried the kitchen lamp with her as she searched the house. No one was there, and all the doors except her own and the linen cupboard were locked.

She returned to the kitchen, putting the lamp on the table. If Tala returned soon, she should have dinner ready. She chopped vegetables and put them into a pot. The sky grew dark in the window, and an owl called to its mate from the giant fir tree. She didn't know where her cousin was, or why she'd left her on her own without a word. She thought about the goose that led her to the pond. If that was Tala, what was she supposed to understand?

It was full dark and the food was ready. Suli was too hungry to wait any longer. She ate alone, listening to the quiet. She left the pot of food on the back of the stove with a plate over it to keep out the mice. It was time for bed, but she dreaded leaving the comforting pool of light of the kitchen lamp.

A fire in in her room would keep the shadows away and provide company, she decided. The kindling took a long time to catch, and Suli was grimed with soot by the time the fire burned steadily, and by then it was long past time for sleep. She washed and got into bed. Her hands and feet were cold. She lay awake listening to the unfamiliar sounds of the old house. A tree branch scraped the wall outside her window, and she held her breath, listening.

Tala expected her to figure things out for herself. She wouldn't have shown her how to heal animals if Suli hadn't asked her first. So if the goose with the white markings was Tala, that meant she could change shape. She remembered her Seeing when she'd first arrived, when Tala seemed to be two people. Maybe this was the reason.

Did that mean Tala was a witch? It could be a different kind of magic, one Suli could learn, too. She'd like to learn to fly. Geese traveled all over the world, across the oceans. She'd be free to go anywhere she liked. Her eyes closed. Maybe leaving her alone was a test, she thought, to see if she was brave enough to be a wise woman.

In the middle of the night, a soft sound woke her. Her heart thudded and she called softly, "Cousin Tala?" but there was no answer. She lay in bed, listening, but all she heard was the silence of the house. She was still listening when she fell asleep.

5

THE LAKE

THE NEXT MORNING, Suli entered the kitchen and found the pot of food from the night before was untouched. Beside it, a pot of porridge simmered, and tea was brewing in the teapot on the table. The kitchen door banged, and Tala came in. "Good morning," she said. "Did you sleep well?" Was there a hint of amusement in her expression?

"No, I didn't. Where were you?"

Tala gave Suli a considering look and then sat down and poured tea into her cup. "I want you to observe and learn for yourself; that's part of my teaching. When you have questions, think of that first."

Suli frowned. "But what if I never understand? How will I learn if I can't ask you a question?"

The corner of Tala's mouth twitched. "I've considered that. Let's see what you make of today's lesson, by observing for yourself. Then we'll talk."

Tala spooned porridge into Suli's bowl, then her own, and sat down. They ate in silence, Suli glancing at Tala from time to time. She couldn't decide if she was angry with her or not.

When she'd eaten and washed the dishes, Suli asked, "What will you teach me today?"

Tala rose from the table, where she'd been shelling beans, and said, "Come with me."

They walked to the edge of Tala's land, where two geese were waiting.

"Good morning, Lamisa. Good morning, Orion. Thank you for helping my student today," Tala said.

Suli greeted them, wondering how they would help her.

"Lamisa and Orion will take you for a walk," Tala said. "Pay attention to what they show you."

Suli opened her mouth to protest, but stopped when she saw Tala's expression. She had to observe for herself. Fine, she'd do it. But later she would have a long list of questions. The first one was: Are you a witch? "Yes, Cousin."

Tala nodded to the geese. They glanced at Suli, then set off on the path. It rose from the foot of the mountain to wind upwards until it was lost to sight.

Suli's irritation grew. She'd come to Tala's house to learn magic, but Tala refused to explain things. How was she supposed to know, without words, what the geese were showing her? And what could geese teach her, besides how to eat grass or insects? If they could teach her to fly, that would be something—but since she had no wings, that wasn't likely. She still didn't understand what the grey goose had wanted from her the day before. She'd flown away with the wild geese. So? If that was Tala, her teaching wasn't working.

If her cousin could become a goose, did that mean anyone could? Or was her cousin a witch, and worse, was she teaching Suli to be a witch? She muttered under her breath. Last night, she'd been afraid. Today, she was angry. She imagined telling Tala she knew she was a witch. She could say, *Unless you explain things, I'll report you.* That would stop her from telling her to observe for herself.

The geese climbed slowly, waddling from side to side, up the steep, rocky path. Every now and then they flew ahead to land further up the path where they waited for her. Suli thought they were laughing at her as she stumbled to catch up. She scowled at them, but they simply turned and continued up the trail.

As she climbed, Suli inhaled the smell of pine needles mingled with the scent of dense undergrowth and damp earth. She called to the geese and pointed to a stream chuckling over stones, gesturing she wanted to rest there, but the geese shook their heads and climbed on.

They'd been walking for over an hour and Suli's calves ached when they came to a large granite boulder. A path ran down into a thick forest of tall pines that filtered the light to a green and moving dimness. As they walked deeper into the trees, Suli heard a roaring sound growing closer. Finally, they emerged from under the trees. Before them lay a sheet of green water under a vibrant blue sky.

At the other end of the lake a waterfall sent ropes of heavy white water crashing into the lake, veiling the water below in mist. At the water's edge, she saw that the water shifted from deep blue to green and turquoise where the shallows revealed the rock beneath. Ducks and geese floated peacefully, basking in the sun.

Suli walked across the short springy grass to the shallows and stepped in, wading behind a shelf of gravel and sand. Lamisa and Orion slipped through reeds into the lake, swimming to join others of their kind. She watched them for a moment, but there was nothing to see. They were simply geese floating on a lake.

She waded happily, squelching her toes in the sandy mud, but she kept her eyes on the geese, hoping there was a reason for the long climb. Suddenly, one of them dived beneath the surface. She watched the bubbles where it went down, but no goose returned to the surface. Instead, a boy's head bobbed up, dark-haired, and his shoulders rose above the water. Suli held her breath. The boy spluttered, shivering at the cold water. He grinned at Suli, then arced over the water, throwing himself at Lamisa with a whoop. He splashed the goose with scoops of water until she turned haughtily and swam away. The boy swam toward Suli, now up to her knees in the shallows. He stood, his wet shirt clinging to him, and called, "Hi, Suli." He looked smug.

Suli narrowed her eyes. "Who're you?"

"Don't you know? I thought you were good at Seeing." He laughed and fell backwards into the water with a splash. "I suppose you don't want to look like a fool."

"Come here and talk to me," Suli said, annoyed. Only after he'd reminded her had she used her Seeing. The boy was Orion.

Orion grinned. "I was going to." He swam to the bank, climbed out, and threw himself on the grass. "What do you want to talk about?" he asked. His breeches and white shirt steamed in the hot sun.

"Are you really a goose?" Suli demanded.

"What do you mean by 'really'?"

Suli's voice was sharp. "I mean did you just change from a goose into a boy?"

"Yes, that's what we do. Didn't Tala explain?" he asked.

Suli snorted. "Tala never explains anything. How can geese be people?"

Orion looked surprised. "We're Sigur's geese from Blue Mountain."

She lifted her hands as if to say, *So?*

He sighed. "A long time ago, people and animals could become each other. Most people have forgotten how, but some of us remember. Sigur is our great-great grandmother. She remembered how to change, and those of us with the talent follow her teaching."

"Oh." Suli was silent, wondering why Tala didn't just explain this. "Are there other animals, or—people who do this?" she asked.

"Some. And sometimes people become animals whether they like it or not. Haven't you ever seen that?" he asked, looking at her as if he'd just realized she wasn't very bright.

Suli had no idea what he was talking about, but she wouldn't admit it. "So—you're Orion?" she asked.

"That's me!" White teeth flashed in his dark face.

"Do you have to come here, to the lake I mean, to change shape?"

His expression became wary. "I don't think I should say any more. It's safer to change here." Then, as if to escape more questions, he dove from the grassy bank into the water.

She thought she could guess what he meant. If he was telling the truth and this was old magic, the kind animals had, it would still look like witchcraft to many. If anyone saw, they could inform on you. She'd heard stories of shape-shifting from the old days, but she'd always thought they were just stories.

Suli sat by the lake, waiting to see if any more of the geese would change, while Orion splashed and clucked and hooted at the ducks and geese. She should ask more questions, but it was hard to think. What should you ask a goose who could become a person? Or was he a person who could become a goose? Which did he prefer? Was it better to be able to fly or to talk to people? She'd like to fly, but eating grass or bugs didn't sound appealing.

In the shadow of a tall pine Suli found a spot of soft grass between its roots. She unwrapped her lunch and ate it. Orion and Lamisa ignored her, swimming and diving on the lake. She was tired after the long climb, and the heat made her sleepy. She leaned back against the tree and fell asleep.

When she awoke, the shadow of the mountain's peak blocked the sun and she was cold. Long shadows stretched across the lake, and the mist from the waterfall was creeping towards her. She stood, brushing pine needles from her dress, and searched the water for Lamisa and Orion. There was no sign of them. They must have left without her.

Suli retraced her steps, looking for the path that would take her back to Tala's house. She was on the path beneath a heavy canopy of pines, surrounded by trees, when a voice spoke to her from the weave of branches surrounding the path.

"Well, well, Dafyd's child, all alone on the mountain, with no one to protect her. Have you come to visit me, young Miss? Or do you plan to just *fly* away?"

Just beneath the sweetness of the voice Suli heard anger. She turned slowly, searching the tangle of branches to see who'd spoken. But no one was visible. "Who's there?" she called, uncertain. "Where are you?"

"Over here. Follow my voice. Imagine! Young Suli, out all by herself, and it's growing dark! You shouldn't be here alone; it's not safe! Come to my house, and I'll get you home." The voice was soft and melodic, but something warned her not to trust it. It came from a dense thicket of hemlocks to the left of the path; to follow the voice, she'd have to plunge into the forest where it was darkest, leaving the path.

"I'm—I'm fine," Suli called. "I can get home, thank you. I must hurry." She began to walk faster, keeping her eyes on the path, hoping it was the right one. She still hadn't seen any landmarks she recognized, but it went uphill. She was almost running now. Ahead the canopy was a lighter green, promising the end of the trees. The voice came closer; it seemed to be pursuing her.

"Wait, Suli, and have supper with me! Stop now. You must be so tired! Stop awhile. I have sweets and milk for you, honey and berries. You can bring some to Tala. Please stop. I'm old, you see, and can't hobble very far. I spend all day baking and cooking—please come visit me. Please. Stop."

The voice pleaded, but malice bubbled beneath. Suli began to run. What if this wasn't the right path? She was afraid the owner of the voice would appear on the path and grab her.

Suli ran as fast as she could, her breath coming in gasps, but no one appeared. Soon she was under a thin canopy of birch and willow, and the late afternoon sun shone through, dappling the dusty path. She ran out into the warm sunlight that still covered the mountainside and recognized the granite boulder where the path began, as though marking a boundary. She bent over a moment to catch her breath. No one was behind her. The voice was silent. Afraid its owner was nearby, she hurried down the mountain as fast as she could.

She made it onto Tala's land just as the sun went down. At the pump, she washed her face and hands quickly. She wanted to run to tell Tala about the voice, but forced herself to stop and think. Geese could become people. That might mean that Tala wasn't a witch, just someone who could change shape. But she had no doubt that the voice she'd heard in the forest, its horrible sweetness barely masking the anger beneath, was the voice of a witch.

6

THE WITCH

Tala sat at the kitchen table. "Well, Cousin, I waited supper on your return." She stood and looked out the window. "Where did you leave Lamisa and Orion?"

Suli dropped into a chair. "They left me, Cousin. I fell asleep after lunch, and when I woke up they were gone. They're probably down at the pond."

Tala shook her head. "No. No one's seen them."

Suli felt her stomach drop as she considered the worst possibility. "Then something may have happened to them on the mountain."

Tala frowned. "Why do you say that?"

"On my way back, I think—no, I'm sure I met a witch."

"What?" Tala's voice was sharp. "Explain."

"There was a voice in the forest. A woman's voice said I shouldn't be alone and asked me to visit her. She knew my name! I was afraid, so I ran down the path." When she'd entered the kitchen, Suli had felt safe, but watching Tala's face go pale, the fear returned, its icy claws digging into her chest.

"By the Sisters! So she's back. Spying on the lake again, I bet.

She must've recognized Lamisa and Orion and taken them. But if this is Orion's idea of a joke, I'll have his feathers for my bed!" The door slammed and Tala was already gone before Suli could run after her.

When Suli arrived at the pond out of breath, Tala had already spoken with the others. "They aren't here," Tala said. "Either they've flown away, on some prank of their own...but Lamisa wouldn't do that." Tala took a deep breath, "If the witch *does* have them, it could all be happening again."

Suli's heart began to pound slowly. "What do you mean?"

Tala stared at the pond, her eyes unseeing. "This has happened before. Some of the flock disappeared a year ago, and have never been seen again. We weren't sure the witch was responsible, but she was on the mountain then too, and there's no love lost between Sigur's people and the witch. Other animals disappeared, too. Some said it was her, others said there was no proof. But if she's back and Lamisa and Orion have disappeared, that looks like proof to me. I have no choice but to stop her. It was my fault I didn't stop her last time."

"How will you stop her?" Suli asked. "How do you fight a witch?" This was her chance to learn what she most wanted to know.

Tala shook her head. "I'm getting ahead of myself. You should eat and go to bed. There will be time for stories about witches later."

"What just happened on the mountain isn't a story!" Suli said angrily. "I need to know what's going on. The witch was here a year ago and part of the flock disappeared. Then she left. Now she's back, and part of the flock has disappeared." Her face was hot. Fear had become anger. "What does she want? Why didn't you stop her before?"

Tala took a deep breath and let it out. "Very well. For more than a year there was no sign of her. I'd hoped she'd gone for good; or stopped being a witch. Foolish of me." Tala shook her head and muttered to herself. She glanced at Suli and her expression softened. "Come," Tala said, taking her by the arm. "We'll eat, and then you'll go to bed."

They climbed the path to the house. Tala walked slowly, as though pushing through dark thoughts.

While they ate, Suli asked, "Cousin, why did you send me to the lake with the geese?"

Tala tilted her head to the side. "You know the answer, don't you?"

Why can't she ever answer a question? "You wanted me to see that Lamisa and Orion change into people. But Orion didn't know what to tell me, so he didn't explain much. I still don't understand."

"Ah." Tala nodded and sat back in her chair. "It's difficult to know how much to say, and how soon. I've been learning about you, too, since you've been here. Many don't understand the difference between magic and witchcraft. And you boasted about going to the Outsiders."

Suli bit her lip. So Tala hadn't trusted her. All the stories she'd heard about changing shape were from the old days; no one ever mentioned witchcraft. But nowadays people would suspect witchcraft first. It was clever to send her up the mountain to see the secret of the geese for herself. She'd believe her own eyes. And since all Suli saw was a boy surfacing from the water with a flock of geese, there was nothing to report. She didn't know whether Tala was breaking the law, but Tala didn't frighten her. She didn't make her feel the way the voice on the mountain had. If that was what a real witch was like, then Tala wasn't one. No matter how irritating or secretive she might be, everything Tala did made sense if she was protecting herself and the geese. Tala might not answer her questions often, but when she did, Suli knew she spoke the truth.

"Tell me more about the witch."

Tala stared at woven patterns in the tablecloth. "She's an excellent example of the difference between magic and witchcraft. Too bad it's too dangerous for you to meet her, or you'd see what I mean. She uses magic to control people and animals. Mostly she uses the Voice."

Suli went still. So that was what it was like to have someone use the Voice on you, the way she'd used it at the bonfire.

Tala nodded. "I know about your using Voice. Your Grandmother wants me to explain it to you."

Suli leaned forward, afraid she would hear she was already a witch.

"The Voice can control anyone—animal or human. It's part of the third kind of magic, Command. A witch uses the Voice to convince a victim her words are his thoughts. The victim doesn't notice someone else has taken control."

"But..." Suli thought about how she'd felt. "I knew they weren't my thoughts."

"Thank the Sisters!" said Tala. "You've had a narrow escape. I'd no idea she was back on the mountain or I'd never have allowed you to go there."

"Wait. Can anyone use the Voice, or is it something only witches do?" Suli didn't dare ask what she feared most: whether she was really a witch.

Tala's dark eyes examined her. "Wise women use the Voice, too. There are times when you must, to help people who don't want you to, or can't stop resisting you. They could be sick or injured or crazed with grief. So you'll learn to use the Voice as part of your training. If you want to protect people, especially from witchcraft, you must use it for defense."

Suli took a deep breath and let it out. She'd have to use the Voice again, and it *was* exactly the same as witchcraft. But Tala hadn't said she was a witch. Then another thought occurred to her, and she felt uneasy. "Is that how you get the goats to stand in line?"

Tala gave her a wry smile. "I don't compel the animals to stay here, or to do anything. It's their choice whether they stay or go. But if they stay, they have to abide by my rules, that's all. I don't enslave anyone, man or beast. The goats and geese could live perfectly well on the mountain without me, but they like it here."

The cozy pool of light from the lamp and the warmth of the fire had calmed Suli. Her stomach was full, and she felt warm and sleepy. The witch seemed far away. But now that her fear had ebbed, her curiosity had awakened. "About the geese: Is the lake special? Can the geese change anywhere, or does it have to be at the lake? Is that why the witch hides and spies in the woods there?"

Tala looked surprised, and nodded approval. "Good questions. Yes, the witch thinks the power to change comes from the Lake, and we've encouraged that belief. She's not very good at Seeing, probably because she uses the Voice to control people. I'm surprised you got away. Usually children can't resist her voice. It must be," she said thoughtfully, "because you can use the Voice yourself." She nodded. "Well, Suli, it looks like you'll get your wish. Since you can use the Voice, it will be your responsibility to protect others from the witch. Remember that."

Suli's stomach twisted. If Tala weren't around, it would be up to her to fight the witch, when she knew so little.

Tala leaned back in her chair. "Have I answered all your questions?"

"Cousin," Suli asked hesitantly, "does my grandmother know you can change shape? Can anyone else in the family do it?"

Tala smiled. "Not everyone has the talent. Your father had it. Your grandmother thought you might have it, too."

Suli's eyes widened. Grandmother had never said a word about changing shape.

Her only memory of her father was of a warm and laughing man who had thrown her up in the air and caught her, telling her she could fly. But Grandmother wouldn't talk about her son, or what had happened to him.

"And it isn't witchcraft? I still don't understand what witchcraft is."

Tala leaned forward, her dark eyes reflecting the firelight. "I've waited to tell you about Sigur's folk until I could talk about it without being accused of witchcraft. I can't wait any longer, not after what's happened." Her white teeth flashed. "Shape-shifting is old animal magic, and one of the things you were sent here to learn. It comes from the time when humans and animals were closer to each other, and has nothing to do with witchcraft. But you need to be careful. Most people don't understand it. You have to promise you won't reveal this to anyone outside the family. You know what might happen if you did, don't you? Do you give me your word?"

"I promise."

"Good. Changing is simply a talent we inherit, but the Outsiders will think shape-shifting is witchcraft; they don't understand there are different kinds of magic."

Suli frowned. If the Outsiders couldn't tell the difference, how would she explain it? "So shape-shifting isn't witchcraft, but the Outsiders think it is. So what *is* the difference between magic and witchcraft: How can I tell?"

Tala nodded. "It's difficult to explain." She sat back, watching the flames dance behind the face in the stove door. "Your grandmother wants you to learn the old ways. All our women need to know how to defend against magical danger. That's part of our work, and our responsibility to family and community. But the old ways are dying out," she said sadly. She stared at the darkness in the open window, where the silhouette of the mountain blocked the sky. "Our villages still follow them, but the towns on the coast don't. They think the Outsiders' ways are better."

Suli was silent. She didn't know what the Outsiders' ways might be, but if they made Tala sad, they couldn't be good.

"So," Tala said, turning to her. "You're here to be educated as a woman of our people should be, to learn the three kinds of magic and to become a wise woman. You'll be responsible for protecting the people and animals in your community. In the old days, more than one foster mother would have taught you magic. But I'll teach you as much as I can."

Suli took a deep breath and asked. "Cousin, have you ever…"

Tala gave her a shrewd look. "You want to know if I've ever used witchcraft, am I right?"

She nodded, her eyes wide. Was she offended?

"It's a good question. I've used the Voice to get away from the witch before. If I'd done that simply to control her—then yes, that would be witchcraft. But I did it to defend myself. Some of what I'll teach you should only be used in self-defense or to help others. That's one way to tell the difference. Witchcraft isn't a specific spell—although when you use Command, the third kind of magic, there's a greater risk that you'll cause harm. Witchcraft is any magic used to control or harm others. That includes the Voice."

Suli shook her head. She wanted a clearer answer. She couldn't always be sure of her own motives, never mind those of other people. Could she use witchcraft without knowing?

Tala stared at the fire. "In the old days, you would have learned other things first, but with the witch here, I can't wait. You need to learn about magical protection. Learning to talk with plants, bees, and other animals will have to wait."

Suli felt a moment of regret; she'd always wanted to talk to bees. But she didn't really understand what Tala meant. "Why don't the Outsiders understand the difference between magic and witchcraft?"

"Magic is difficult to explain to those who can't do it. That's why the Outsiders in the towns are so frightened of what is, after all, simply women's knowledge. They can't tell the difference between magic that pollinates the orchards and heals animals and magic that causes harm. Their fear infects the villages, and so we live in dangerous times, with dangerous people around us."

"Like the witch?"

"Like the witch," Tala agreed. "But there are worse threats."

"What do you mean?"

Tala gestured toward the mountain. "It's easy to be on guard against her, at least for you, isn't it?"

Suli nodded. The witch's voice had sounded false. She hadn't been tempted to come closer.

"There are others who aren't so obvious, who cloak evil intentions with fair words. It's much harder to tell when they mean you harm, unless you're good at Seeing. Many are fooled. The witch practically announces herself. Of course, some people are still fooled." Tala shook her head sadly. "After all these years, she still doesn't see she's her own worst enemy, and that all her spells and charms have gained her nothing. Nothing but loneliness and fear."

Suli looked at her curiously. She wanted to ask her teacher how she knew so much about the witch, but Tala had risen from her chair.

"We both need sleep. At dawn, I'll search for Lamisa and Orion. Have I answered all your questions?"

"Nearly," Suli said. "I'm glad you explained about changing shape. How do I know if I can do it, too?"

Tala smiled. "You don't need to know everything tonight. You've had enough adventure for one day. But Suli," her expression grew serious, "If I'm not here when you get up tomorrow, you should stay inside the house and bar the doors after feeding the animals. Use your Seeing before you let anyone inside."

Suli nodded and went to fill a bucket of water at the pump. She heard the kitchen door slam and saw Tala striding down the path to the pond. She was worried about Tala, now that she trusted her. Tala had never made her feel afraid the way the voice in the forest had, and she could See that Tala meant well. She was going to fight a witch, and Suli couldn't help. She'd only begun her training.

She looked up at the mountain that rose behind her, blocking the sky. Somewhere in that darkness was a witch who knew her name and where she'd sleep tonight.

7

ALONE

THE NEXT MORNING, when Suli opened her shutters, dark rows of clouds hung above the distant hills. The air was damp, promising rain to come. The house was silent. Suli pulled on her woolen leggings and went into the kitchen to start breakfast. The stove was cold, and when she called Tala's name, the silence grew deeper. She was alone in the house.

Her throat tight with fear, she went out to do the morning chores. When the animals were fed and the goats milked, she fetched the kindling basket and lit a fire in the stove. She fed the fire patiently until it caught, then set the porridge to simmer. She took dishes from the sideboard and set the table. Unable to stop herself, she went to the top of the path and looked down at the pond. Neither Lamisa nor Orion was there.

A knot twisted in her stomach. Something could have happened to her cousin. The witch might've trapped her, the way she had Orion and Lamisa. Whatever dreadful thing she did to the missing geese last year, she could be doing again. Suli had heard all the witch stories: tales of turning people into animals, of cooking and eating children, of robbing children of their memories, or imprisoning them inside a stone. She wished she knew which of the stories were true.

She returned to the kitchen and ate her porridge, and washed her bowl. Maybe the geese knew something. She left the house and descended the steep path to the pond. The geese huddled in a clump at one end, their heads resting on each other's backs. They knew something was wrong.

"Have you heard from Lamisa or Orion?" Suli called out. Several of the geese shook their necks and honked a few despairing notes. "Has Tala come back?" Again, the geese shook their heads.

Slowly she climbed the path back to the house. Five crows sat on the ridge beam of the roof. Two more perched in the fir tree nearby. Silently, the black heads turned to watch her as she walked to the garden. *It's as if they know something*, she thought, glancing at them uneasily. She sat down and began to weed half-heartedly. When she found uprooted clumps of her cousin's pennyroyal in her hand, she decided she was doing more harm than good. A fat drop of rain fell in the dirt beside her, and then another, and soon the rain was pelting down. She ran for the house, passing the goats huddled under the eaves of their shed.

She made nettle tea and drank it, staring out the kitchen window at the rain. If Tala hadn't returned by nightfall, she'd have to decide what to do.

❧

THE DAY PASSED SLOWLY, and her fear grew. She considered going for help, but where? She didn't know anyone in Weatherstone. If she traveled back to her own village, she'd be admitting she couldn't solve her own problems. To ask for help would prove she didn't have the courage or wisdom to be a wise woman. She couldn't do that, not yet. Besides, her cousin could return while she was gone. So Suli took care of the animals and waited.

It grew dark, and she jumped at faint sounds. She went outside to look down at the pond. Staring hard, she thought she saw movement amidst the shadows in the copse of trees, and a dark figure. She told herself that if someone were standing there, they'd be soaked to the skin, but it didn't help. Maybe rain couldn't touch a witch. She returned to the house and barred the door.

When evening came, she decided to check on the geese one more time. In spite of her fear, she wrapped the old shawl that hung on the kitchen door over her head, and carried the kitchen lamp to the pond. The geese huddled under the trees, silent, their feathers fluffed up against the rain. In the dim light thrown by the lamp it was hard to see, so she counted them to be sure. Orion and Lamisa weren't there. She trudged uphill on the slippery, muddy path.

Safe in the house, Suli barred the parlor and kitchen doors and shuttered all the windows, latching them closed. She blew out the kitchen lamp and took a candle with her to her bedroom. Now that the doors were barred, Tala couldn't get in, but Suli was afraid there was someone watching her in the darkness. If the witch could trap Tala, she must be powerful. Wouldn't she want to prevent Suli from telling anyone else she was back?

She slept uneasily, waking to listen for any sound above the soft murmur of the rain. Something woke her in the middle of the night. She listened intently, hoping to hear Tala calling for her to unbar the door. But all she heard was the laurel tree, tossed by the wind, its branches scraping the wall outside her bedroom window. Her heart beat painfully.

Suli heard a muffled sound by the parlor door. She sat up, straining to hear. Angry with herself for being afraid, she threw off the covers and stepped onto the cold floorboards.

She went to the parlor door and looked out the round window beside it. The garden was bathed in the grey light reflected by the clouds. Nothing moved. She didn't dare open the door.

Back in her bed, she pushed her icy feet under the covers and sat staring into the darkness, listening for any sound. Finally she lay back and dozed. Near morning, the hens' squawking woke her. She thought it must be Tala this time, but no one called. She fell back asleep.

When Suli finally woke the next morning, the rain had moved on; only tattered white clouds passed overhead on a clean wind. She unbarred the kitchen door and stepped outside to feed the animals. Footprints circled the house, coming close to the windows and doors. Heavy boots had pressed deep into the mud. Tala wore rope-soled sandals. Someone else had been there, standing in the rain, trying to get in.

She scattered grain for the hens and let the goats out to graze. When she returned to the house, she saw the visitor had left something else. A folded sheet of paper, with her name on it, had been pushed through the handle of the kitchen door. She stared at it for a moment in horror before opening it to read: "If you want Tala back, you must come and live with me in the forest."

Her hands shook, and she dropped the note. Bending over, the blood pounded in her head. Suli took a deep breath to steady herself. She stared at the paper, the letters swimming before her eyes. The fear she'd felt in the forest washed over her again.

If she went to live with the witch it would ruin her life. Perhaps Tala would be freed, and she could help her escape. But Suli didn't believe the witch would free Tala. Since the witch had caught her, the witch must be better at magic than her teacher. She'd be a prisoner of the witch, but everyone would assume she'd become her apprentice willingly. They'd say they'd known all along that Suli would become a witch: Like mother like daughter.

No matter what happened after that, even if she escaped,

she'd never be safe. People would whisper—or worse, accuse her. She'd be shunned and suspected for the rest of her life.

She saw no other sign the witch had been there, but she was afraid the witch could appear at any moment from behind a shed or tree. She forced herself to go to the pond.

Suli called to the geese, "Have you heard anything?"

The geese shook their heads, honking mournfully. She trudged back to the cottage and barred the kitchen door again, despite the sunny day. She didn't know what else to do. She stared out the window. More crows sat in the giant fir tree; she was sure they were watching her. Were they spies for the witch?

Tala had finally begun to explain things. Suli had been about to learn advanced magic, and now her teacher was gone. Now she had to protect herself from a witch long before she was ready. She knew so little about advanced magic.

Apprentice or not, she was the one who could get Tala back. The witch wanted her, not Tala. All she had to do was go to the forest, find the witch, and Tala would go free. Maybe. But Suli would never become a wise woman after that. No one would believe she'd had no choice; no one would ever trust her again. They'd say she was drawn to witchcraft because she was witch-spawn and her blood was tainted. And she couldn't fight the witch, not yet, so what could she do? She wanted to help Tala, but not at the cost of ruining her own life. She sat at the table with her head in her hands.

8

LEARNING TO FLY

IN THE YARD, the shadow of the chimney was short and dark, the sun directly overhead. If she was going to do something, Suli thought, she should do it now, in broad daylight.

Over and over she replayed the scene in the forest, hearing the anger beneath the sweetness of the witch's voice. Why was she angry, and why did she want Tala's apprentice? Maybe just to get back at Tala, but Suli thought there was something more. The witch had seemed eager to charm her. She wanted something from Suli, but what? She suddenly remembered the voice that had whispered to her from the trees, the night she'd first arrived. It must've been the witch, waiting for her. Somehow she'd known Suli was coming here.

Suli needed her teacher. She couldn't fight a witch by herself; she didn't know enough. And maybe not even Tala could fight the witch, since the witch had captured some of Sigur's people the year before and had Tala now.

All she knew for sure was that she couldn't live with the witch, not even to help Tala. But what other plan did she have? She couldn't learn magic without a teacher and without knowing advanced magic, Suli couldn't protect herself from the witch, or help Tala. There had to be someone else who could teach her. Maybe a wise woman from a nearby village could help her…

Loud squawking came from the tall fir tree in the yard. The crows were making a racket.

Rap, Rap! Someone knocked on the window. Heart pounding, Suli rose and turned to look out the window.

It was Orion, in human form. His face was dirty, his shirt torn and muddy. He smiled and pointed to the door. "Suli, it's me!"

Her Seeing confirmed it was Orion. She unbarred the door.

Orion came in, his face haggard, his clothing torn. "Don't worry," he said, "it's really me. The witch held us captive, but we escaped. I need to talk to Tala. Where is she?" His eyes darted nervously around the kitchen.

"How did you get away?"

"The Voice wore off, and once we could change, we untied the net. Where's Tala?"

"She isn't here. She went to look for you and hasn't come back," Suli said.

Orion sat down abruptly, the shock plain on his face. "Tala is missing? I don't believe it!"

She brought the teapot to the table and poured him a cup. "It's true. After you and Lamisa disappeared, I heard a voice in the woods. I ran away and told Tala, and she went to look for you. I haven't seen her since. The witch must have her." She couldn't tell him about the witch's note. He'd expect her to go live with the witch.

Orion crossed his arms, hugging himself. "The witch is evil. Someone has to stop her."

Suli sat down and asked quietly, "How did the witch catch you? Where's Lamisa?"

Orion hunched his shoulders and looked away. "The witch used the Voice on us, and we came when she called. Then she threw a net over us and staked us to the ground behind her cottage. Lamisa flew off to tell the Elders. Do you know how to fight a witch?"

She shook her head. "No. That's why I need to find someone to teach me."

"Nevertheless, you got away from her," Orion said thoughtfully. "Only wise women can do that. Even if the witch hadn't thrown a net over us, we can't resist the Voice. But you did. You can help Tala. I'd like to, but I won't go near the witch again." He shivered.

"If only this had happened later!" Suli said. "Tala was finally explaining things; she said Grandmother thought I could change —just like you do. If I knew how, I could fly to the mountain to look for Tala. But I don't know anything!"

Orion smiled. "Is that all? I can teach you that, as long as you have the talent. We could search the mountain together. But on the ground remember to stay human. The geese are susceptible to the Voice; that's how I got caught."

She smiled uncertainly. "Really? You just said you wouldn't go near the witch."

"Well," Orion's face clouded. "I'll search the mountain for Tala, but I won't go near the witch."

That was fine with her. She was excited: if she could fly, she could find out what the witch was doing. And she could ask others to help her. If she could fly! A few days ago, she would have scoffed at the idea, but after seeing Orion change, she knew it was possible. Once she could fly, maybe she'd find Tala and free her. "Are you sure you can teach me to change? My grandmother didn't know for certain, she just thought I might be one of your— Sigur's people."

"Only one way to find out. It's not hard, if you have the talent," said Orion, his face serious.

Suli rose to her feet. "What do you want me to do?"

"Let's go to the pond."

The geese floating in the pond honked and cried out with joy when they saw Orion, but they grew quiet when he explained where he'd been.

Then Suli and Orion stood in the shallow end, facing each other. The muddy bottom squelched between Suli's toes.

"Watch what I do." Orion closed his eyes. There was a blur in the air, as though wings blocked the sun. A brown and white goose stood where he'd been a moment before.

The sunlight flickered again, and human Orion reappeared, his brown eyes twinkling. "Now you try. Close your eyes. Feel your body becoming like the water, fluid and free. Can you feel it?"

She nodded, imagining she was part of the water. Her hands were clammy with nervousness. This was why Grandmother had sent her here. She was going to change shape. What if she failed? Or worse, what if she changed and something went wrong and she couldn't change back?

"Think about wings sprouting from your back," Orion said. "Feel how they spring from your shoulder blades." He waited a moment. "Can you feel them lifting?"

She could. Feeling foolish, Suli lifted her arms, imagining them covered with long white feathers.

"Now say to yourself, *Hala, Bala, Idala*," Orion said.

Suli repeated the words. A wave of energy passed through her body, leaving a tingling sensation. She felt strangely light, as though her bones had become hollow.

"Open your eyes," Orion commanded.

She obeyed, and looked at Orion, still standing in the shallow end of the pond. He smiled encouragingly. Then she looked down at her feet. They were too close and—they were pale pink. The webbing between her toes was clearly visible. Feeling dizzy, she quickly closed her eyes.

"You'll feel better in a minute," Orion said.

Even with her eyes closed, she could tell he was smiling. She opened her eyes and examined her white wing feathers dappled with grey. The sunlight on the water dazzled her. "I'm a goose?" she asked.

"Yes." Orion smiled broadly. "You're a goose all right."

"Am I speaking goose?" Suli asked.

"Of course."

"But you're human and you understand me." She looked across the pond. The other geese floated together, watching.

"You can't speak human language with a beak instead of a mouth," Orion said. "But you can understand both with practice, no matter what your form. Go on, start swimming. I'll be right behind you."

Clumsily, she waded into deeper water. Her legs were oddly placed beneath her, but once she was floating, they propelled her effortlessly. She sailed forward, enjoying the satiny feel of the water, and turned to look for Orion. He was a goose now, swimming behind her.

"Nice, isn't it?" he said.

Not only could she understand him, she could tell he was smiling, in spite of the beak. She looked at the flock of geese floating nearby. They all had expressions on their faces she'd never noticed before. "I didn't have to learn how to swim—will I be able to fly?"

"Yes," Orion said, "but you'll need to practice first."

She paddled happily across the pond, honking, "Wheee! I'm a goose!" She barreled across the water with the others scattering quickly to get out of her way.

Orion followed. "Congratulations! You're one of us now. See? Changing isn't difficult. But we'd better practice flying."

"Wait, Orion, does this mean everyone in my family can change? Can my brother, Eb? Can my grandmother change?"

Orion shook his head. "I don't know. Just because one person inherits the ability doesn't mean everyone does. Your grandmother must have known others who could, or she wouldn't have known the signs. But now," he continued briskly, "you'd better to learn to fly. A goose running away from danger looks pretty silly. I'll show you how to take off."

Suli nodded, but she was thinking how awkward it would be if she could fly and Eb couldn't. It wouldn't be fair. It was bad enough she could do magic and he couldn't.

Orion swam to the other side of the pond. He flapped his wings and lifted into the air, barely rippling the water's surface. After flying once around the pond, he landed beside her, explaining what she had to do.

She flapped her wings violently. Twice she lifted a few feet above the water, only to fall back into the pond with a loud splash. It was harder than it looked.

The other geese tactfully looked away. Suli was clumsy and awkward. Her wings weren't at the right angle for the air to flow beneath them and lift her up.

"You're trying too hard," Orion said gently. "Just relax. When you begin to flap your wings, imagine you're already aloft."

"What if I forget what I'm doing and fall?" she asked.

"Instinct takes over. Your body knows what to do."

She snorted. All her body knew was how to stay on the ground. She tried again. This time her wings caught the air and lifted her up and up. She was gliding over the pond, the cool wind in her face. She turned into the wind and circled the pond, wings motionless until she needed to change direction. Orion joined her in the air, coaching her to rise, descend, and turn.

She felt the air beneath her, holding her up. Now that she could fly, she didn't want to stop. She couldn't stop grinning, or at least it felt like she was. All she wanted to do was stay in the air. Why would anyone remain earthbound if they could fly? Orion signaled to land, and she followed him down, braking on the water.

The other geese crowded around her, crying noisy congratulations.

Flax swam up. "I'm so glad you've changed, sister. I wanted to talk with you, but I don't like to change anymore."

"I'm glad too," Suli said.

The others murmured, "Welcome, sister, welcome to the family."

It was easy to tell them apart now, and to read their expressions; most were smiling, welcoming her to the flock. They were perfectly normal, perfectly nice, just the same as other people. Some had white and grey feathers, as Suli did, some were brown or white, but they were all people just like her. She was one of them.

She had never suspected changing into an animal was possible. She could fly! And talk with geese like her, and swim and dive as they did. When she'd left home to learn magic from Tala, she thought she'd learn spells, not something that would transform her completely. For the first time since she'd arrived, she was happy. The geese accepted her; she belonged to them, and they to her. She'd become someone else: someone with the power to leap into the sky. She could fly anywhere. It was better than magic.

Orion swam up. "Tala will be so proud of you. Now we'd better decide what to do about the witch."

At the reminder, Suli's happiness disappeared. Tala was a prisoner. Whatever she knew, of flying or of magic, she'd have to use to fight a witch.

"We'd better change back," Orion said. "It's dangerous to stay in winged form when we don't know where the witch is." He climbed onto the grassy bank and stood still, closing his eyes. There was the strange blurring of the light, and then a boy in sopping wet breeches and shirt smiled at her ruefully. "It's a nuisance, having to dry your clothes all the time. But we can't pop up all over the countryside without clothes."

"To change back: close your eyes and imagine you're human

once more. Now say: '*Idala, Bala, Hala,*' and imagine your feet are on solid ground," Orion said.

Suli felt a pang of regret; she didn't want to go back to being earthbound, but she followed him up the bank, closed her eyes, and did as he said. She looked down to see two bare brown feet. She wrung the hem of her wet dress. "I need to change my dress."

They climbed back to the house. Suli showed Orion the footprints and he shook his head, looking grim.

"It's a good thing you barred the door last night," he said, after he'd done the same. "The witch knew you were here, but she couldn't get inside. I wonder why she didn't use the Voice. Did you hear her last night?"

"A sound woke me, but no one called. I was listening in case Tala came back." She shivered.

Orion nodded. "I'll put the kettle on, while you change."

The kitchen was empty when she returned. Suli pulled a chair beside the stove to hang the wet dress on the clothesline above it, the drops sending tiny jets of steam into the air with a sizzling sound.

She sat down to rub her hair with a towel. Now that she could fly, she could search the mountain for Tala herself. But if she found the witch, what would she do?

Orion returned wearing dry clothes, his wet hair combed. He checked the kettle but it hadn't boiled yet.

"Orion, there's something I don't understand—maybe you'll know."

He turned. "What?"

"The other day, a grey goose with white markings around her eyes wanted me to follow it, so I did, down to the pond. It left with a flock of wild geese. Was that Tala? And if it was, what I was supposed to understand?"

Orion nodded. "Yes, that was Tala. She often flies with the wild geese, or the Free Folk, as they call themselves. She likes the freedom they have to travel from place to place without belonging anywhere. I don't know why she wanted you to see that, except she says she learns from them."

"Learns what?"

Orion's expression was thoughtful. "That might be an excellent thing to find out. They might be able to help."

"How?" Suli asked.

"Human magic doesn't work on them. They know better than to listen to humans." His voice sounded bitter.

Maybe that was the answer; find someone to teach her the magic she needed to know. "If the wild geese know magic that protects against the witch, I want to talk to them," she said, rising to her feet, "If I leave now, I can be back before dark."

"Better not. That's what happened the last time—we went to look for the one gone missing, and then someone else disappeared…promise me you won't go looking for the witch."

He didn't know about the note, or that she didn't want to go anywhere near the witch. "I promise. What happened the last time the witch was here?"

Orion brought two cups and the teapot to the table and busied himself pouring tea. For a moment, she thought he'd refuse to answer. But he handed her a cup and said, "We're especially vulnerable to the Voice when in winged form. A year ago, almost twenty members of the flock disappeared that way. We still don't know what happened to them, but everyone thinks the witch was responsible. Crows disappeared, too. The Elders couldn't decide what to do. Tala wouldn't act against the witch without proof."

Suli shivered. "Did the witch kill them?"

"We don't know. But they never came back."

"Why does the witch hate us?"

Orion smiled when she said "us." "Tala said she resents us because we can change," he said.

"I'll ask the wild geese to help us."

Orion didn't look up. "Suli..." he began. He wouldn't meet her eyes.

He looks so miserable, she thought. "It's all right. I can do this by myself. My Seeing will protect me. Tala said perhaps the Voice doesn't work on me. Stay here and rest."

Orion met her eyes. "I feel like a coward."

"But you're not. You were trapped by the witch, not knowing what would happen to you. You need time to recover. I'll be all right. Where can I find the Free Folk?"

Orion raised an eyebrow. "At the lake, of course."

9

THE FREE FOLK

SULI STEPPED INTO THE YARD, closed her eyes, and changed, leaping into the warm air.

The late afternoon sky was a clear blue. She glided over the land at the foot of the mountain and considered what Orion had told her about the Free Folk. They avoided humans and looked down on Sigur's geese because of their human taint. They might not help her. Still, they let Tala fly with them, and that gave her hope.

Flying up the mountain's side, Suli reveled in the strength of her wings and the sense of lightness and power they gave her. She rose in the bright air of the summer day as though she weighed no more than thistle down. The farms and forests were green beneath her, the Blue Mountain River flowing past. She understood why many of the geese chose to spend all their time in winged form.

It didn't take long to reach the lake. Suli avoided the forest where she'd heard the witch, flying to the end of the lake where the wild geese floated by the waterfall.

The geese were ghostly in the mist, visible one moment then disappearing the next. Those in the sunnier part of the lake dived for fish, while others dozed on the grassy bank in the warm afternoon sun. Heads turned to watch as Suli descended. She folded her wings and settled on the surface. Two ganders, their heads grey with age, swam towards her.

They stopped a few feet away. Suli bowed her neck and called to them, "Greetings, Free Folk. I'm Suli, Tala's cousin."

One of them replied haughtily, "Greetings, Suli. I'm Tilfrost, leader of this flock. What do you seek here?" It was a polite way of asking why she was trespassing on their territory.

"I'm looking for Tala. She's been missing a day and a night."

Tilfrost snorted. "I've heard Sigur's geese are like human children—afraid to leave the tiny cages they call homes, too frightened to roam freely on the wind as we do. Tala flies with us because she is not like the rest of you; she needs to feel the wind under her wings and to see the stars on the horizon change. How do you know she's not flying free right now? Why should you try to find her?" He looked down his beak at her.

"Some other time that might be true," Suli said diplomatically, "but the witch has returned, and we think she's trapped Tala. Have you seen the witch?"

Tilfrost and the other gander spoke softly, their heads bent together. Then Tilfrost raised his long neck and said, "This is grave news. We do not concern ourselves with humans, but your witch harms the winged folk, too. We've not seen Tala. I cannot help you. The Free Folk do not meddle with humans. If you were wiser, you wouldn't either." And with that, Tilfrost swam away.

"*Wait! You must help me!*" Suli cried desperately, and realized too late that she'd used the Voice.

Tilfrost ignored her, except for one disgusted glance. He glided away hooting angry disapproval. The crows called shrill warnings to each other, back and forth across the lake.

The other gander had watched without moving. Now he swam up to her.

"You should not have done that, young lady. Tilfrost has very strong opinions about humans and by using the Voice, you've proven him right. You won't change his mind now. I'm Timber." He looked uncertainly at Suli. "You must be a wise woman, too. Or are you a witch?"

Suli felt embarrassed and ashamed. She shook her head. "I'm sorry. I didn't mean to use the Voice…I'm an apprentice, learning to be a wise woman."

Timber frowned. "Hmph. You need teaching, child. You need Tala. Do you know how to heal?"

The change of topic caught her off guard. "I know a little. Why?"

Timber looked unhappy. "One of my little ones is sick. I hoped you could help me."

Suli had never healed an animal by herself, but Timber looked so worried. "I can try."

"Thank you." He dipped his neck. "Follow me." They swam to the bank and climbed out. Suli followed him beneath the trees, their webbed feet soundless on the carpet of pine needles. "Here she is," said Timber.

A small gosling covered in pale down sat in a nest of leaves between the roots of an old tree. *She doesn't look well*, Suli thought.

"Can you do anything?" Timber asked.

"Let me See," she said. She clucked soothingly to the child and looked out of the sides of her eyes, as Tala had taught her. She thought she knew what to do, but she needed to use her hands.

"I need to change into a human," she said to the gosling. "Don't be afraid."

The gosling stared wide-eyed at human Suli when she sat down beside her. Suli put her hands lightly around the delicate, fluffy child. Suli used her side-Seeing. *There* was the sickness; she concentrated on burning it away.

When she'd done all she could, Suli opened her eyes and gently stroked the gosling. The child's eyes were brighter, and she looked better. Suli rose and changed back into a goose. "I've done what I could," she told Timber.

"How do you feel, sweet one?" Timber asked.

The gosling staggered to her feet and fluffed out her feathers, smiling. "I'm better, Papa!"

He honked with relief and laid his head against hers. "I'm glad. If you feel well enough, go tell your mother."

The child scampered off to the lake. "Bye!" she called to Suli.

Timber bowed to Suli. "I'm in your debt, Suli of Sigur's people. If I can ever do anything for you, you have only to ask."

Suli smiled. "I'm happy to help. And there *is* something you could tell me. I've heard the Free Folk are safe from the spells of the witch. Is this true? If you told me how you do it, I could protect my flock."

Timber preened his feathers thoughtfully and then shook his head. "There is no secret. A fully-fledged adult of the Free Folk doesn't need protection. We don't listen to the words of humans or other dangerous animals. A gosling, yes, is vulnerable to the words of wicked folk. But we guard them from the lies of humans, hawks, or snakes—any creature that might lure them away from their mothers. I'm sorry."

Suli looked down at her webbed feet, disappointed. She'd been counting on finding some way to protect herself, preferably advanced magic.

"But don't you realize," Timber said, looking at her curiously, "that you don't need our help? You used the Voice on Tilfrost; that means you can resist it. That's how wise women protect everyone. You can use the Voice and can Heal. Why don't you simply use the third kind of magic against the witch?"

She was about to explain she didn't know how when a cry sounded above her. A brown goose glided down to land beside her. "Orion! Is something wrong?"

Orion laughed, shrugging his wings. "No, but I felt bad, letting you come alone. One of the Free Folk told me you were here. Do they know where Tala is?"

"No," Suli said. She decided she wouldn't tell him what Timber had said. She wanted to think about it first.

"I *would* like to repay you for healing my daughter," Timber said. "Is there something else I could do?"

"Yes, if you're willing," Suli said. "Since the Voice doesn't work on you, could you look for Tala on the mountain? And ask others to help?"

"I will," Timber said. "Goodbye." He bowed and returned to the lake.

"It's growing dark," Suli said to Orion. "Let's go home."

White and red stars had risen in the evening sky by the time they landed by the pond. The geese honked softly and gathered around them.

The geese called Suli's name hopefully. She climbed up the bank to change, and waited, shivering in her damp dress, while Orion explained where they'd been and that there had been no word of Tala. "But some of the Free Folk have promised to look for her."

Wilo, who was the eldest, said, "It's happening just as it did before. The witch has taken her." The other geese nodded sadly.

Suli hadn't forgotten what Timber had said, that she could protect others using the Voice. But until she knew how, she wouldn't pretend she could. The wind blew fat drops of rain into her face. "Everyone must stay away from the mountain and the lake, while the witch is there," she told the flock.

The geese agreed, and Suli and Orion said goodbye and climbed the hill to the house. It was frustrating; she knew no more than she did that morning, not about the whereabouts of Tala or the witch, nor how to protect herself from the witch's magic. Being told to use the Voice didn't explain how to do it. It hadn't worked on Tilfrost or Timber. But they were immune, Timber had told her. Would it work on someone else?

Suli entered the kitchen, Orion behind her. The fire in the stove was almost out.

"Lamisa?" Orion called. There was no answer. "I don't think she's back."

Suli took the dress from the line above the stove and went to her room to change. The dress, warm from the stove, felt comforting on her chilled skin.

She returned to the kitchen and put the wet dress on the line, before kneeling to add wood to the stove.

Orion came in from outside. "Lamisa's not back yet, which suits me. She'll be angry we went to the mountain." He dropped vegetables into the sink and began to wash them.

Suli set two places on the table, looking at the night sky and the mountains framed in the window. "Should we be worried?"

Orion shrugged. "Those meetings can take forever. Everyone has to have their say and then they vote, over and over. If she's not back tomorrow, I'll worry."

She sliced the bread into thick chunks and put a bowl of greens on the table. "Where do you think Tala is?"

"Dunno." Orion diced turnips and carrots, and then crushed juniper berries with the side of his knife, scraping the juice into the simmering pot.

"Her cottage is too obvious. I think the witch has trapped Tala somewhere secret," Suli said. "Tomorrow we should send search parties to fly over the valleys of the mountain."

Orion shook his head. "We should wait until Lamisa is back." He put the rest of the vegetables into the pot and moved it to the hotter part of the stove. "The Elders may know something we don't."

Suli bit her lip. Her worry for Tala increased with every hour that passed. The witch was waiting for Suli to give herself up, perhaps growing angrier by the minute, and she might take her anger out on her teacher. Tala was probably hungry and cold, trapped somewhere; she couldn't wait for help forever. The flock wouldn't search for her. They were so used to Tala taking care of them, they couldn't act on their own. And Orion did whatever Lamisa told him. Suli didn't care if Lamisa was training to be an Elder; Orion should think for himself. "As long as they stay in the air, everyone will be perfectly safe," she argued.

"There's another reason I think we should wait," Orion said quietly. "I just spoke with the leader of the crows while I was feeding the animals. The crows have already done what you said; they've flown over the secret valleys and they didn't find her. If they can't find her, I don't think we will."

"The crows? Why are they searching?" her voice rasped. Suddenly there were unshed tears in the back of her throat. Tala had to be on the mountain. Where else could she be?

Orion glanced at her and poured a glass of water, handing it to her. She drank and took a deep breath.

He tapped the wooden spoon against the side of the pot and laid it down. "The last time the witch was here, she stole the crows' babies," he said. "They never found out what she did with them. The ravens and songbirds are worried, too. They rely on Tala for protection. With her gone, the witch can do as she pleases. They won't go near the lake."

Suli sat at the table. The crows weren't watching the house for the witch. They'd been keeping an eye on it because they worried about Tala, too.

"Crows, ravens, and songbirds all listen to humans. They find our singing and talking interesting. That makes them vulnerable."

She thought about the crows watching her from the roof beam of the house. "Do crows know magic?"

He rubbed his chin thoughtfully. "They know something. They have great stories about witches. You should ask Kaark."

"But I can't talk to them."

"Well, you don't know their language, do you? The soup's ready." He ladled vegetables into her bowl and sat down.

She dipped her spoon into the bowl and blew on it. Maybe the crows could help. They hated the witch, too. "Could I learn Crow? Would they teach me, do you think?"

"They might."

She tasted the vegetables, flavored with juniper berries and bits of smoked fish; it was very good. They were silent until their bowls were empty.

Orion pushed away his bowl away with a contented sigh, and threw a leg over the arm of the chair. He's too comfortable, Suli thought. We both are. We're warm inside, with full bellies, while Tala may be hungry and cold and alone. But I can't live with the witch.

"Would *you* teach me to speak Crow?" Suli asked.

Orion nodded, swallowing a large mouthful of bread. "Sure—Crow talk is easy. Crows understand our speech, too. But I should warn you: They'll make fun of you." He made a face. "They think humans are funny."

She looked down at her bowl. What would a wise woman do? "I'll search for Tala at first light, but if I can't find her, I'll need someone to teach me magic. Once I know how to talk to crows, I can ask for their help."

"That's not a bad idea." Orion rose. "I'll wash and you dry. And I'll be in the guest room tonight. You shouldn't be here alone."

She nodded, glad of the company.

That night, Suli lay in bed listening to the rain drumming on the roof. Rain spattered down the chimney, making the fire hiss. The wind fingered the cracks in the shutters and doors and blew rain against the windows. As she fell asleep, Suli heard the cries of the Free Folk flying over the roof in the storm. She hoped they were searching for Tala.

10

TALKING TO CROWS

THE NEXT MORNING the wind had moved on, but rain fell steadily from the grey sky, churning the yard to mud. When Suli entered the kitchen, Orion was there with the porridge already simmering on the stove.

"Can we talk to crows today?" she asked.

Orion shrugged. "I haven't seen any this morning, but we can still start your lessons. I can teach you the basics myself."

"Good. I want to search for Tala from the air, but it's hard to see in the rain."

"Lamisa would want you to stay here, with the witch back," Orion said.

"Lamisa isn't my teacher. Tala is."

The rain continued, darkening the sky until they had to light the lamp before they ate breakfast. Then they put their dishes in the stone sink, and the lessons began.

Orion demonstrated the basic calls. First the "I am here" or "look at me" call. "It doubles as hello when you're addressing a stranger," he said, and made a loud croaking sound. She tried to mimic it. "Almost," he said. He gave the cry again. "Now you."

Suli tried to imitate the sound over and over again until

Orion was satisfied, and then he taught her more calls, and wing and beak language as well. She was surprised that crows had a large vocabulary, and said so.

"You shouldn't be surprised," Orion said, frowning. "If you learn nothing else, you'd better realize that animals are just as smart as humans, especially the winged folk. They've been around longer than humans and have their own wisdom. You should respect that."

Suli rolled her eyes. "Yes, Orion."

They spent most of the gloomy morning practicing. Just before noon, the sun broke through the clouds, sending shafts of light across the yard. The boughs of the trees glowed green, the pine needles adorned with glistening jewels that spattered the ground with heavy drops. A chorus of birdsong began. Shapes flitted from branch to branch.

"Let's see if any crows will talk to you," Orion said.

"I'm not that good yet."

"I understand you perfectly," Orion said. "Anyway, there may not be any about. And if there are, they're going to make fun of us for needing their help to do magic."

They stepped into the muddy yard. The goats had already gathered in a line, waiting. "Orion! Did anyone feed them yesterday?" She'd forgotten her chores the day before.

He waved his hand dismissively at the goats. "Yes, I fed them. Don't worry about them, they always find something to eat."

Suli ran to the outbuilding, her feet making a sucking sound every time she lifted them from the mud. Orion followed and took the pail of grain from her. "I'll do it. Go ahead and call the crows. Stand by the fir and give the 'I am here' call."

She moved beneath the dripping tree, jumping when a drop hit her head or ran down her face. The needles underfoot smelled of resin and damp earth. She stared up into the branches and repeated the call three times, her voice growing stronger each time.

Answering cries came from down the hill by the pond, growing nearer, until two large crows landed on the branch above her. One said, "We're here, too! Who are you?"

She tilted her head back to see them. She tried to sound confident, as a wise woman would, and said in human speech, "I'm Suli, Tala's cousin. I'd like to learn Crow."

The first crow fastened his eye on her and said in Crow, "Hello, Suli, Tala's cousin. We've seen you before."

Suli bowed slightly, the way she did to the goats. When she straightened up, the crows' hunched shoulders were shaking. Were they laughing at her? She didn't know the words to ask them what was funny.

Orion joined her under the tree. He looked up at the crows with a quizzical expression. "Hello, Kaark, Ebon. Is something funny?" he asked in Crow.

"That trick she does!" the second crow said. "It's wonderful! Do it again!"

Orion turned to Suli and translated, then asked, "What did you do?"

"All I did was bow, like this." She bowed to Orion and the crows laughed harder, bouncing up and down on the branch.

The first crow struggled to speak. "That looks ridiculous! We don't bend that way. Humans! I hope," he croaked helplessly, "we don't give offense." The second crow was leaning so far over he was in danger of falling off the branch.

Orion said impatiently, "Yes, yes, we're happy to amuse you, Kaark, but Suli has a question for you, when you're sensible. She wants to learn your language. And we should talk about Tala."

Kaark stopped laughing and turned one bright eye on him. "What about Tala?"

Suli decided Kaark must be the leader. "She's missing, and we think the witch has her. We'd like your help to find her."

The crows exchanged glances and straightened up, settling their wings. Kaark nodded and said, "We know. Our scouts have searched for two days. We have our own score to settle with the witch. What more would you ask?"

Orion nodded. "Thank you for searching. The other favor we'd ask is this: Could one of your flock teach Suli to speak Crow? She wants to learn."

Kaark stared hard at Suli. "Why would a human child want to learn our language?"

Suli understood all the words. She replied slowly, using human words when she had to. "I need to know how to defend myself, and everyone else, against the witch. Orion says crows know magic. Will you teach me?"

"Magic, eh? Are you really a witch in training, Suli?" Kaark asked. His voice sounded harsh and cold. "We saw you use the Voice on the Free Folk. Only a witch would do that."

Offended, she said, "I'm not a witch! I want to *fight* a witch. That's why I need to learn magic. Without Tala, I have no one to teach me."

The two crows started laughing again and ignored Orion's requests to stop laughing and answer the question.

"I beg your pardon, Suli," Kaark finally said, wiping his eyes with his wing. "My name is Kaark, and I'm flock leader. Come outside after your nap today, and someone will teach you." Then he and the other crow flew away, chuckling.

She turned to Orion. "I don't see what's so funny!"

Orion shook his head. "No human does. You'll just have to put up with it if you want to talk to them." He started to walk toward the henhouse. "Let's get the rest of the chores done before lunch. Then we should stay inside until your lesson."

She was about to argue, but he was right. What would she do if the witch leaped out from behind the chicken coop?

Suli remembered the dark figure standing under the trees by the pond, and how afraid she'd been. She hurried to help Orion finish the chores.

❧

IT RAINED DURING LUNCH, but after Suli's nap, the sun came out. She was sitting in the garden, pulling weeds, when two crows landed beside her. One was Kaark; she recognized a pale feather on his back. The other was a stranger. She greeted them in Crow, but didn't bow; she didn't want to be laughed at again.

"Hello, Suli," Kaark said. "This is my son, Coalfeather. He has searched the mountain, but saw no sign of the witch. He can tell you himself."

Coalfeather bobbed his head and began to speak, but Suli stopped him. "I'm sorry. I don't understand all the words."

Kaark said, "You should change, Suli. You'll understand us better in winged form."

Suli closed her eyes and changed. The air felt silky against her feathers, and she saw details in the shifting leaves she hadn't noticed when she was human. It was easier to read the faces of the two crows now: Kaark was trying not to laugh, but Coalfeather looked solemn.

Coalfeather repeated, "Pleased to meet you, Suli. Tala has always helped us, so when we heard Tala was missing, I went to look for her, but saw no sign of either her or the witch. My father has told me about your request."

This time she understood every word. Words came more easily too. "What about the witch? Did you see her?"

"No, her house is empty. There's no fire, and no animal has seen her."

It might be a good sign that the witch had disappeared, but where was Tala? "Has Tala ever disappeared before?" she asked.

"Only once—the last time she fought the witch."

She suddenly felt cold. Maybe Tala had fought the witch and lost.

"Suli," said Kaark, "I've thought about your request. With the witch here, we need a wise woman to protect us, and you need

Crow wisdom to survive. Coalfeather is our most learned teacher. He's agreed to teach you. He's more forgiving of humans than the rest of us; he doesn't even find them amusing!" And with that, Kaark burst out laughing and flew away.

She frowned. "I wish he wouldn't laugh at me."

"Don't mind him," Coalfeather said, sighing. "Let's begin. There are Crow ways you will find useful. But first, I need to know more about you. Why do you want to be a wise woman? My father says you want to fight witches. That's an odd ambition for a girl. He also said you used the Voice the way a witch would, to command the Free Folk."

She looked at Coalfeather uncertainly. If she gave the wrong answer, would he change his mind and decide not to teach her?

"Are you afraid you might become a witch? Or afraid people will think you are one?"

Suli stared at him in surprise. "Yes," she said, deciding the truth was easiest, "I have to prove I'm not a witch. Everyone said I'd become one, just because I accidentally used the Voice. But I hate witches!"

Coalfeather hunched his shoulders and hopped away, then back. "Using the advanced magic of a wise woman will make it *more* likely some folk will call you a witch. So if proving to others that you're not a witch is the important thing—"

"It's not," Suli interrupted.

"Then what is?" he asked.

She looked into the crow's intelligent eyes and knew she couldn't fool him. "I *did* think if I became a wise woman it would prove I wasn't a witch. But I understand better now, what being a wise woman means. I know what I want to do—and what I can do."

"Which is?"

"I can change things! I can make plants grow and heal sick animals. I can resist the Voice, and I can *fly*. I can help others because of those things. If the only way to stop a witch is to learn advanced magic, I'll learn it. If I can stop the witch from hurting people, it's worth being called one. Is that what you want to know?" she asked, challenge in her voice.

Coalfeather seemed to relax, folding his wings flat against his back. "It's important we *both* understand why you are learning magic." He hopped away and said more briskly, "And it will help me teach you. Let's begin."

She exhaled. If that was a test, she'd just passed it.

Coalfeather paced back and forth, explaining he would teach her the knowledge crows passed on to their children. "Humans interfere too much with the way of things. They try to change what does not need to be changed. That's one reason we distrust them. We watch humans carefully, but we refuse to become dependent on them. It's why my father laughs at them. Otherwise, there is the danger of becoming like them.

"The winged folk who talk and sing, my own people among them, are fascinated by the fact that humans do those things, too. That's why the witch's Voice is a threat to us."

Suli frowned. "What about Tala? She uses magic."

"Tala's a friend. She helps us without interfering in our affairs. We trust her."

"I want to be like her," Suli said. "I want to help and not interfere. Once I know magic, I'll protect everyone."

He smiled at her fierceness. "Good. But remember, you've only begun to learn, and the witch can control anyone—human or winged. Don't try to fight her."

"I won't—yet. But I can resist the Voice and I..." she hesitated, "I've used it twice, accidentally. I think I can use it for defense, if I had to. I could protect the crows."

Coalfeather stopped pacing and tilted his head on one side. One bright eye stared at her. "I will tell the Council you have offered to do that. Now," he ruffled his feathers and folded them back sleekly against his back, "There are important stories you should know. Stories about Crow magic. This one happened in the time before I was born..."

Suli listened eagerly while Coalfeather spoke of animals that tricked or escaped their predators by using their Seeing. She waited for instructions for using magic, but none came. After an hour of listening, she knew Crow very well, but she was restless. Soon it would be time for the evening meal.

"I like your stories, Coalfeather," she finally interrupted, "but I don't see how they help me fight the witch. If crows are so wise about magic, why don't they use it? In the stories you've told me so far, all they do is trick or outwit their enemies."

He gave her a stern look. "I'm teaching you to be a wise crow," he said, flattening his feathers in reproof. "Before you fight anyone, before you use the Voice, be sure it's necessary. That means you must See what's going on. Then you'll know whether you should do anything at all. Crows prefer to understand the situation first. We use the third kind of magic only when there's no alternative."

Suli nodded impatiently. All she knew about the third kind of magic was that it included the Voice. It was easy to agree that using the Voice was wrong. What else did he mean?

He smiled. "This will make more sense later. Just remember to use your Seeing first. It's always better not to use the third kind of magic."

"All right," she said, not willing to reveal her ignorance. "But can we fly to the mountain while you teach me? You said there's no sign of the witch. Maybe we'll see Tala."

Coalfeather sighed. "That's unlikely, when all our scouts haven't found her. But it should be safe enough while we're in the air. If it will help you pay attention, yes, we can fly to the mountain. But don't stray. Stay near me."

"Yes."

"Then follow me." He leapt into the air, with Suli right behind him.

11

THE THIRD KIND OF MAGIC

Suli and Coalfeather flew side-by-side, rising on the warm air from the valley floor. When Tala's house was just a tiny dot below them, Coalfeather spoke.

"Perhaps a story about the third kind of magic will make this clearer," he said. "Once upon a time, when powerful Crow princes ruled all the lands, there was a Crow prince with a hoard of magical objects. Witches are attracted to magical objects the way magpies are attracted to shiny things. Magic wands, helmets that make you invisible, boots that carry you long distances, or rings that cause you to vanish; they all use the third kind of magic, and witches crave these things for their power. Prince Obsidian had collected a trove of magical items from throughout the land. A witch wanted three of them in particular. She decided to steal them, so she traveled to his castle, disguised as an old woman."

"Crows have castles?" Suli asked doubtfully. She was watching the shadows of the clouds pass over the trees below, her own shadow moving faster. She'd never heard of a time when Crows ruled all the lands.

"It's a story," Coalfeather said. "Pay attention. When the witch appeared at the castle gate, the sentry asked her what business she had there. She smiled and turned him into a frog."

Suli looked at him skeptically. "How did she turn him into a frog?"

He flapped his wings impatiently. "It's a story. As I was saying, the witch got inside the castle and found the treasure room. She took the three magical treasures and hid them under her cloak. She stole a magic ring, a holly branch that never dies, and a cap with an eagle feather. She was leaving the castle when the Prince himself stopped her and demanded to know what she was doing there.

"The witch said, 'You don't need these things, but I do!' She vanished from sight and he heard her voice saying, 'Take me home!'

"The Prince was angered by this brazen theft, and ordered scouts to search the country for the witch. Weeks passed, and finally a little girl reported seeing the witch in the woods.

"The Prince flew there himself. He wanted to spy on her to find out how she used his treasures. He'd owned these three things without knowing what they did.

"He stayed in the woods, behaving like any other crow, watching and waiting. Finally, one morning he saw the witch go by, wearing the cap with the eagle feather. She carried the holly branch that never dies and two buckets. He flew after her, taking care not to let her see him. She stood before a great boulder. She took the holly branch and tapped the stone three times, saying, 'Water be fresh, water be free, hear my call and come to me.' At the third tap, water gushed from the stone. She collected it in the buckets. She tapped the stone once more and the water stopped, but a pool had formed on the forest floor. She picked up the buckets and carried them away.

"The Prince flew down and drank water from the pool. It was clean and good. He was amazed something so useful had lain unnoticed in his storehouse.

"He continued to watch the witch; he saw her put on the gold ring. Instantly, she disappeared. He heard rustling in a tree, and saw two blue eggs floating away from a nest. The witch was invisible. Now he knew what two of the magic objects did. The holly branch created water anywhere, and the golden ring made you invisible."

"You're going to say he stole them back now, aren't you?" Suli said smugly. They were approaching the lake, and the sound of the waterfall grew louder.

"No," Coalfeather said, "That's not how the story goes. Prince Obsidian decided to let the witch keep them. Do you know why?" he asked.

"No." She frowned.

Near the top of the mountain, Coalfeather turned and began to descend toward the lake. Suli flapped her wings to catch up.

They flew over the forest, and Coalfeather turned his head. "Let me tell you about the third object. The next day, Prince Obsidian followed the witch to the market. She still wore the cap with the eagle feather. In fact, he'd never seen her without it; she never took it off. She was chatting with a friend when a stranger approached and asked if she knew how to get to Malmio. The witch said, 'Yes, I know how to go to Malmio.' But before she could give directions, she disappeared. The cap had carried her there. When she returned, several minutes later, she was furious. She tugged and pulled at the cap, cursing all the while, but it wouldn't come off. She didn't possess the cap; the cap possessed her. She thought she'd gain power by using it; instead, she was in its power. Now do you understand?"

"No," Suli said, distracted. They were above the place in the forest where Suli had heard the witch's voice. She scanned the trees below for any sign of her. "Do you know where the witch lives?"

"Follow me," he said. He swooped low, away from the lake. A moment later, they were above a clearing. They circled a small cottage set beneath the branches of encroaching trees, but there was no sign of anything alive below.

He called, "I don't see anything. Let's go to the lake, where it's safer."

She followed him.

They circled the lake cautiously before they glided to a stop and braked, landing on the tall green grass. Suli sat, folding her wings. The lake shimmered peacefully in hazy sunlight.

Coalfeather hunched his shoulders, his head bowed in thought, and began to pace. "It's important you understand this story. Any magic that can control someone is part of the third kind of magic. When you use it, you change the balance in the world. That extra power has to come from somewhere—usually from the person using it. By using magical objects, the witch became weaker. The cap used her power in order for its magic to work."

She frowned in concentration. "What about the Voice? That's power over someone else; does that make you weaker?"

"Yes, that's the best example. When a witch uses the Voice to control someone, an imbalance is created. Magic is about cause and effect. If you create the imbalance, you face the consequences. Witches who use the Voice grow weaker."

"Then what happens?" She held her breath.

"You pay the debt. You've created an imbalance, and the power is used up. The more you use the Voice, the more it weakens your Seeing. If you're a witch and you use the Voice to control others, in time you won't be able to See or Heal. You gradually lose your abilities and you won't be able to understand what's going on around you."

Suli shivered. Why would anyone risk losing the ability to See? She relied on it all the time. Losing it would be like going blind. She hadn't realized that the third kind of magic would weaken her ability to See. She'd always thought the magic of Command was dangerous because someone more powerful could defeat you, not because it drained your own power. "Why would anyone ever use the Voice, if it's so dangerous?" Suli asked.

"Humans are tempted by power. To change how the world works or to command others is irresistible to them. That's why crows don't trust them.

"Let me tell you the end of the story. Thanks to the witch, Prince Obsidian now knew he didn't need the magical objects. The witch had saved him from trying them himself. Crows fly fast and far; we don't need a cap to go where we wish. And because we can fly, we can usually find water. And we can disappear without using a golden ring."

Coalfeather disappeared right before her eyes.

Suli inhaled sharply, staring at the grassy bank where he'd been a moment before. "Where did you go?" she called. "Come back!"

Coalfeather reappeared. "You see? I never moved. We have our own magic. We don't need magic rings."

She said admiringly, "Teach me how to do that!"

He shook his head. "We don't teach humans our magic; it's against the Law. Tala knows this skill, but she learned it by using her Seeing. If she thinks you should know it, she'll teach you." He tipped his head on one side to look at her with his shrewd black eye. "This skill is an illusion, not power over someone else. The most important lesson to learn today is that you don't need to control others. You don't need to use the third kind of magic. Use your Seeing, or animal magic, to evade, or hide from a threat. It's safer."

She wasn't sure she knew the difference between animal and human magic, and she didn't know how to use the Voice—not on purpose, anyway—so how could she understand? "Just because it's safer?" Beneath her feathers, her skin prickled in the heat. It was hard to concentrate. She stepped delicately into the water, paddling to float in place. She dunked her head to cool off, and looked back at Coalfeather.

Coalfeather walked to the edge of the bank and sighed. "I just explained this. What if a magic wand or a ring has the power to control *you* as well as other powers? That's often the case. Magical objects use the third kind of magic, and there's a price to pay. It's difficult to explain this even to crow fledglings, until they have more experience. If you must use magic, use your Seeing—and your own common sense. That's the best way. Most of the time, magic isn't necessary."

Coalfeather paced, thinking. "Perhaps if we practice, this will become clearer. I can't teach you to be invisible, but I *can* teach you to see me while I am." He bobbed his head and disappeared. "Now," his voice came from somewhere on the bank, "Change back. You must do this as a human."

Suli climbed back onto the bank and changed. She wrung the water from her dripping hem, sighing. "All right, I'm ready."

"Concentrate on what's around you. Look from the corners of your eyes. Can you find me?"

She lowered her lids and let her eyes go out of focus, squinting out of the sides of her eyes. Shapes and colors were distorted, but she saw new details, too. She glanced away from the bank where Coalfeather had been a moment before, and then back again, not looking directly at it.

"I can see you!" she exclaimed. "That wasn't even hard!"

He hopped towards her, smiling. "I thought you'd be able to do it. You already have the knack of Seeing; you just need to develop it."

"Would that work on any invisibility spell?" Suli asked, sitting down on the grass with her back to the sun. Her dress was already drying in the hot sun. "Could I see you if you used a magic ring?"

"No, that's the point," Coalfeather said. "A magic ring makes you invisible by changing you. You might discover that being changed is not a pleasant thing. The third kind of magic bends things out of their true shape..."

Some instinct made Suli turn to look behind her and use her side-Seeing to scan the edge of the forest. Coalfeather turned to see what she was looking at.

A cloaked figure had stepped out of the trees. It moved towards her, holding a sack. The figure ignored her glance, certain it was invisible.

"The witch!" Suli cried, "The witch is here!"

Realizing she'd been discovered, the witch ran toward Suli and grabbed her arm, trying to pull the sack over her head. Suli kicked at the witch's legs and scratched her hands to make her let go. "No!" she cried, trying to use the Voice, "No! Let me go!" The words had no effect. The witch was tugging the sack over her head. "Stop!" Suli called. *Why isn't it working?*

Coalfeather aimed his claws at the gleaming eyes beneath the witch's hood. "Awk! Awk!" he cried, and in a moment the air was full of crows, raking the witch's arms and hands with their claws.

Suli pulled the sack from her head. Thwarted, the witch gave a frustrated cry and ran for the trees. The crows followed, diving at her until she was hidden by the trees. Coalfeather landed beside Suli, who was breathing hard.

"We'd better warn the others," she said.

Coalfeather smiled grimly. "At least we found the witch."

12

SCRYING

"YOU WERE LUCKY," Orion said. "What possessed you to take Suli to the lake, of all places?" He sat beside Suli on the bench by Tala's kitchen door.

Coalfeather paced in the silvery dirt. He shrugged. "The witch hadn't been seen for days. Now we know she's still there." He hopped closer to Suli. "And we know that Suli cannot yet use the Voice for protection." He dropped his voice. "You need someone to teach you, Suli. I cannot do that."

She'd hoped he hadn't noticed her failure. "But you said to use animal magic instead! I don't know what I did wrong; I don't even know how I used the Voice the first time."

Coalfeather bobbed his head. "Most of the time, yes, you don't need the third kind of magic. But when you're dealing with a witch—." He made a rumbling sound. "This is why the animals rely upon wise women. Only they can use the Voice for protection."

She felt she'd let him down. She'd wanted to protect the flock and the crows, but now she knew she couldn't. Without her teacher, how could she learn? And they still didn't know where Tala was.

Coalfeather began to pace again. "Do not be too hard on yourself. You did see through the witch's invisibility spell."

"Thanks to you," she said. "And the witch would have taken me, too, if you hadn't called the crow scouts to attack her. They put themselves in danger for me, and so did you. Thank you, Coalfeather."

"I knew our scouts would see what was happening and come," he said calmly. "We weren't in danger—you were. The witch wants you, for some reason."

"Coalfeather," Suli began, "about your scouts…" She hesitated.

"What about them?"

"I bet some of them watch the house, don't they?"

Coalfeather ruffled his feathers. "Yes."

"I couldn't help noticing," she said. "Could they give us warning if the witch comes here?"

He shrugged, and his feathers fell back into place. "Perhaps. But I must ask the Council first. My father will say we're becoming human nursemaids."

"I wonder…" Orion began.

The kitchen door banged open, and a dark-haired woman in a white dress came down the steps. Suli thought she'd never seen before, but after a moment she recognized her: it was Lamisa, in human form. "Why are you all sitting out here in the dark?"

"Didn't you hear us talking? The witch almost got Suli!" Orion said.

"The witch?" Lamisa's face was pale in the grey twilight. "What do you mean? Was she here?" She came down the steps to stand in front of them.

"They were at the lake," Orion explained. "The witch tried to kidnap Suli, but the crows chased her away!"

Lamisa sat down heavily next to Suli. "By the Sisters! Hello, Coalfeather. Thank you for your help."

Coalfeather bobbed his head and said, "I have to leave, Suli. It's past time I returned to my family. I'll come tomorrow to continue your lessons. Keep an eye out for the witch!" He flew away.

"And Suli speaks Crow now?" Lamisa asked. She shook her head. "The geese told me what you've been up to while I was gone. We'll talk about it over dinner. Flying to the lake! Such foolishness! You're lucky you escaped. Come inside."

Lamisa climbed the steps, but she paused at the door and said to Suli, "The Elders have instructions for you. We'll talk after dinner." She went in.

Suli sighed and went to the pump to wash while Orion waited his turn. "Who exactly are these Elders, anyway?" she asked.

"They enforce the laws and give advice to all of Sigur's people. I suppose they're our leaders. When she finishes training, Lamisa will be an Elder, too, very important in the flock." Orion smiled. "I'm the only one here who isn't a magical mucky-muck or training to be something important."

Suli was silent. She'd assumed that Lamisa was simply another member of the flock. There was a lot she didn't know about Sigur's people. Lamisa might be more important than Tala, someday. "When did Lamisa come back? Did she tell you what the Elders said about Tala?"

Orion shook his head, drying his hands. "She arrived after you and Coalfeather flew away, and she won't say a word to me. She says you have to hear it first, since it affects you the most."

Lamisa wouldn't be rushed. All she would say during dinner was that the Elders wanted to find Tala urgently, and Suli would help them.

After dinner, the candles were snuffed and the lamp turned down to a pale glow. Suli, Lamisa, and Orion sat before the fire in the hearth. The wood crackled and popped. Shadows danced and moved around them. Suli felt sleep stealing over her.

"Do not go to sleep," Lamisa commanded. "I want you to look into the heart of the fire. Concentrate: Do not look away, do not blink. Keep staring into it until you begin to see shapes."

Suli sat up straight.

Lamisa's expression was stern, her face shadowed by the fire. "Look into the fire and see if you can find Tala."

Suli glanced at Orion. He stared down at his hands twisted together in his lap.

She forced herself to look into the fire. There was something there, in the very center. She shook her head. Why did they think she could do this?

"Look into the fire," Lamisa repeated. "Tell me what you see."

Suli blinked. In the yellow center of the orange and blue flames, shapes had appeared; Tala, and another woman she guessed was the witch. From their gestures, she saw they were arguing. She felt a strange sensation behind her eyes, like cool water in her head.

"Can you see her?" Lamisa asked.

She nodded and said hoarsely, "Yes."

"What's she doing?"

"She's arguing with someone—the witch, I think. I can't hear them."

Orion sat up. "Is she all right? Is she in danger?"

Suli looked at him curiously, "Can't you see them, too?"

Orion shook his head. "No, only a wise woman can do scrying."

She gave Lamisa a questioning look.

"No, you're not a wise woman yet, but the Elders thought you could do this. Your Seeing is better than that of many wise women with years of experience. Look back at the fire. Tell us what you see."

The feeling of cool water filled her head. She felt alert, peaceful. The tiny figures moved. She saw the witch raise her arm as though to strike Tala. But suddenly Tala wasn't there; the dark shape of a goose flew over the witch's head. "She's getting away! She's changed, and she's flying away!"

Orion stood up. "Where is she?"

Suli shook her head. "She's gone now." But something else appeared. A small figure had joined the witch. It turned, and Suli realized with a start it was herself. Suli-in-the-fire walked into the witch's house, and the witch had hold of her arm. She was living with the witch, taking her orders.

Her horror must've shown, for Lamisa asked, "Is something wrong? What else do you see?"

The vision in the fire disappeared, and the coolness behind her eyes was gone, too. "I saw two women. One changed into a goose and flew away. I don't know where they were." But she did. The witch was on the mountain, and Suli was living with her. She couldn't tell them that. Not until she decided what to do.

Lamisa smiled. "This is good news. Wherever she is, Tala is probably flying back to us right now. You did well, Suli."

"Oh, let's go to bed!" Orion said. "I'm falling over. Maybe Tala will be here in the morning."

"Maybe," said Lamisa. "But let's latch the shutters and bar the doors first. We're staying here tonight, Suli. You shouldn't be alone."

On the way to her room, Suli stopped Lamisa in the hall. "What else did the Elders say about me? How did they know I could do that?"

Lamisa glanced toward the door where Orion had disappeared and led her back to the kitchen. A faint glow outlined the face in the stove. Charred logs crumbled with a soft sound in the hearth. Her face was serious in the dim light. "If Tala doesn't come back," she said quietly, "you'll have to be the wise woman and take care of the flock without the rest of the training. You can resist the witch, and the geese can't. They gave me other instructions too, but..."

"What other instructions?"

"Let's wait and see if Tala comes back. It's better for her to decide these things."

"What things?" Suli asked.

"I've said enough. Go to bed."

Suli stumbled down the dark hall to her room, wondering what Lamisa meant. How could she be a wise woman without training? Were they just going to leave her here alone at the mercy of the witch? Strangers on the other side of the mountain thought they knew more about her abilities than she did herself. They *had* known she could scry in the fire. Everyone seemed to be telling her what to do and how to do it. They expected her to protect them, but she'd proven today that she couldn't use the Voice.

She could refuse. They were asking too much. And what if they wanted her to live with the witch? Was Tala free in the vision because she'd gone to live with the witch? Maybe *that* was what Lamisa wasn't telling her. Maybe the Elders knew that was the price to get Tala back.

She'd been sleepy in front of the fire, but Suli felt wide awake, her heart beating faster. The Elders thought she could handle the witch without Tala. After her failure at the lake, she was certain she couldn't.

She took a deep breath and lay down. If they expected her to live with the witch, well, she wouldn't do it. She'd run away first. They couldn't force her to ruin her life by living with a witch. No one could.

13

TALA RETURNS

THE NEXT MORNING, Suli was awakened by the cries of geese flying over the roof. She ran to the window and threw open the shutters. Sigur's geese were flying around the house, and there were wild geese among them. In the center flew the grey goose with the white markings on her head. Tying her dress, Suli rushed out the kitchen door.

She was coming down the steps when the entire flock landed in the yard. Lamisa and Orion were there; they must have flown to look for Tala early that morning. They changed, and then the grey goose became Tala. Her clothes were torn and dirty.

"Cousin!" Suli cried. "Welcome home."

Tala smiled, but her face was grey with exhaustion. She bent down to answer the geese's questions, the noise of their gentle honks and cries filling the yard.

"*Awk! Awk!*" Suli looked up to see Kaark and Coalfeather landing. The crowing and honking were so loud, Suli gave up trying to understand and held her hands over her ears. Tala patiently reassured everyone she was unharmed, although she looked pale and exhausted. Lamisa took her arm and pulled her toward the house, with Suli trailing behind.

Once they were inside, Suli thought, they'd hear the story of where her cousin had been. But Tala said only, "I was in a dangerous place and I got back alive, and that should be enough for now." Orion opened his mouth, but Tala raised her hand. "No more. I need to eat and sleep."

"We thought the witch held you prisoner," Orion said. "We were worried."

Tala looked grim. "I'll tell you what happened, but at a time of my own choosing."

"I'm glad you're back," Suli said. "I need to know how to fight the witch."

Tala cocked her head to one side, reminding her of Coalfeather. "May I eat first? Or do you need to know everything this minute? I've been looking forward to sleeping in my own bed for days."

Suli bit her lip and nodded, happy just to have her teacher back. She was relieved, too; now no one would ask her to live with the witch.

The four of them sat down to eat. The geese remained in the yard to be close to Tala; they no longer took her presence for granted.

After she'd finished the leftover stew and eaten a bowl of porridge, Tala pushed her bowl away, sat back, and looked around the table.

"The witch has come back," Tala announced, "and the main reason is because of Suli. She's here for you."

"What do you mean?" Suli asked, startled. "I don't even know her!"

"But she knows you: She's decided my apprentice will tell her everything she wants to know about changing and the powers of the lake."

"I don't understand."

Tala leaned forward. "The witch heard you were coming here,

so she decided to come, too. Do you remember meeting an older woman, a stranger, after it was arranged that you'd come here?"

Suli tried to think. She'd never left her village before coming to Tala's house. It had to be a stranger coming to the village, and there were so few. Then she remembered the woman at the market, a week before her birthday.

Suli was at the market with Eb to sell the pig she'd raised herself. She didn't notice the woman until she leaned over the pen to inspect Suli's young sow.

"Is she yours, young Miss?" the woman asked in a kindly voice. Suli looked up to see a woman whose age was difficult to tell, in spite the grey in her hair.

"Yes, ma'am. She comes from a long line of sows that produce good litters. We've not lost one as long as I've been alive."

"Ah. And how long is that, exactly?" the woman asked, smiling.

"I'll be twelve next week," Suli replied.

"Time to begin your apprenticeship, then. Maybe you'd like to come study with me?" the woman asked. She looked at Suli intently.

Surprised, Suli had stared at her. It was a strange thing to say. Apprenticeships were usually arranged within families. "Thank you, no, Mistress. It's already arranged." She had thought the stranger didn't need to know she was waiting to hear from the Elders.

"Ah. And who will be your teacher?" asked the stranger, who hadn't given her name as she should have.

"Suli! Here's a man who wants to buy!" Eb called, interrupting. She turned her head to look, and when she turned back the woman was gone.

Everyone around Tala's table was watching her, waiting. "Yes," Suli said aloud. "A woman came to look at my pig on market day. She said I should apprentice with her and I said, no, it was already arranged." She frowned. "But I didn't know I would be coming here. I didn't tell her your name."

"It doesn't matter," said Tala, "she already knew it. She knew your father, and she knows we're related." She sighed heavily. "Yes, it makes sense now."

Suli asked slowly, "How did the witch know my father?"

Tala met her eyes. "Your grandmother and the witch's mother are sisters, Suli. The witch is also your cousin."

"Does that mean—," Suli waited a moment to see if Tala would be angry, "—does that mean that you and she are...?"

Tala nodded. "Yes. The witch is my sister, Magda."

۽

WHILE TALA SLEPT, Suli, Lamisa, and Orion went down to the pond. The geese were excited, chattering away, going over the details of Tala's return. Suli sat on the bank watching them. They think we're safe now, she thought dully, just because Tala's back. She knew better. The witch was after her, and none of them were safe.

Lamisa and Orion, in human form, sat together nearby. They spoke in whispers, glancing at her now and then. She glared back, daring them to say something. It was like being blamed for her mother all over again. It wasn't her fault. *What do they think I'm going to do? Invite her here?* They'd known the witch was Tala's sister the whole time and hadn't told her. She'd thought they trusted her; they expected her to protect them, whether she knew how or not. And now they probably blamed her for bringing the witch back. Well, it wasn't her fault; she hadn't done anything to make the witch come. But she did feel guilty. Would everyone, including the crows, shun her when they knew why the witch was back?

"*Caw! Caw!*" sounded above her. Coalfeather landed beside

her, his black feathers glinting purple and blue in the sun. "Hello, Suli," he said.

"Hello," Suli said, not meeting his eyes. She wondered if he would blame her, too. His expression was serious. Maybe he'd already heard the news.

"Why do you look so sad? Tala is back," Coalfeather said. "I came to tell you: The Council has agreed to assign scouts to the house. With our wise woman back, we don't need so many guards to protect our nests. However, my children must be fed every hour now, and with Tala here, you don't need me, so I'll be gone for a few days. Stay away from witches!" He bobbed his head and flew away.

Suli smiled, watching him fly away. Coalfeather had told her more about magic than anyone, and he'd saved her from the witch. Kaark was a character, but she knew she could trust him, too. They were her friends. Which was more than she could say about Lamisa or Orion. They stood a few paces away, trying to catch her eye. She glared at Orion, and he came over. "We know it's not your fault the witch came back," he said softly.

She stared at the geese in the pond. "Why didn't you tell me she's Tala's sister—and my cousin?"

"Because it's none of our business," Lamisa said, joining him. "It's a family matter. There's more to the story. Your father and Magda were friends. But we don't know the details; you'd still have to ask Tala. Would you really have wanted to know, without Tala to explain?"

She hung her head, feeling confused. "Yes. It's my family, after all." But she spoke softly, and she didn't look up when they walked away.

She watched the geese in the pond, remembering that the witch had called her *Dafyd's daughter* in the forest. She'd forgotten that until now.

For the first time since she'd come to Weatherstone, Suli wondered about her father's life with the flock.

14

PRINCESS FIG

SULI SAT on an old grain sack to protect her dress from the dirt while she worked in the garden. Her dolls sat beside her to keep her company. Everything would be fine, now that Tala was home. She inhaled the scent of the yellow roses on the fence and picked up the doll in the blue dress.

"Good morning, Scarlet," Suli said, the doll in blue dancing to greet the red one. Princess Fig was visiting her friend, Princess Scarlet Runner Bean. Fig dismounted from her silver horse in the garden surrounding Scarlet's castle. The horse walked away to crop grass and eat roses.

"How have you been, my dear?" Fig inquired.

"Just terrible! The castle is at sixes and sevens," Scarlet replied. "The goblin escaped the dungeon and he's overturned tables and broken crockery in the kitchen, and thrown pillows and blankets out of my bedroom window!"

"Goodness! Can't your Hero stop it?" Fig asked.

"We don't *have* a Hero right now! The last one left when he was offered his own castle, thank you very much!"

Fig thought for a moment. She walked over to where an elder bush grew by a low wall. She whispered something to the bush, and cut a stick from it. "You and I will make the goblin return to the dungeon together," she said.

"But we're princesses!" said Scarlet, who was a bit timid.

"It's your castle, isn't it?" Fig said.

"But how?"

"Let's find out what it wants."

They went through the palace's kitchen door, in search of the goblin.

It wasn't hard to find. They could hear the sound of a terrible commotion coming from the Library. The goblin was ripping up books and throwing them in the air while the housemaid tried to stop him. "Whee!" the goblin cackled. "Whee! I'm free, and I can do anything I like!"

Fig surveyed the scene before her. Books with broken spines, their pages torn out, lay in piles all over the floor. A few had been thrown through the window to land in the box hedge outside. The goblin grinned, exposing green pointed teeth. He was bald as an egg, and his sagging grey skin looked as though it had lain at the bottom of a pond for weeks. He wore a grimy old tablecloth.

"Stop this at once!" Fig roared. She had a very loud voice, as her parents had often remarked.

"Ha! A little Princess! Why should I?" The goblin leaned over her with a nasty grin. His breath smelled of dead rats and pond scum.

"Because if you don't, I shall trap you forever inside a book and keep you in the library to pay for this. You won't be able to groan or wail or rattle chains or *be a nuisance in any way*!" The last words were said so softly that none but the goblin heard it.

The goblin looked at her in surprise. He asked doubtfully, "You can't really do that, can you? You're a Princess!"

Suli, as Princess Fig, smiled mysteriously and said, "I have magical powers. I can brew secret potions, and I know a spell to trap you inside any object I name. The great wizard Mirador was my tutor. If you defy me, your life will be nothing but a sad whimpering inside a book. Do you defy me?" Fig raised the stick of elder wood before the goblin's face.

The goblin stepped back. He hadn't known any Princesses besides Scarlet, who always cried and ran away every time he groaned at her. This little creature with the menacing wand wasn't afraid of him at all; perhaps he should do what she said.

"No! Princess, I don't defy you. Please don't trap me in a book!" the goblin pleaded, cowering.

Fig nodded haughtily. "Very well. Return to your dungeon, and I won't punish you. But if you leave it again, I shall come back and put you in a stone and throw you in the duck pond!"

The goblin raised his hands. "No, Mistress, please! I'll go back to the dungeon. I quite like it, you know. It's dank and dark, and there are lovely chains to rattle. I only wanted to see what it was like out here."

Suli pointed the wand at him.

"But I'm going!" he said hastily. The goblin hurried back to the dungeon. The two Princesses, and the butler, and the maid gathered the books together to inspect the damage.

"I wish you had a spell to repair the books," said Scarlet sadly. "Some of them are ruined—the pages are torn to bits!"

"I do know a spell," Fig said. She frowned in concentration.

Her friend blinked. She'd thought Fig's talk of spells was all bluff. Did she really know magic?

Fig picked up the cover of a book that had lost its pages. Suli waved her stick saying, "*Repair yourselves!*"

Pieces of paper flew from every corner of the room and joined together. Finally, they dived at the spine of the cover and inserted themselves neatly inside. The book was good as new.

The faces of the butler and the maid went pale. Fig smiled her mysterious smile and said, "I really did have a wizard for a tutor, you know."

Scarlet nodded dumbly, her eyes wide.

"So let's fix the rest of the books!" Fig turned to the next one in the pile.

A shadow blotted out the library.

Tala was standing over her. "Is that what you think magic is?" she asked. "Presto with a wand and everything is fixed?"

Suli was embarrassed to be caught playing with dolls. "Well, that's how it is in fairy tales," she said. "It's only a story."

Tala snorted. "People want to believe magic will cure everything, but the opposite is true. Magic might cause even more problems. Can you think why?"

Suli flushed red. "But you've barely taught my any magic at all! How would I know?"

Tala's eyebrows rose. "Really? I thought I had."

Suli thought, this wasn't the third kind of magic, so what was the problem? She folded her arms and asked, "Why would magic cause a problem?"

"Because you don't know what the unintended consequences might be," Tala said. "For example, those books in your story. If a book is smart enough to repair itself, what else could it do? How did it know which pages belonged to it? You gave the book intelligence and self-awareness. If a book has both of those things, do you think it will let you carry it around to read it? What if it doesn't want you to?"

She blinked. "But—the spell was only supposed to do one thing!"

"That's just it. You thought the spell did one thing, but you gave an object magical powers."

She remembered Coalfeather's stories about magical objects and suddenly thought she understood. "You don't know what it might do."

"Exactly," Tala said. "That's why using the third kind of magic is dangerous. You can't always foresee what you might set in motion."

Suli shaded her eyes to see Tala's face. Tala was constantly warning her and making gloomy pronouncements; why couldn't she explain things properly? "Well, I'm in no danger. I don't know *how* to do the third kind of magic."

Tala did not smile. "You will. Tomorrow, you'll finally get your wish. I'll teach you to use the Voice."

15

ANIMAL MAGIC

THAT NIGHT, when Suli came inside to set the table, Tala told her they would talk about the different kinds of magic after supper. "You must know the dangers before I teach you to use the Voice tomorrow."

Suli stopped setting out bowls to look at her. "Coalfeather warned against using the third kind of magic. He said to use animal magic instead. But then he said there was no other way to protect against a witch, and that's why wise women must use it."

"Did he teach you any animal magic?" Tala asked, raising an eyebrow. "I thought that was against their law."

She could See through the invisibility spell, but that wasn't the same as knowing how to do it. "No," she admitted.

"To stop a witch you must use the Voice. Seeing isn't enough. But before you learn it, you must understand the risks." Tala turned back to the stove.

Suli finished setting the table with clammy hands. At least both her teachers agreed about the risks of using the Voice.

Orion and Lamisa came in and sat at the kitchen table, talking quietly. Suli sat down across from them and they fell silent, not meeting her eyes. So they did blame her.

Tala brought the food to the table and said a blessing. They ate in silence.

Orion stole glances at Suli, but when she tried to catch his eye, he looked away.

"Do you think Magda will come after you here?" Orion asked Tala, when the silence grew oppressive.

Tala swallowed before replying. "I doubt it. She and I have the same argument over and over. She knows she won't hear anything different from me. But Suli must be careful; she shouldn't go anywhere alone."

Orion threw her a worried glance. Lamisa got up to do the dishes and Orion went to help. When they were done, they said goodnight and left.

Suli put a pillow on the hard chair close to the fire. The smell of wood smoke reminded her of evenings at her grandmother's house. She felt a rush of homesickness, and wondered what Eb and Grandmother were doing at that moment. She looked out the window. The mountain was a black silhouette in the window, framed against pale blue bands hanging in the western sky. Birds called as they settled in the trees to roost. She felt a long way from home.

Tala sat opposite her, in the rocking chair. The fire crackled, the scent of apple wood filling the room. Tala rocked slowly, matching the rhythm of her words to the motion of the chair. "You mentioned animal magic. Animals are skilled at sensing and watching what goes on around them. Our ancestors learned from them, by observing them in turn. The skills of illusion, concealment, and changing shape are all old animal magic. You can learn these skills, too, by observing them."

"Coalfeather said animal magic is safer."

"Animal magic doesn't try to control others; it's for camouflage or escape. Most human magic is safe, too. Seeing usually does no harm. Healing *does* change the other animal or plant, but in a helpful way. Command, or the third kind of magic, interferes with the way things are. That's where the danger lies.

"But I'm getting ahead of myself," Tala said. "The first kind of magic is basic Seeing, the art of looking into the hearts of others, to know whether someone lies or intends harm. Every girl in the villages should know how to do this."

Suli nodded.

"The second kind of magic is Healing. If you become very skilled, you will See how water, earth, animals, and plants work together. When you use your Seeing to care for animals and plants or people, that's Healing."

Suli nodded impatiently. She already knew this.

"The third kind of magic is not taught to everyone," Tala said, "and for good reason. Command is dangerous in the hands of someone who wants power for its own sake. If you use Command to control or hurt others, you become a witch."

Suli swallowed. "So your sister, Magda—"

"Was taught the third kind of magic, as I was, but instead of helping others, she chose to force others do her will," Tala said harshly.

The wood popped, and the flames made a hissing sound. Suli shifted uneasily on her chair. "Coalfeather says anyone who uses the third kind of magic loses the ability to See. Why would anyone risk that? If I lost my Seeing, I'd be frightened."

"It depends. If you use the Voice to harm someone—then yes, it drains your power. If you use it to help or protect someone, there's little risk. You're *blocking* or *stopping* the misuse of power. Wise women must risk something for their power."

Suli bit her lip. Then she asked what worried her most. "How will I know if I'm using it to harm? How can I be sure?"

"A good question. Seeing reveals how things work. It's practical knowledge. But there's also energy, a power that comes from doing things the right way. The energy of Seeing is like water bubbling up from a spring. If you don't use it correctly, the spring runs dry. And if you twist this energy, the way a witch does, you run the risk of losing it completely. A witch loses even the most basic Seeing; in time, she can't understand what's going on around her. Then all that's left is to try to control everything. Do you understand?"

Suli thought she didn't want to use the Voice, ever. But Tala said she had to, to protect everyone. That was why she'd come here. "So if I use the Voice against the witch, what will happen to my Seeing?"

Tala smiled faintly. "As long as you're doing it to protect yourself or someone else, nothing. The third kind of magic relies upon Seeing, too; you See what someone desires or fears, and you create illusions to attract or frighten them. If you use that to control the thoughts and actions of others, you're on the wrong path. A witch."

Suli released the breath she'd been holding. "Is that what happened to your sister?"

Tala didn't answer, but stared into the fire. An owl called softly to its mate in the giant fir, and the wind brushed the branches of a tree against the house. Suli was growing too hot; she shifted her chair further from the fire.

"Let's talk about the Voice," Tala said softly. "The Voice makes your listener feel safe; that's when you slip inside their mind to take control. Sometimes this is necessary to help the listener, but Magda does this to harm." Tala said the last words as though they hurt her. "You've resisted it once, but to protect yourself and others, you must to learn to block it completely." She leaned back, her chair still, as though she'd finished what she had to say. Shadows cast by the fire deepened the lines in her face, and there was sadness in her eyes.

"But…I got away from her Voice," Suli said. "I saw through the sweetness. I knew it wasn't real. Is that what you mean?"

Tala nodded. "Partly. But she didn't yet know what you want, so you had no reason to believe her. What if she offered to teach you everything she knows about magic, to answer all your questions; would you have listened?"

Suli rubbed her eyes, and tried to think. It was true she wanted to know more than Tala had told her. "I don't know," she said. "I wouldn't trust the witch now that I know what she is, but if I had just met her—I might."

Tala nodded. "That's the problem, to learn when to be on guard. At the market, you were listening to her, and you would've been in danger if your brother hadn't interrupted you. You were too trusting of strangers then."

"So how do I know when not to listen?"

"You already know. You simply have to pay attention and you weren't at the market. The Voice, and the stories it weaves, can confuse and distract you. That's what I'll teach you first—to see through the Voice, so you can protect the flock, the crows, and the wild geese, too."

Suli glanced at her teacher and saw she was smiling. "Orion told me about your trip to the wild geese. That was good thinking, to try to gain their help, though you shouldn't have tried to use the Voice. I'm proud you helped Timber's daughter. That's what a wise woman would do."

A warm feeling spread through her. Tala had never praised her before.

Tala rose from her chair. "I need to sleep. There's something I'd like you to do before you go to bed."

"Yes, Cousin?"

"I'd like you to apologize to Orion and Lamisa tonight. It wasn't their fault they didn't tell you about Magda. I told them not to interfere in my family business, and they did as I asked. If you're going to be angry, be angry with me. But part of your training is to understand why I didn't want to tell you right away. Wise women have to be careful what they reveal to others."

Suli frowned at her, trying to decide what she felt about being kept in the dark. Sometimes she thought Tala used "it's part of your training" as an excuse to do as she pleased. She sighed. It didn't matter. She had to obey Tala in order to learn. "Yes, Cousin." She walked to the door.

"Suli?"

"Yes?" She turned.

"I'm sorry, too. I should have told you sooner." Tala shook her head. "I thought I was protecting you, but now I know that's not what you need."

Suli smiled. "Thank you, Cousin."

16

THE VOICE

THE NEXT MORNING, Suli waited on the bench outside the kitchen door. The glare of the white overcast sky hurt her eyes, so she kept her eyes on the ground. She imagined running away. Now she knew that by using the third kind of magic, she'd be controlling others against their will, and risking her ability to See. She'd thought she'd be triumphant when she finally learned how to fight a witch. Now that the time had come to use the Voice, she was afraid she'd fail, or worse, that she'd succeed and the flock would never trust her again. And she could lose her Seeing.

Tala came down the steps to stand before her. "I'll start by using the Voice on you, so you know what it's like," she said. "Remember, I'm trying to change your thoughts and feelings. Pay attention to that."

Suli nodded, determined not to let Tala know she was afraid.

Tala spoke softly, her voice rising and falling.

Suli couldn't quite hear the words. She rose to her feet and walked across the yard to the rain barrel. She took the ladle, dipped it in the water, and drank.

Tala called, "Please come back. We're not finished."

Surprised to find herself by the barrel, Suli walked back. "I'm sorry, Cousin, I don't know how I got there. I must've been thirsty," she said.

"Did you notice what I said to you?"

Suli looked down and shook her head. "I couldn't understand you."

Tala smiled wryly. "That's because you confused my words with your own thoughts. I said you were thirsty and you needed a drink of water from the barrel."

"I didn't even hear the words!" She'd failed already and hadn't even noticed.

"Let's try again," said Tala. "Focus on the words and try to block out the rhythm of my voice."

Tala's murmuring sounded like water chuckling over stones in a stream. Suli fought to concentrate. This time, she caught a word or two. But when her cousin stopped speaking, she was standing on one leg, her arms held out for balance, with no memory of how that happened. She lowered her leg and said gloomily, "I thought I understood more words this time."

Tala nodded. "It takes time and practice. You didn't do the first thing I suggested—to twirl in a circle, so there's hope." A smile flickered on her face. "You'll get better. Again."

They practiced for the rest of the morning. Tala murmured in a soft, melodious voice, and Suli tried to resist her suggestions. By the time the sun was overhead, she was hungry, tired, and frustrated. It felt as though she'd been fighting the Voice for days. Tala said they'd take a break to eat. "Although you should learn to resist when you're tired and hungry, too, when your resistance is lowest. But perhaps not on the first day."

Suli washed at the pump and walked down to the stream to retrieve the jug of lemonade cooling there. Orion brought a fish he'd been cooking on a grill by the pond, and Lamisa joined them. The four sat down to a meal of freshly picked greens from the garden and Orion's fish.

"So Tala's teaching you the Voice?" Orion asked, before swallowing a large mouthful of fish.

"Orion! You shouldn't talk about it," Lamisa scolded.

"Why not? Everyone knows. The crows will talk of nothing else. They say Suli is learning to be a witch!"

"They can't really believe that," Suli said. "It must be one of Kaark's jokes."

"No, I think they're worried. They don't trust humans at the best of times, and they know Tala is teaching you advanced magic," Orion said.

"Well, I'll tell Coalfeather it's all nonsense. He'll…" Suli began.

"It's not nonsense," Tala interrupted.

"What do you mean?" Suli asked.

"It's not nonsense for them to worry about what I'm teaching you," Tala repeated.

"But you're not teaching me to be a witch!"

"Nevertheless, don't say anything that might appear to be a lie. What I'm teaching you *is* the same as what the witch does, so better you don't say anything at all. Let them wait and see. Actions speak louder than words." Tala sipped her lemonade.

Suli frowned. "But I don't know how to—"

"Not yet," said Tala. "But after our nap, you'll use the Voice. This is important. You need to know how it feels, from both sides. You may have to use it to protect the flock someday—as well as those blessed crows!"

Lamisa and Orion glanced at each other and then kept their eyes on their bowls until they'd finished eating.

Suli went to her room, but couldn't sleep. She lay on her bed, staring at the leafy shadows on the wall. What would the crows think when they saw her use the Voice?

When she rose from her nap, Tala was waiting outside. "Ready for the next lesson? Good. Let's go down to the pond." Tala strode down the path, her sandals leaving whorled patterns in the dirt.

Suli followed, running to keep up. "Why the pond?" she asked breathlessly.

"I want you to use the Voice on the geese. They've agreed to let you practice on them."

Suli's stomach twisted and she fell behind, walking slowly. The geese had lost friends and family because of the Voice. Entire families had disappeared. How would they feel if she used it on them? How could they trust her again?

Tala was at the bottom of the hill. Suli ran to catch up and joined her reluctantly. Most of the flock huddled at the far side. Lamisa, Orion, Wilo, and Flax floated by the bank, waiting for them.

"Orion has volunteered to go first," said Tala briskly. "Come out, please, so Suli can focus on you."

Orion climbed out of the water, and stood waiting a few feet away from Suli, the water dripping from his feathers. He tilted his head to one side, waiting.

"Now remember what I told you. Notice what they want the most. Then use that to suggest why they want to do what you say. It's as if you are singing a lullaby to charm them to sleep. The rise and fall of your voice relaxes them. Suggest something that will help him, something for his own good. Like this."

Tala began to chant in a singsong way, but more slowly than before, so Suli could hear it. "Now you try."

Suli nodded and tried to imitate Tala's chant. She told Orion he was safe; he was floating in the pond under a blue sky, and everything was wonderful. She murmured on, telling him to change and jump into the pond.

And suddenly, he did. Orion changed into a boy and jumped into the pond. He stood in the shallow water, his breeches wet, staring at Suli in surprise. "What happened?" he asked.

"I told you to change and jump in the water," Suli said, afraid of his reaction.

"Oh," he said.

One by one, Suli used the Voice on Lamisa, then Flax, then Wilo. Wilo resisted the longest; she was the oldest of the flock, and had the most experience. But she, too, drifted off to sleep when Suli suggested it.

After Wilo fell asleep, Suli sat down on the grass, not meeting anyone's eye. She felt dirty, contaminated by the Voice. Tears stung her eyes. She didn't want to be like the witch, and now she was.

Hidden within the bulrushes a few feet away, Coalfeather was almost invisible, but she knew he was there. She wondered if he'd ever speak to her again, now that she'd proven she was a witch.

"You did very well," Tala said quietly. "I didn't expect you to control everyone so well on your first try. If you need to protect yourself or the flock, now you know you can."

She looked up. Tala was a dark outline against the white sky. "It's wrong!" Suli said thickly. "And it feels awful."

Tala knelt down and took Suli's hands in hers. She looked into her eyes and said, "Yes, it is. And it's good that you know that. But sometimes you have to do something that feels wrong to prevent something even worse from happening. Come back to the house."

Tala stood and said loudly, "I'm grateful for your help, Orion, Lamisa, Wilo, and Flax. Suli will be able to protect us all, some-day. You've helped her learn. Thank you."

They climbed the path. Suli glanced over her shoulder, wishing she could talk to the geese. She searched the reeds for Coalfeather, but didn't see him. The geese floated together, talking softly amongst themselves, casting sidelong glances at her. She turned and followed Tala up the path.

At the house, Tala sat down on the bench by the door and gestured for Suli to sit beside her. She waited a moment, her eyes on the blue hills in the distance. "I know you're upset. You fear becoming like the witch, but that's not what I'm teaching you. The Outsiders say this is witchcraft and dangerous, but they're wrong. This is what wise women have always done to protect others. Your grandmother didn't send you here to become a witch. Or do you think she did?" Tala turned to look at her.

Suli answered reluctantly. "No. But I still don't understand why—"

"I've explained this," Tala said. "If you went to the village and used the Voice on a woman in the market to get your loaf of bread for free, that would be wrong, and would make you a witch, or at least set you on the road to becoming one."

Tala's voice grew husky. "Or if you convinced the geese they were never human and must hide to escape danger—." She broke off, clearing her throat. There were tears in her eyes.

"Is that what happened to the rest of the flock?"

Tala nodded. "Magda said as much. She told them they had to hide with her or be killed."

Suli frowned. "Why? Why would she do that? The Voice feels evil. *She* must be evil."

Tala shook her head. "May I remind you that you have used the Voice twice now when provoked? Were you evil, too? What about now?"

Shocked, Suli didn't know what to say.

Tala said quietly, "Magda didn't use to be evil. Once she was just like you or I. But she's bitter, angry after all these years at your father and at me. She doesn't seem to care about anybody except herself. I still hope one day she'll realize her mistake."

"Why is she angry with my father? He's dead."

Tala took a deep breath. "She's angry at those who can change, because she can't. She's angry with me most of all because your father was her best friend until he learned to change; then he spent all his time flying with me. We had all played together before that, you see. But when we learned to change, we separated from those who couldn't fly. Dafyd spent all his flying. Magda said I stole Dafyd away from her, but that wasn't true. The truth was," she said with a sad smile, "that your father loved flying more than anything else."

"More than he loved my mother? More than he loved Eb and me?" she asked. Her grandmother never would talk about him.

"Perhaps not more than he loved you," Tala said, "but he loved it more than his safety."

"The witch didn't..." Suli began. A terrible thought had occurred to her.

Tala shook her head. "No, no. Magda had nothing to do with your father's death. We think he was shot by hunters while flying with the Free Folk." Tala reached out and touched her hand briefly.

Suli's father had died because he loved to fly. That was sad, but it had happened a long time ago, when she was small. She was more surprised than sad. Tala was finally telling her what she wanted to know, and she didn't know what she should feel. Her father and the witch had been best friends, but when he'd learned to change, he left her to fly all the time, even with the wild geese. And Magda still blamed Tala.

"If the witch hates you because you can change, then she must hate me, too, because of my father," Suli said. "And because I can change."

Tala pursed her lips. "I don't know. She was angry with your father for leaving her behind, but I don't think she hated him. He married your mother, you and Eb were born, then one day he didn't come back. This was a long time ago."

"But you said she came back to Blue Mountain because of me," Suli pointed out. "Maybe she wants to revenge on me, because of my father."

Tala rose to pace slowly. "Magda wants to learn my secrets from you," she said heavily. "But her anger is still directed at me. She wants to use you to hurt me."

That didn't sound better than being hated. "How did the

witch trap you?" Suli asked. She was afraid the flow of answers would dry up. "Did she use the Voice?"

Tala looked grim. "She tried, but the Voice doesn't work on me. If you practice long enough, it won't work on you, either." She stood still. "I suppose you need to know, in case she tries the same thing. I searched the forest to see if I could free Orion and Lamisa. I didn't want to fight Magda, but I'd vowed I'd never let her hurt the flock again. She used Lamisa and Orion as bait, knowing I'd come. She trapped me a pit, in one of the hidden valleys. She caught me with a net, not magic."

"Why didn't you change and fly away?"

"The net was tied down tight with ropes. She planned it thoroughly. Human or goose, I couldn't escape the net, and she never came close enough for me to use the Voice. No one saw me in that pit."

"How did you get away?"

"The mice of Blue Mountain found me. They gnawed through the ropes and took a message to the Free Folk. Timber and others came to help; they lifted the net, and I flew away with them. Thank the Sisters she let Orion and Lamisa go without harming them."

"They should have helped you!" Suli said.

"They didn't know where I was. Don't be too hard on them. They're much more vulnerable to the witch's powers than you or I. Remember that; not everyone can do what we can. It's our responsibility to protect others, not the other way round." Tala sat down again, adding, "When you're fully trained, you'll be responsible for protecting the flock.

"Now," Tala said briskly, folding her arms, "if I've answered your questions, let's talk about how you felt when you used the Voice. You must use it when you have to, or you'll be at the mercy of bad folk. That includes people who think wise women are witches. Promise me," she looked at her sharply, "that you will use it to defend yourself, the flock, or any animal in trouble.

Being a wise woman means protecting those who can't protect themselves."

Suli looked away. She didn't want to promise, not yet; the Voice felt wrong. She hadn't understood that to fight a witch, she'd have to use the same magic the witch used. She didn't want to use the Voice.

But that was why she was here. She sighed and met Tala's eyes. "I promise. I'll protect myself, the flock, and other animals from the witch, even if it means using Voice. But is that all I need to know about the third kind of magic?"

"Of course not," Tala said. "But the rest can wait until tomorrow."

17

THE OUTSIDERS

Light spread across the mountain slopes above Suli. The leaves of the apple tree and bean stalks glowed, touched by the rising sun. Suli inhaled the spicy scent of chrysanthemums, and felt something was different that morning. Maybe she was different. She picked up the doll lying in the dirt, its blue dress soaked with dew. "If you use the same magic the witch does, what does that make you?" she asked Princess Fig. The doll stared blankly, offering no opinion.

Using the Voice felt wrong, but wise women needed it. If she had to choose between letting the witch hurt someone and losing her ability to See, she'd use the Voice. If the witch came today, she'd fight her. She finally knew how. But understanding the risk and accepting it didn't mean she *wanted* to use it.

"Caw!" Kaark and Coalfeather landed on the grass beside her.

"Are you still speaking to me?" Suli asked, pleased.

Kaark sang in his creaky voice:

> Grickle grackle grickle,
> Crows aren't fickle.
> Eating fruit or flies,

Crows use their eyes.
Hopping, eating, flying
Crows know truth from lying!

He stopped singing and tilted his head to look at her.

"Does that mean you know I'm not a witch?" Suli asked.

"We're still your friends, Suli," Kaark said. "Even though you act like a witch." He laughed harshly.

"That's not funny," she said.

"Ignore him," Coalfeather said. "He's trying to provoke you."

She felt a flash of anger. It wasn't something to joke about. But before she could reply, Kaark flew away.

Coalfeather turned his bright eye on her. "Crows will trust you, witch Suli," he cackled loudly, strutting across the dirt in imitation of his father.

She laughed and threw a handful of grass at him. He hopped away.

"*Don't* become like your father," she said, leaning back on her hands. "I couldn't stand it."

"Luckily, that's not possible," Coalfeather said dryly. "Ignore him. Believe it or not, he wants you to learn as much as you can, as quickly as you can."

"I'll try," Suli said. "So you'll still teach me?"

"That's why I'm here."

🐦

TWO WEEKS PASSED, and except for the occasional lesson with Coalfeather, Suli hardly left Tala's side. When Suli asked why she had to learn so quickly, Tala told her to keep her mind on her lessons.

She learned charms to keep insects away and which plants would clear water to make it drinkable. She learned to perform illusions that would fool ordinary folk—but not a wise woman—

and different ways to use the Voice. Then Tala changed her mind, and said she should learn to talk to animals.

"You mean all animals speak one language?" Suli asked, excited.

Tala sat on the bench in the yard, knitting a shawl in grey and green wool. "No," Tala said, counting the rows. "Pidgin is the common language all animals use to talk to each other. Each has their own language among their own kind, but when a mouse wants to talk to a crow, he uses the pidgin. Once you know it, you can speak to anyone in an emergency."

"Oh," Suli said. The idea of talking to any animal she wished was wonderful, but what emergency was Tala expecting? There seemed to be something she wasn't saying.

"I'll give you the basics, but we don't have time for you to practice as you should. I only hope you'll remember it if you need it."

A prickle of fear crawled down the back of her neck when Tala said things like that. Tala kept hinting that they didn't have much time, but wouldn't explain why. She was too busy counting her stitches to notice Suli's worried expression.

Suli had thought she'd be happy and proud once she learned advanced magic; instead, she was worried. "It's as if she knows she isn't going to be here," she told Coalfeather during one of their lessons. "As though she were going away. What do you think?"

Coalfeather tucked his head under his wing to preen. She thought he was hiding his expression while he decided what to tell her.

They were sitting by the pond at sunset, watching the geese swim. Tala said it was important she continue to learn from Coalfeather, and they had an hour to talk before dinner. Suli sat on the bank, her feet tucked beneath her. Autumn was coming and the nights were growing cool. She closed her eyes, savoring the earth and water smells of the pond.

Coalfeather's head emerged from beneath his wing, and he spoke carefully. "There's been trouble in a village nearby; a witch-hunt. Once they start, they always find at least one, whether there are any real witches or not."

Suli shifted uneasily. The prickle of fear on her neck was back. "Will they arrest Magda?"

"I don't know. These Outsiders don't understand about magic. They make mistakes. They're just as likely to arrest Tala. You need to be careful, Suli. If anyone asks you about Tala or her teaching, don't say anything."

Her breath stopped in her throat, and her heart beat fast. The orange disc of the sun sank behind the far hills and blue shadows stretched across the pond, turning the air cold. Tala had said the same thing, that the Outsiders couldn't tell the difference between magic and witchcraft. That meant no one was safe, not even Tala.

Only a few months ago, Suli would have written to the witch Investigator herself if she thought Tala was a witch. Now she knew the world was more complicated than she'd imagined. She'd been foolish to believe the Outsiders understood magic.

"Don't worry," Coalfeather said. "The trouble may not come here, and if it does, Tala is the greatest wise woman in the villages. She won't let harm come to you. And you've done very well yourself. You escaped the witch without training, and you can see through crow magic. You can use the Voice if you have to. You may not believe it, but you're already a skilled wise woman yourself. Don't forget that you can use the Voice. You may need it to save yourself, or the rest of us, from the witch."

Suli might lose her teacher again. She couldn't catch her breath. "But I'm still an apprentice!"

Coalfeather nodded. "I know, you're young and haven't had much time to practice. But you have allies. If Tala is taken away, the crows will help. Even the Free Folk will help us, when my father tells them he trusts you, and that Dafyd was your father."

Suli was silent. Despite her fear, she was touched. When Coalfeather had said "help us" instead of "help you," something inside of her relaxed. The crows were on her side.

❧

That evening, Lamisa made a soup that smelled wonderfully of garlic and spices, and Orion built a fire on the hearth. Tala went outside to check the bread in the beehive-shaped oven. Suli laid the table. Here was her chance. She went to Lamisa and asked softly, "Have you heard of a witch hunt in a nearby village?"

Orion was stacking wood by the stove and turned to look at her. "How did you hear about it?"

"Coalfeather told me."

Orion glanced at Lamisa.

"You should ask Tala about this," Lamisa said. "It's not for us to discuss."

Suli's face grew hot. They were shutting her out again, just as they'd done about Magda. "I'm tired of your secrecy," she said. "I don't even know whether to trust you."

"You can trust us," Orion said in a reasonable tone, "but we aren't your teacher, and we don't know anything about witch finders. Ask Tala."

"Ask me what?" Tala said, coming through the door with a basket. The fresh-baked loaves filled the air with the tantalizing aroma of warm bread. Orion's stomach growled.

Suli stammered, "There's a witch hunt in a village nearby."

"Hmph!" said Tala. "Lamisa, bring the soup. Orion, Suli, sit down. We're ready to eat."

When everyone was seated, Tala said the blessing. She broke off a piece of bread, the fragrant steam rising in her face, and passed the basket to Lamisa. "So what is this about hunting witches?"

Suli kept her eyes on the embroidered pattern on the tablecloth. "They say an Investigator is here looking for witches. Did you hear about that?"

"Yes," Tala said curtly. "But it's not your concern."

"But you said yourself the Outsiders can't tell the difference between magic and witchcraft," she argued. "What if they come here and decide you're a witch, and you're teaching me witchcraft?" Once she'd said it, she knew that was her worst fear.

"They won't bother about you, Suli, you're too young. As for me," Tala said, "we won't borrow trouble by worrying. If it happens, it happens."

"But shouldn't we have a plan? I want to know what to do!" Suli protested.

Tala spoke gently. "I meant what I said. You don't have to worry. It's my job to protect you and the rest of the flock. If I think you need to be involved, I'll tell you. Right now your job is to learn as much as you can, as quickly as you can. Will you promise to do that?"

Her mouth was dry. She nodded. Tala hadn't reassured her at all.

"Good," Tala said. They ate the rest of the meal in silence.

Orion rose to take the dishes to the sink and Tala said, "I'll be teaching Suli before the fire tonight. We'll do the dishes. Thank you both for all your help."

Lamisa and Orion looked surprised. Lamisa joined Orion at the door. "Good night, Suli. Don't worry."

Suli smiled weakly at both of them. "Good night, Lamisa, Orion. I'm sorry."

Orion smiled. "See you tomorrow."

When the last bowl was set out to dry, Suli sat in her chair by the fire. Tala was rocking slowly across from her.

"Let's work on your scrying," Tala said.

18

THE INVESTIGATOR

THE NEXT DAY, Tala worked Suli as hard as ever and said no more about the rumors. At odd moments, Suli would remember Tala might be arrested, and she'd forget what she was doing. She did everything Tala asked, but all the while her fears grew.

They spent the morning outside while Tala explained how to read signs that foretold the weather.

"I've been waiting for a good day for this, and I've been rewarded," Tala said dryly. The damp, cool air smelled of wet earth. Dark clouds piled against the mountain and the sky grew dark. A flash of lightning appeared above them on the mountain, followed by the crack of thunder. The wind pressed their skirts against their legs, then veered, setting the skirts flapping.

"The storm's almost here," said Tala. "Did you notice how the clouds darkened and changed shape? Let's be inside before the rain begins. It's time to eat anyway."

Suli nodded and ran to the stream to get the milk jug. As she bent over the rushing water to pull it out, a bird screamed in the branches above her. She straightened and saw Coalfeather and a blue jay arguing loudly. To her surprise, she understood them both; the jay spoke Crow, but with an accent.

"No, I won't!" he screeched at Coalfeather.

"You should tell her—it could be important!" Coalfeather insisted.

"It's not my business. I probably shouldn't have told you! What humans do to each other is none of my concern," the jay said. It leapt from branch to branch as though searching for the best place to scold Coalfeather.

Coalfeather extended his wings and called, "Really? These humans can protect us from the witch's Voice—that protects your babies as much as mine. You should be grateful, you cranky old gossip!"

"Well, I like that! See if I say another word!" And with that, the blue jay took off into the air, screeching as it went.

Suli called to Coalfeather, perched on the branch of a linden tree. "What was that about?"

Coalfeather was a dark shape against the green leaves, swaying with the branch in the wind. He looked worried. "It may be nothing, but I want to speak with Tala right away." He launched himself off the branch and flew toward the house.

"He could've told me, too," she grumbled as she struggled to lift the heavy jug from the stream. "I thought we were friends."

Suli climbed the hill, cradling the jug in her arms. She was several yards from the house when the rain began, fat drops sending puffs of dust to hang in the air until the rain was pelting down. Coalfeather was on the kitchen windowsill. She ran the last few feet to the kitchen door, just as he flew away. She set the jug on the table, grateful to be out of the rain. "What did Coalfeather tell you?" she asked Tala, out of breath.

"You'd better change your dress," her teacher said, stirring a pot on the stove.

Suli ran to her room and put on her blue wool dress and brown leggings, and threw a shawl over her shoulders. In the kitchen, she hung the wet dress over the stove. The rain pounded on the roof, drowning out other sounds. Tala sat waiting for her at the table.

Suli sat at the table, and Tala said the blessing. The rich smell of wet earth and grass came through the window, sharpening the flavors of the cold potatoes and the vegetable soup. Suli stole glances at Tala's face while she ate. When Tala stopped eating to watch the downpour through the open window, she asked, "What did Coalfeather tell you?"

"Finish eating. I'll tell you after I decide what to do."

Suli sighed and finished her food in silence. Then she pushed back from the table. "Have you decided yet?"

Tala frowned and dropped her spoon into the empty bowl. "Yes. Don't worry. It may sound worse than it is."

Suli bit her lip. Tala's reassuring words made her more afraid.

"The jay told Coalfeather that a witch Investigator has arrived in our village, at the request of the Mayor. Someone sent a letter saying there's a witch here."

Suli was silent a moment. "Well—that's true, isn't it?"

Tala shook her head. "It's never a good thing when the authorities look for witches. They can't tell the difference between women's work and witchcraft."

"But if they investigate Magda, maybe she'll leave and go somewhere else. Then we don't have to worry…"

"Suli," Tala interrupted, "the letter isn't about Magda. It's about me. The letter says I'm the witch."

❦

THAT AFTERNOON, Suli was trying to sleep in spite of loud thunder, when someone knocked loudly on the kitchen door. She rolled out of bed and ran to the kitchen. A young man dressed like a farmer handed a sealed envelope to Tala. Then he bowed and ran down the hill before she could utter a word.

Tala slid a finger beneath the wax seal and pulled out a sheet of paper. She read aloud: "An accusation of witchcraft has been made against Tala Wing. You will be provided with an opportunity to present a defense. Tala Wing and her apprentice must report to the Grain Exchange in Weatherstone tomorrow, the 22nd of Apple Moon, at the second hour after dawn, to provide evidence." She read the rest in silence then said, "Bring my writing desk from the parlor."

When Suli brought the wooden traveling desk into the kitchen, Tala was sitting at the table with her head in her hands. She looked up, her face grey, and opened the desk, removing paper, pen, and ink.

This is really happening, Suli told herself. *The Mayor and the people of the village of Weatherstone are accusing Tala of being a witch, and they'll think I'm one, too.*

Tala wrote a list of things for Suli to do if she was taken away. When she was done, she poured sand over the paper to blot the ink, then carefully poured it back into a little blue jar. "They won't put me on trial right away; they have to gather evidence first. If it's only one person with a grudge, well, that doesn't look good, so the hearing will decide if there's any real evidence. They'll search for others who'll confirm that I'm a witch."

"But why would anyone do that? And who would accuse you in the first place?" Suli asked, her voice rough. She was trying to hide how frightened she was.

"Jealousy, mostly. It's hard to keep shape-shifting a secret, and people resent anyone who can do something they can't. It's a hard lesson, but people can be spiteful."

Tala turned the paper so Suli could read the list. "I can only write about things that won't be misinterpreted. You must memorize the rest. First and most important: If the Investigator questions you, don't say a word about shape-shifting; don't try to explain it, and don't say you can talk to animals. Do you understand? If you tell them anything like that, they can hang me as a witch."

Suli nodded, feeling the blood drain from her face. Her knuckles were white where she held the edge of the table.

"Second, but just as important, don't talk about Magda." Tala raised her hand to stop her protest. "I know you think that would help me, but it won't. Once fingers start pointing at other women, this will turn into a full-blown witch-hunt. That means every wise woman in the surrounding villages will be suspected. The Investigator could bring them all in for questioning, and he could kill them all. Tell me you understand this." Her voice was harsh.

Suli swallowed hard and nodded, not trusting herself to speak. Her eyes smarted from unshed tears.

"Then there's the question of whether you can go home to your family. The Investigator writes that he wants you to remain here so he can question you. He says you can live with your cousin, my sister, in her cottage on the mountain." Tala gave a mirthless laugh.

"They can't force me to stay with the witch!" Suli said in disbelief.

Tala's face softened and she said, "That's what he wants you to do. I'm sorry."

"Sorry? Why are you sorry?"

"Because I must ask you to obey. If you argue or run away, it will add to the case against me. Please, Suli, do this for me." There was sadness in Tala's face, and Suli thought she saw fear in her eyes. The stern teacher Suli had come to love was afraid, too.

Suli pushed her chair back from the table and stood up. "But she wants to use me against you! She'll try to learn your secrets!"

Tala closed her eyes, and Suli noticed how tired she looked. She said tiredly, "I don't have any secrets, not from Magda. There's nothing you can tell her that I haven't already told her a thousand times." Tala opened her eyes. "She refuses to believe me. Nothing you say to her will harm me—but if you argue with the Investigator, or run away, or tell the Outsiders anything about

Magda, they can use it against me. Please, Suli, do this for me. I know you want to help."

Tears finally spilled from Suli's eyes. "But I'll be her prisoner! I'll be at her mercy, and no one will be able to help me. You'll be locked up. You can't predict what she'll do to me. She might hurt me because of my father."

Tala shook her head. "No. She wants you to tell her things, so she'll try to win you over. Your resemblance to your father should help. I don't think she'll hurt you. And you don't need me to protect you: You can protect yourself. I've taught you as much as I could in these last few days. Now it's up to you." A smile appeared for a moment on her face. "The crows will help you, too. They're quite fond of you, you know. I'm not afraid for you."

"But I can't protect myself from the witch!" Suli said, her voice breaking.

"Yes, you can. You know enough now. The only question is whether you'll be too afraid to use what you know. You haven't had time to practice, to learn to conquer your fear. You'll have to learn this without me. Ask the crows if you need help. There may be others who'll help you, too. It will be up to you to know when to ask for it."

"No! I don't know enough! Besides, if I live with the witch, everyone will think I'm one, too!" Suli felt her face grow hot, the blood pounding in her head. How dare Tala say she'd be all right? Of course she was afraid: Tala was the only person in Weatherstone she could count on, the only person she trusted besides the crows. And she was disappearing again.

"I know this is hard for you; it's hard for me too, my dear. I don't want to go—but it will be worse for everyone if I don't. And if you don't live with Magda, they'll think we both have something to hide."

"Maybe the blue jay is wrong, maybe they have the story wrong, maybe the accusation was about Magda…"

"No, Suli!" Tala spoke sharply. "The accusation was *from*

Magda. I almost expected something like this; she'll denounce me and try to use you against me. You can't allow your anger to cause you to say anything that suggests there's a witch here—or anywhere. Tell them you know nothing about magic or witch-craft. Say I've been teaching you to grow vegetables and to take care of goats and geese! Tell me you understand this!"

Suli stared at her, shocked. She'd never seen Tala so angry. Then she understood: Tala was afraid of what she might do. What she told the Outsiders might result not only in Tala's death, but in the deaths of other women as well. Suli's anger dissolved beneath a wave of fear. How would she know the right thing to say? "I understand, Cousin," Suli said in a low voice. "But I'm still afraid."

Then Tala did something she'd never done before. She stood up and came around the table to put her arms around Suli. Tala murmured softly, "We're all afraid. I know you'll do the best you can. That's all I ask." Tala let her go and her teeth flashed in a sudden smile. "You'll be able to fool them. You have more skill with the Voice than Magda ever had. Remember that. Magda won't suspect you're a better wise woman than she is."

Suli didn't believe that, but she smiled weakly. "What else can I do?"

Tala walked to the window and stared at the rain. "We'll call a Council with the flock, the Free Folk, the crows, and any other animals who will come. But now there's something else I want to teach you. Stand up, please."

She rose to face her teacher, a dark outline against the stormy sky in the window, her face in shadow.

"I wanted to wait until you had more confidence, but..." Tala shrugged. "There's a way to disappear when someone is looking right at you. You make them see what you want them to see. Do you understand?"

Suli shook her head.

"I'll show you." And Tala disappeared.

19

THE COUNCIL

AT THE POND, Tala asked the ducks, geese and wild birds to carry messages, saying there would be a Council at sunset.

Coalfeather landed in a tree nearby, and Suli went to stand beneath him. "Hello, Coalfeather," she said dully.

"Hello, Suli, how are you?" he asked.

Suli frowned and looked over her shoulder. Tala was bending down to speak to one of the geese. "I'm worried about Tala. And I'm scared—Tala wants me to live with the witch!" She said this in a fierce whisper so Tala wouldn't hear.

Coalfeather bobbed his head. "I understand," he said. "But remember, Tala is wise. And you're much better at magic than the witch. I don't want you to get a big head, but you're smarter than the witch, too. It would never occur to her to try to talk to the Free Folk, or to learn Crow."

"But that's because I can change," she said. "That helps me understand what you say."

"Yes, that helps, but other humans, who can't change, learn our language anyway. That old besom is so arrogant she thinks only humans matter. She'll learn differently. Soon, I think." He was smiling.

"What do you know?" she asked suspiciously.

Coalfeather smiled at her with affection. "I *know* you can rely on us to help you, Suli. I also know that you can handle the witch yourself. You'll see."

"Maybe," she muttered. "But what about the hearing? What will happen to Tala?"

His smile disappeared. "That I don't know." He bobbed his head and flew away.

Tala had come over to stand beside her. "Everything all right?" she asked.

Suli wanted to shout "No!" but she nodded instead and they walked up the hill together.

❧

AT SUNSET, all the animals gathered around a fire built between the pond and the orchard. Suli sat next to Tala in the circle. Lamisa brought messages from the Elders, Timber represented the Free Folk, and Kaark and Coalfeather were there for the crows. The geese from the pond sat together, listening intently. Squirrels, mice, jays, songbirds, skunks, rabbits, moles and even the goats were there. All spoke the pidgin so everyone could understand.

"The witch has been a threat to every creature near the mountain for too long," said Lamisa. "The Elders say it's time to put a stop to it. They call on every animal of good will to help Suli when she goes to live with the witch. She's the one who will stop the witch from harming anyone ever again."

Suli stared at Lamisa, thinking she hadn't heard her correctly. "What are you talking about? Tala is the wise woman! She's the one who can stop the witch."

Lamisa regarded her calmly. "I have given their message."

Suli looked at the faces of everyone in the circle. No one else seemed to think it absurd.

Tala nodded. The light of the fire cast shadows under her cheekbones, and there were deep lines between her brows. "I'll be in jail during the investigation, and Suli must live with Magda; that's what she's wanted all along. But," Tala raised her hand before Suli could protest, "this is our great chance. While Magda thinks she's learning my secrets, Suli can discover hers." Tala turned to Suli. "She won't harm you: you're too valuable. Don't reveal how good you are at Seeing. Don't let her know you can use the Voice, or that you can scry. Above all, don't let her know you can change! The longer she's ignorant of your abilities, the safer you are, and the more you'll learn."

"I don't understand. I'm only an apprentice. Why does everyone expect me to fight the witch?"

"I don't expect you to fight anyone," Tala said. "Fighting is not the answer. Watch, wait, and learn. You may discover that kindness and understanding are your best defense."

Suli shook her head. What was Tala talking about? Not only was she abandoning her to live with the witch, but Tala wanted her to be nice to her as well?

"Will you promise to remember what I've said?"

"I'll remember," Suli said. "But I don't understand."

"As long as you remember. I hope you'll understand when you need to. Now, let's decide who will help you on the mountain." Tala's eyes searched the circle. "Are there volunteers?"

The animals looked at each other, their eyes gleaming yellow, red, and green in the firelight. They waited, but no one spoke. Finally, Kaark stepped forward and said proudly, "The crows will watch over Suli and carry messages. We are honored to help."

Suli blinked back tears and smiled. The crows were brave to help her. Kaark and Coalfeather smiled and bobbed their heads. She turned to look at Lamisa and Orion standing behind the circle. Orion stared at his feet, and Lamisa wouldn't meet her eyes. A group of mice chattered softly. When they realized Suli was watching them, they fell silent.

Tala waited a moment more and smiled sadly. "I know you're all afraid of the witch, and I don't blame you. But if the time comes that you can help Suli, I hope you will. Kaark, I thank you and your people for your generous offer. I ask that some of your messengers be sent to me while I'm in jail.

"This is a dangerous time," Tala continued. "The Outsiders threaten our people, human and animal, and the way we help each other. If they start a witch hunt, the help the wise women gave you in the past must end. It will be too dangerous. But if the witch becomes harmless," she smiled at Suli, "it will be a great thing. Now--does anyone have more to say?"

The animals were silent.

"Then the Council is ended. Come, Suli." Tala rose and left the circle, and Suli followed her, climbing slowly up the path in the dark. She lagged behind, remembering her vision in the fire. The vision of Tala escaping and coming home had proven true; would the vision of living with Magda prove true as well?

Tala said Suli had to live with Magda, because if she ran away it would add to the case against Tala. But once Tala was convicted of witchcraft, Suli would be branded a witch's apprentice—and she might be in danger of hanging, too. On the other hand, even if the Outsiders said Tala was guilty, no villager would believe it. No, it was living with Magda, the real witch, that would ruin her life. She'd never be safe from accusations again. She thought she'd left the name-calling and rumors that she was a witch behind, but someone could bring it up at the trial. If she lived with Magda, wouldn't that prove the suspicions were true? It was too much to ask. Tala couldn't expect her to give up all hope of a normal life, just to make one ignorant Outsider happy. She couldn't do it.

❦

THE NEXT MORNING, they rose early.

Suli's stomach squirmed unpleasantly and her hands were clammy as she packed her possessions into the sack she'd brought from home. Should she tell Tala she couldn't do it? It would be so much worse to announce in public that she wouldn't live with Magda.

Tala stood in the doorway, repeating her instructions. Suli should talk about the garden, about taking care of the goats, about tending the geese. Tell them she cooked, cleaned, and weeded, and that Tala had taught her sewing.

"Sewing?" Suli raised her head.

"No, you're right, better not. You don't have a sampler to show. Tell me how you'll send messages."

Suli sat on the bed and recited, "I'll tell one of the crows when I need to send a message. They'll take it to you, or to Coalfeather, or to Timber at the Lake. I can't talk to Lamisa or Orion when they are in human form, because the townspeople will notice. And of course, I can't talk to them when they're geese. It would look suspicious."

"Very good," said Tala. "Now tell me what you'll do at Magda's house."

"If she frightens me, or tries to harm me, I'll use the Voice to tell her to go to sleep," Suli said.

"Good. What else?"

"If she becomes too dangerous, I can disappear. Only I'm not sure I can do it."

"You can. What else? What if she tries to hurt the geese?" Tala was frowning, her arms folded tightly across her chest.

"I'll use the Voice to tell the witch she doesn't want to hurt anyone. If I can't control her, I'll fly to the Lake and warn everyone." She was nervous, but her voice was calm. It was as if someone else had memorized the list. And all the time she thought, *I won't live with Magda; I can't.*

"Good. But you *will* be able to control her with the Voice. Don't change unless it's a last resort. Once she knows you can change, she'll be more dangerous, and you'll have lost the advantage of surprise. If she asks for the secret of changing, tell her..." Tala paused then said sadly, "she needs water from the Lake and a charm. You can make something up." Suli saw there were shadows under Tala's eyes. "Are you ready? It's time to go."

Suli nodded, and slung the sack over her shoulder. In a few hours she'd have to decide. If she lived with Magda, she'd be called a witch for the rest of her life. The only other choice was to run away.

20

THE HEARING

TALA WALKED BRISKLY DOWN the path to the village. Suli followed, running every few steps to catch up, her sack bumping against her back. Coalfeather followed them at a discreet distance.

In the town square, a crowd was gathered before the open door to the Grain Exchange, the only building large enough to hold everyone in the village. They stepped into the dim light. A long center aisle ran between wooden benches. Half of the villagers were already seated, their voices echoing in the barn-like space.

The fusty smell of old grain sacks and wet wool filled her nose. The dust of a thousand sacks of corn, barley, and oats floated in the air, drifting in and out of the shafts of light that fell from the high windows. The corners of the room lay in shadow.

Some of the villagers whispered and pointed as they passed. Three women sitting together nodded and smiled at Tala. Others threw fearful glances their way, muttering to their neighbors. When Tala and Suli reached the end of the aisle, they stood before a long oak table, where the Mayor and the Investigator sat facing the villagers. A bailiff and a clerk sat at each end. The bailiff winked at Suli in a friendly way, but the Investigator frowned as though she, too, were guilty of something. .

Tala addressed the Mayor. "I've come as you asked, but this is a fool's errand. The accusation is false."

The Mayor nodded, his face carefully neutral. "This is Master Haring, the Investigator come to hear evidence. You and your apprentice may sit there." He waved at the empty bench in the front row. The rows behind them quieted, but many in the back kept talking.

They sat down and the Investigator rose, clutching the lapels of his shiny frock coat. His hair was limp, and the red veins on his nose might've given him a cheerful look, Suli thought, if his mouth weren't twisted in a frown.

The Mayor rose, too, and banged the table with a polished stone until the crowd quieted. He called loudly, "People of the village of Weatherstone, this hearing will determine whether Mistress Tala Wing can be fairly accused of witchcraft." He sat down and nodded at the Investigator.

The Investigator turned toward a dark corner where two figures sat in the shadows. "Who brings the evidence?"

One of the figures rose and walked toward the table. By the time she had moved into the light, Suli had recognized Magda. This was the first time she'd seen her clearly since that day in the market, but the grey hair pulled into a knot at her neck was the same. Magda was dressed like a respectable townswoman, in a shiny black dress, glasses hanging from a long silver chain. In contrast to Tala's thin angularity, Magda's face had been softened and melted by the years. She seemed a comfortable, grandmotherly sort of woman, and Suli was afraid she'd fool the Investigator. Magda glanced once at Tala and looked away. "I bring the evidence," she said.

A murmur arose from the crowd as those who recognized Magda whispered to their neighbors. The muttering continued as the news that the accuser was the witch herself made its way to the back of the hall.

"State your name and tell us the nature of your evidence," the Investigator said. He sat down and nodded at the clerk, who dipped his quill in the inkpot and began to write.

"I am Magda Wing. The evidence I bring is of witchcraft. Tala can change her shape at will."

Low voices murmured in the hall. Some of the villagers stood to get a better look at Magda.

"Your name is Wing also?" The Investigator asked. "What is your relation to the accused?"

"She's my sister," Magda replied.

Suli heard a few gasps, quickly replaced by silence. Everyone wanted to hear what Magda would say next. Suli glanced at Tala, whose dark eyes never left her sister's face. She wondered how it felt to know your sister's accusation might cause your death.

"What evidence do you have that your sister can do this?" The Investigator asked.

Magda's calm expression never changed. She was confident she'd get what she wanted, Suli thought.

"I myself have seen her turn into a goose. She's been doing this since we were children. There are others like her, who practice witchcraft together. All of them can change into animals."

Loud gasps and whispers greeted this news, and it was repeated to those who couldn't hear. Suli twisted around to watch the crowd. Not everyone looked surprised. The three women who'd smiled at Tala watched Magda with stony expressions, an angry look in their eyes. Suli guessed they were the wise women from other villages; they knew about Magda.

Suli glanced at Tala. Her face was white and her lips were pressed tightly together. Tala stared so intently at her sister, she seemed to be speaking without words.

"That's not evidence," the Investigator said. "That's simply an accusation. Siblings often accuse each other, because of some old grudge. How do I know you speak the truth? Can anyone else corroborate what you say?"

"I will," said a voice from the dark corner. A woman pushed her way past the seated villagers to get to the center aisle.

Suli leaned forward to see who'd spoken. It was the woman she and Eb had met their first night in the village, the one with a greedy heart. The woman's new clothes were gaudy and tight on a well-fed body, and there was a look of triumph on her face. *Can't they see she's lying for money?*

"You will testify that Tala Wing is a witch?"

"Oh, yes," the woman said, coming to stand beside Magda. She smiled and clasped her hands in front of her, setting her gold bracelets jingling. "I've seen Mistress Wing change into a goose, *and* into a goat. She placed a curse on my goats. They no longer give milk!"

Laughter, snickers, and mutterings came from the crowd. Clearly some didn't believe her. "Why would Tala bother with your goats, woman?" A man called loudly.

"If you fed your goats properly, instead of being so stingy," a woman called, "your goats wouldn't be dry!"

The Investigator ignored them. "Do you have any witnesses to what you claim?"

The woman's face fell for a moment, but then she smiled again. "Oh yes! My goat boy saw it, too! He saw her change into a goat!"

This was too much for the villagers. "Her goat boy is simple! He couldn't testify to his own mother!" someone called out.

"She's lying! She always hated Tala!"

The murmurs of the crowd grew louder. Suli's heart lifted at this show of support. Many of the villagers, it seemed, knew Magda's reputation, and suspected she'd accused her sister out of jealousy. Suli glanced at Tala to see her reaction to these hopeful signs. Tala patted her hand, but her expression never changed.

The Investigator raised his hands to quiet the crowd and turned back to the woman, with a frown. "What is your name?"

"Mistress Parker, if you please, Your Honor," she said. She curtsied, making her necklaces and bracelets rattle.

The Investigator glanced meaningfully at the clerk, who had stopped writing to stare at the woman. He hastily wrote down her name. "You claim you saw this woman turn into a goat?" He pointed at Tala.

"Oh, yes!" Mistress Parker said, nodding vigorously.

"Describe what you saw, when and where it happened." He sat down again.

Suli's heart sank. He was taking Mistress Parker seriously, despite the villagers' protests.

Magda's face wore a frozen smile as the other woman spoke; she probably thought she'd won. Suli fumed in her seat. She longed to call out that Magda was the real witch and that this was a plot to get revenge on her sister. If Tala hadn't warned her to keep silent, Suli would have accused Magda herself. There was no real evidence; it was all malice and lies.

When Mistress Parker finished her tale, which involved spells, the full moon, and water from the lake, the Investigator motioned for her to sit down. She took a seat on the empty bench across the aisle from Suli, who frowned at her. It was a ridiculous story, but the Investigator hadn't objected. Magda was winning.

Suli's face was hot with anger. The whole thing was absurd. She wouldn't let Magda get away with killing her sister. If Tala thought that by living with Magda Suli would help her case, then she had to do it. Everything Tala had told her had proven to be true. She had to believe this was too. Somehow, she had to stop Magda's plan.

"Do you have any evidence that your sister is a witch, besides the assertion that she can change shape?" The Investigator asked Magda, who still stood before the table.

Magda smiled. "I've heard my sister boast many times that she can make animals and people do her will. She uses the Voice to control them."

The talking in the hall grew louder. Suli turned to look at the crowd. Some stared at Tala with suspicion. Magda was persuading them.

"And yet, all we have is your word and that of Mistress Parker here."

"What further proof do you require?" Magda asked in a respectful voice. "I've done my duty by telling you of the danger this woman poses to the village, even turning in my own kin, at the risk of harm to myself. I'm only trying to do what's right," she said, her voice taking on the rising and falling cadence of the Voice.

No! She's using the Voice. We have to stop her. Suli glanced over her shoulder at the wise women, but they gave no sign. Tala sat unmoving, a look of resignation on her face. Anger made Suli's heart pound and her hands tremble. Why weren't the villagers defending Tala? Why didn't she defend herself? Couldn't they see what would happen?

"Your Honor, you should gather more evidence and hear from those who are afraid to say anything publicly," Magda coaxed. The Investigator appeared confused by her words. "It's dangerous to testify against a witch. Let them come to you in private, at the Mayor's house, and I'm sure you'll hear more evidence than you will in this public place. Also, Your Honor," Magda lowered her eyes modestly, "I'm willing to take the child, to see that she comes to no harm while you gather evidence. I'm the child's cousin, and I'm sure her family would be relieved a relative is looking after her." She smiled at the Investigator. He nodded.

Suli had rehearsed what she would say: She'd ask to go home, saying her Grandmother was ill and needed her. But she couldn't now. It would look like she was distancing herself from Tala, as though she thought she was guilty. She'd appear disloyal, and Magda would seem generous by comparison.

"Very well." The Investigator spoke to Tala. "Mistress Tala Wing, you'll be held at the jail while we investigate your case. Mistress Magda Wing, you have custody of the child, Suli Wing. We may need her testimony later, so don't go too far."

"I'll be ready whenever you need me," Magda said, curtsying, with a smile. She'd gotten what she wanted. Suli had to go with her.

Tala looked so terribly sad. She rose and hugged Suli. "Take care of yourself. I know you can. Don't worry about me." The bailiff led her away.

Tears spilled from Suli's eyes; Tala was innocent, but she was going to jail. Magda had won, for now. But *she* wouldn't let her get away with it. She'd fight Magda and make her pay. Coalfeather and Tala had taught her enough. Tala needed her help, and she would give it; that's what wise women did.

Then Magda was there. She grabbed Suli's hand, pulled her to her feet, and led her away.

21

ON THE MOUNTAIN

MAGDA DRAGGED a sullen Suli behind her all the way up the mountainside. The sun was setting when they came out of the forest into the clearing where Magda's house crouched beneath ancient trees. Bats flitted across the darkening sky, swooping in graceful arcs.

Worn out by all that had happened since she'd risen at dawn, Suli didn't protest when Magda led her to the low shed next to the house and opened the door. Magda pointed to a hammock slung from the rafters, a ghostly shape in the darkness, and said, "You'll sleep there." Suli stepped inside, and the door closed swiftly behind her. A key turned in the lock. The witch hadn't even left her a candle. She stood still, waiting for her eyes to adjust.

Slowly the darkness solidified into shades of grey, and a line of pale light appeared where the walls met the roof. Cold air seeped into the room. She stumbled over to the hammock and fell into it, swinging awkwardly, too exhausted to do more. There was no blanket. She lay awake, staring at the unfamiliar shapes in the darkness, wondering what the witch would do to her. She might hurt her. But the worst thing was that everyone would suspect her of learning witchcraft from her. Exhausted, cold, and hungry, she fell asleep.

In the middle of the night Suli woke, shivering from the cold. She stumbled toward the door, groping for her sack, and when she found it, she pulled on her leggings. Then she piled all her clothes on top of her in the hammock. She was still cold, but her teeth stopped chattering. Just before dawn, she fell asleep.

When she woke the next morning, the sound of birds singing in the trees made her feel less alone. Kaark would have spies nearby. Dim light fell from the crack between the mud walls and thatched roof. Suli put her clothes back into the sack and swung slowly to and fro, sitting in the hammock. She felt stronger after her sleep, ready to cope with the witch.

Rows of apples sat drying on shelves against the wall. Bunches of herbs hung from the rafters, and sacks of oats gave off their familiar smell in a corner. There must be mice in here, she thought, so she wasn't really alone. She rose and searched for anything she could use as a blanket; she didn't want to spend another night without one. But she found nothing.

The key rattled in the lock. Magda was framed in the doorway, light streaming in around her. Today she wore a brown homespun dress with a sacking apron over it. "Had a good sleep, m'dear?" she asked in a syrupy voice.

"It was cold last night, Cousin, and I had no blanket," Suli said in a plaintive voice.

"Oh, you poor thing! I quite forgot!" Magda's words were undercut by her swift malevolent glance. Suli pretended to be fooled and smiled.

"And—may I have a candle?" Suli asked in a small voice. "I'm afraid of the dark." Magda already thought she was stupid. If the witch thought she was timid, too, she might give her more freedom.

Magda barked with laughter. "A great girl like you? Of course, I'll find a stub you can have." She gestured for her to follow.

Outside, Suli blinked at the daylight and looked about her. A dense thicket of weeds, vines and nettles surrounded the clearing. Ash and fir trees leaned over the house as though trying to choke it. Why had Magda chosen to live in such a gloomy place?

The garden was a stone's throw from the kitchen, a jumble of plants mixed together. Unlike Tala's garden, the plants weren't thriving. Tall nettles and hemlocks mingled with the vegetables, fruits, and flowers. The tomatoes and squash were puny and pale. The witch hasn't given the plants what they need, Suli thought. Maybe she's lost her Seeing.

"After breakfast," Magda said, as they walked toward the cottage, "there are chores for you. My harvest is ripe, and it's time to put up food for the winter. Since you're my apprentice now, you'll help."

Suli could see that Magda was proud Suli was her apprentice. "Will you teach me things, too? Like Tala did?"

Delighted by the question, Magda smiled broadly. "Of course! I'll teach you all kinds of things, whatever you'd like. I know magic Tala never dreamed of." She glanced at Suli, speculation in her eyes. "And I'd like to know what Tala has taught you, too. That way I'll know what you've already learned."

This was her cue to say what she'd rehearsed. "I worked in the garden and took care of the goats."

"Goats!" Magda exclaimed. "Well, you won't be wasting your time on goats here, I assure you, young Miss. But you can help in the garden."

Magda led her to the cottage door. A water pump stood a few yards away, and another small shed, chained and padlocked shut, stood just inside the trees. Suli wondered what was in it. As if she could hear her thoughts, Magda narrowed her eyes and said, "Wondering about that shed? I wouldn't, if I were you. You might find yourself locked inside it, young Miss. And there's something nasty in there."

Suli stumbled, shocked that Magda could tell what she was thinking. Maybe she hadn't lost her Seeing after all.

"In here," Magda said roughly. She pushed Suli through the door into an ordinary-looking kitchen. Dim light filtered through a large window covered by drooping pine branches. "You can start the fire and make the porridge. You know how to cook, I suppose?"

Suli nodded silently and opened the door to the firebox. She looked around her. "Where do you keep the steel and flint?"

"Oh yes—here." Magda took them from her apron and handed them to her. "I keep 'em close. Flints have magic in them. Can't have them lying about," she explained.

Suli stared at her, confused. Every housewife had her flint and steel in a drawer or on the mantelpiece. Were Magda's flints special in some way? Her hands trembled with nervousness; Magda watched her closely while she blew on the flames to coax the kindling to catch.

"I'll have those back now," Magda said. She put the flint and steel in her pocket. "Oats are on the shelf." She pointed. "While you boil the water, I'll fetch the milk from the larder." Magda went back outside.

Suli went to the window to see where the witch had gone, but Magda had disappeared. Suddenly she heard wild squeaking, as though an animal were in pain at her feet. She followed the sound to a cage on the other side of the stove. Two grey mice were shrieking desperately in pidgin, "Help us! Before she comes back! She's going to feed us to the snake!"

"What snake?" Suli asked in pidgin, before she realized it didn't matter. She began untwisting the wire that held the cage closed. "Can you find your way home from here? If I go outside, she may see us."

"Yes, yes, only hurry! Today's the day she feeds the snake!"

Suli cut herself several times on the sharp wire twisted around the door before she finally got the door open. The mice ran under the stove, calling, "Thank you! Thank you!" She rewired the cage door loosely, so Magda would think they'd escaped by themselves.

By the time Magda returned, the oats were simmering on the stove. She placed a brown jug on the table. "Here's the milk. Now I've got to see to my geese and chickens. I'll be back by the time the porridge is ready," she said.

Suli stirred the pot and moved it away from the hottest part of the stove so it wouldn't burn. Magda hadn't noticed the mice were gone. It was odd that she hadn't heard any sounds to indicate Magda had chickens and geese; surely she should have heard the geese honking or roosters crowing. The animals couldn't be nearby.

Suli dropped the spoon with a clatter and stood perfectly still, struck by the thought: *What if Magda's geese are the ones who had disappeared?*

She stuck her head out the door to listen, then went down the steps. She walked around the house, but the dense trees and brush blocked her view in every direction. All she could hear was the chatter of birds.

"*Caw! Caw!*" She looked up in time to see Coalfeather land on a branch at the edge of the clearing. Glancing nervously behind her, Suli hurried over.

"How are you, Suli? Has the witch harmed you?" Coalfeather asked.

"I'm fine," Suli said. "The worst she's done is made me sleep in her storage shed without a blanket. But listen!" Her eyes flashed with excitement, "The witch said she was going to feed her chickens and geese. I think the missing geese might be here!"

Coalfeather tilted his head and said doubtfully, "But she was gone for a long time. Where were the geese then?"

"I don't know. But I'll find out where they're kept. Tell the others. Maybe they can see them from the air."

They heard a warning cry of "*Awk!*" in the distance.

Coalfeather said, "She's coming. If I can't come, I'll send someone else. A crow will always be within call."

Suli nodded and ran back inside to pull the porridge off the stove. Once she added water, it was perfect.

She laid out bowls and spoons. She'd had no dinner the night before, so she quickly drank a bowl of the creamy goat's milk. She'd seen no sign of goats, either. All the animals must be together.

Magda came through the door, her boots clomping loudly. She sat down and gestured for Suli to bring the porridge. She ladled it into the bowls, and they began to eat.

"Tell me, Suli, what did Tala teach you about her geese?" Magda stopped eating to watch her.

"Her geese?" Suli repeated, her face carefully blank.

"Yes, you ninny, the geese who live in her pond. What did she say about them?"

She'd expected this question, and had her answer ready. "I didn't have to feed them. They looked after themselves."

Magda narrowed her eyes. "I think she told you more than that. But I can wait. Come."

Leaving her food half eaten, Suli followed her out the door.

Magda walked into the jungle of the garden and turned to face her. "It's time to harvest the nettles. They must be cut down, washed, and the fibers combed into strands so I can weave them on my loom." She pointed to a cluster of nettles, some taller than Suli, growing by a stream. "Use that scythe to cut them down, before you wash them in the stream." She smiled unpleasantly. "You may get stung a little."

A rusty scythe lay on the ground, the weeds growing through it. Suli could barely lift it, and when she tried to swing it, the momentum nearly knocked her off her feet. Magda watched, arms folded across her chest, but made no move to help.

Suli said, "Perhaps I could use my knife?"

Magda shook her head. "Some of these stalks are old and

tough; I doubt a knife would work. Still, you're welcome to try. I'll be in the house. I expect all of this to be done by noon. You can wash them after lunch." Magda began to walk away, but stopped. "And if you remember what Tala said about the geese, come find me. There may be easier work in the house. But you'll have to talk about Sigur's people."

Suli stared at her, wide-eyed.

She waited until she was sure Magda was inside before dropping the scythe and walking around the house, searching until she found Magda's heavy boot prints leading to the forest. She took out her knife and cut a notch in a nearby tree so she could find the path again. Then she returned to the nettles, staring at them gloomily.

"What are you doing?"

Startled, she looked over her shoulder. Magda was watching her from an open window.

"I was thinking, Cousin. It might be faster to carry the nettles to the stream as I work."

Magda disappeared from the window. The kitchen door opened, and the witch marched angrily toward her. "Were you this much trouble when Tala asked you to do something?" she asked, hands on her hips.

"No," Suli said seriously, her expression innocent. "Tala said I was good with the animals. I fed the goats. You have goats, too, don't you?"

"Hmmph! I bet you'd like to see my goats, wouldn't you, young Miss? Well, you won't, not until I know I can trust you. Get to work. I want to see the nettles piled by the stream, ready to be washed. Then you can weed. The garden is completely out of control. I'll be checking on you. I want to see you moving! I have to get the snake's dinner."

Suli picked up the scythe, her heart beating fast, and held her breath, listening.

She heard a loud crash from the kitchen. "Stupid mice!" Magda yelled.

For the rest of the day, Suli cut and piled nettles in the stream until her hands were swollen and raw from the stinging leaves. That night, while she gingerly drank her bowl of thin soup, Magda asked about the geese again. Suli shook her head. Magda locked her in the shed, saying if Suli didn't talk about the geese soon, Magda would use magic to loosen her tongue. Suli lay in the darkness, hungry and cold, with her hands swollen and throbbing. But she was no longer afraid. She was certain Magda was losing her ability to See, and that the missing geese were hidden somewhere nearby.

22

DAFYD'S WHISTLE

THE NEXT MORNING, Suli was sent to work in the garden again. Magda threatened to beat her if she didn't clear the weeds quickly. "Follow me!" she barked.

"Yes, Cousin," Suli said obediently. She yawned, rubbing her eyes. She'd woken several times in the night, muscles cramped with the cold. Magda still hadn't given her a blanket.

Magda surveyed the pile of nettles Suli had left to dry in the sun. Then she pointed to the rows of corn, beans, and squash, overrun with weeds.

"Pull up the weeds and throw them on the garbage pile." Magda gestured to a midden of dead branches and plants, some of which had started to take root and grow.

"I could arrange the plants so they help each other grow," Suli suggested meekly. "Perhaps the midden is too close to the garden? The weeds are reseeding into your vegetables."

Magda was offended. "You think you know more about making things grow than I do?" she asked, her face turning red. "I have powerful spells that tell them what I want to do! Someone has put a curse on my garden, that's why it's not healthy! Oh, and by the way," she added, her eyes glinting, "I have a snake guarding it. I hope you're not afraid of them." She smiled maliciously and walked away.

Suli let out a deep breath. So the snake was in the garden; she'd keep her eyes open. She stepped gingerly into a row of beans. Unless the midden was moved further away, the weeds would win the fight. Magda couldn't tell she was harming her plants; perhaps using the Voice had weakened her Seeing, just as Tala had said. Suli's confidence grew.

She decided to help the plants first. That's what wise women were supposed to do: Help the life around them. Maybe she could rearrange things without Magda noticing.

She became absorbed in weeding and replanting the vegetables, and the morning slipped away.

The sun was climbing toward noon when Suli finally saw a long black snake sunning itself on a rock. "Excuse me," she said in pidgin, "are you the snake guarding the witch's garden, by any chance?" She didn't want to offend it.

"That's what she thinks, anyway," the snake said lazily. "As if I'd work for a witch. I'm just here for the free food. Who are you? I don't think I've seen you before."

"No, I've just arrived. My name's Suli. The witch brought me here to be her apprentice."

"Really? Why would you want that? She's not very good at magic. She can't even speak to animals like you do."

"It's a long story. Tell me, do you know about the witch's geese?"

"Geese? No, dear, I just live in the garden and eat the mice she brings me. I don't travel much."

"Oh. Well, it's good to meet you. You'll probably see me working in the garden."

"That's nice." The snake appeared to go back to sleep.

After a hasty lunch, Magda sent Suli back to the garden, ordering her to pick any vegetables that were ripe. She tried, but the harvest was poor. The squash and tomatoes were scrawny and pale, and the beans had mildew on them. She only collected a few basketfuls. Magda muttered that she'd expected better from Tala's apprentice, and Suli decided that if Magda expected her to produce vegetables out of thin air, she'd lost not only her Seeing, but her common sense as well.

Later that afternoon, Magda's voice came from an open window. "Suli, dear, come here. I have something to show you."

Dear? She stood up, brushing her hands. The voice had come from the window where Magda had yelled at her the day before. Suli entered the kitchen and walked warily down the passage to the back of the cottage.

"Where are you, Cousin?"

"In here," came Magda's voice.

Suli walked slowly until she came to an open door. Magda sat on a bed, a box open on her lap. Dim green light filtered through the leaves on the window. "Come here, dear, I've something to show you."

Why was Magda suddenly being nice to her? Wary, Suli walked slowly toward her.

"I'd like to give you a present, to show you how pleased I am you're my apprentice."

Suli concentrated: Was Magda using the Voice?

"Your father, Dafyd, made this. He and I were great friends once. Hold out your hand."

Suli hesitated and then stretched out her hand. Magda put a wooden whistle, the length of Suli's index finger, on her open palm. "He made me this when we were about your age," Magda said, staring past her. "He said it was magic, and that only mice could hear it. Go ahead—try it."

Suli blew the whistle. It made no sound. "*Is* it magic?" she asked, half-believing.

Magda laughed. "No, he was just pretending. It never did anything. But I'd like you to have it, to remember your father. I miss him. You look so much like him, especially your eyes. Only your hair is brown, and his was black." Magda smiled sadly and handed her a leather cord. "Here's a cord to hang it on. I used to wear it so."

In spite of herself, Suli was pleased. She smiled and took the cord.

"Your father was kind to me once, but then, he was kind to everybody. He'd spend hours chattering away to the songbirds, or trying to lure a mouse with a piece of cheese so he could talk to it." Magda smiled. "He and I would go down to the river and lie in the grass, and he'd talk to the otters or the swans while I'd fish for our dinner. I'd help him call the animals sometimes. The animals always recognized him and would crowd around to see him."

Suli stared at Magda in astonishment. This was more than anyone had ever told her about her father. "Did you talk to the animals, too?"

Magda came back to the present with a start and frowned. "I learned a little then. But after Dafyd left—no, I don't talk to animals."

Suli could See that Magda resented the animals now, because her father had cared about them. Still, it was kind of Magda to give her something so precious—something her father made for Magda when they were friends. She could almost imagine Magda as a child playing with other children. Maybe Magda wasn't evil, just angry and sad. She wasn't so different from other adults Suli knew.

"Do you like it?" Magda asked.

"Yes!" Suli said. "Thank you, Cousin. I've never had anything that belonged to my father. You're the first person who would even talk about him."

"Is that right? Nothing from your father at all?" Magda watched her closely.

Suli went still. Magda wanted to know if she could change. Of course, Magda would suspect she'd inherited the ability. She stared at her feet. "It's a wonderful present, Cousin. I'm very grateful. I really don't have anything from my father. He died when I was very little, you see." She hoped she appeared to be fighting back tears.

"Yes, well." Magda's expression was thoughtful. "I'm glad you like it," she said briskly, closing the box on her lap. "Now let's take a look at the garden and see what you've done."

❧

SULI WORKED in the garden for the rest of the day. Magda left her alone, but after dinner, Magda asked her about the geese again. When Suli said she knew nothing, Magda locked her in the shed without a word. She wasn't sleepy, so she swung back and forth in the hammock, thinking. The witch wasn't as scary as she'd expected. Magda hadn't really hurt her, aside from the nettles and the freezing shed. But Magda was still angry at Tala and Suli was no closer to finding the geese.

❧

THE NEXT DAY, Suli worked all morning, moving the weed piles to a new midden that Magda couldn't see from the house. Noon had gone by, and there was no sign of lunch, when Suli caught sight of a young crow watching her from deep within the branches of a spruce tree. She thought she recognized Ebon and guessed he was keeping watch. He flew down to where she sat weeding, hidden by rows of corn. "Hello, Suli. I'm Ebon. Coalfeather sends greetings." She nodded, wondering why he hadn't come himself. "

"We flew over the forest, as you asked, but we didn't see the geese. They must be well hidden."

"Thank you. Where's Coalfeather?"

Ebon preened a feather. "He's carrying messages for Tala."

Her eyes stung with unexpected tears, and she wiped them

away angrily. She was being silly. After all, Ebon's presence proved she wasn't she wasn't really alone, and Tala needed Coalfeather's help more than she did. "I'm grateful for the crows' help, Ebon. At least they aren't frightened of the witch."

Ebon laughed. "The witch does frighten us, but crows are brave." He bobbed his head and flew away.

Distracted, Suli had forgotten to ask about Tala; she'd remember next time. She was too tired and hungry to think clearly. Magda had sent her into the garden before she'd eaten half her bowl of barley that morning and it was long past time for the noon meal. She tried a few nearly-ripe snap beans, but it didn't help. She decided to rest for a few minutes. She leaned back against an oak, where Magda couldn't see her, closed her eyes, and fell asleep.

When she awoke, the late afternoon sun slanted across the garden. For a moment, Suli didn't know where she was. Then she remembered: She was alone on the mountain with Magda. She wished she had someone to talk to. She fingered the cord around her neck and took out the whistle, rubbing her fingers over the pale, smooth wood. She put it to her lips and blew.

A sudden movement beneath the leaves by her right hand caught her eye. Shiny eyes appeared.

"Hullo," Suli said softly in pidgin, "who are you?"

A mouse climbed atop the leaves and stood on its hind legs, regarding her boldly.

"Hello, Mistress Suli," the mouse replied in pidgin, "Thank you for freeing my people from the witch's cage."

"How do you know my name?" Suli asked.

"I saw you at the Council at Tala's house. I'm Andragora," said the mouse with a bow, "Queen of the mice on the mountain. You aren't safe here. You should run away."

"But Tala wants me to stay here," Suli said.

Andragora frowned. A second mouse emerged and whispered in her ear.

Andragora nodded and said, "We don't like it, but we won't interfere with Tala's instructions. If Tala wants you here, she must think you can kill the witch. You helped my people, and we'll help you. Use the whistle to call us if you need us. We're everywhere."

Suli fingered the whistle. So it did work! But why did everyone think she could stop the witch? "Wait! Before you go: Can you get into the witch's storage shed?"

A guarded look passed over Andragora's face. "Why do you ask?"

"The witch locks me in at night. I may need your help to get out, or to send a message."

Andragora conferred with the other mouse. "That's easily done," she said. "Be careful. The witch is coming!" She bowed with a sweeping gesture, and with a rustling of leaves, Andragora disappeared.

"Suli!" Magda called from the other side of the garden. "Suli! Where are you? Come back to the house for dinner."

She rose, brushing the leaves from her dress, and walked toward the cottage. Behind it, the moon was rising in a darkening sky.

She had the beginnings of a plan. If she could get out of the shed, she could follow path into the forest. Maybe she'd learn the fate of the missing geese that very night.

23

INSIDE THE MOUNTAIN

SULI WASHED her hands at the pump and entered the kitchen. The enticing smell of onion soup set her stomach growling. "How can I help?"

"Sit down. You can do the dishes," Magda said.

Suli sat down. Instead of serving the food, Magda sat across from her. "Before we eat, I need to know what Tala has taught you." Magda smiled, but the smile didn't reach her eyes. "Everyone says my sister is the best wise woman in the mountain villages. I'm sure she's taught you many things. Tell me some of them."

Suli was hungry and tired from working all day on little food; she didn't feel alert enough to be clever. "She taught me to work in the garden…"

Magda interrupted. "Yes, and you minded the goats. You've told me that a dozen times. I'm not a fool, young Miss. Tala wouldn't waste time on you if you were as dim-witted as you pretend. I want to know the *magic* she taught you." Magda's smile was threatening, an animal baring its teeth.

Suli looked at her empty bowl. "I wasn't with Tala very long, so I didn't learn much. I know a charm to ward off pests from the tomatoes and squash."

"A charm." Magda repeated, her voice soft with menace. "I know perfectly well she taught you real magic. You will tell me everything she taught you, right now. I'd bet a gold natto she taught you how to change."

Suli looked up, her eyes staring, mouth open wide, the very image of dumb confusion. "Change what?" she asked.

Magda shoved her chair back and leaned over the table so that her face was inches from Suli's. "You know exactly what I mean," she said softly. "Change into a goose, or a winged person, or whatever they call themselves."

"Who?" Suli asked, her voice trembling.

"Sigur's people!" Magda spat the words, straightening up. "You know all about them, don't you? You'd have to, living at that house. You *will* tell me the secret of how they change." She gave her a sly look. "If you tell me, I might go to the judge and tell him I was mistaken about Tala." She waited. "This is your chance to save her."

For a moment Suli was tempted, but she could See that Magda was lying. Magda had no intention of helping Tala. If Suli admitted she knew about Sigur's geese, it could make everything worse. Or she could admit she knew, but tell her the lie about the lake water and the incantation. That might distract Magda for a few days.

But Magda had waited long enough. "Tell me! Tell me now or I'll hurt the geese. I can do what I like to them, you know. They're only geese to me, not people. I could kill one as easily as that!" She snapped her fingers before Suli's face.

Suli rose from her chair, backing away from Magda. "So they are here."

Magda smiled unpleasantly. "Suddenly you know what I'm talking about! Good! You can protect those precious geese, and save Tala at the same time. All you have to do is tell me how to change. How do I become one of them?"

The hungry look on Magda's face frightened Suli far more than her threats. "There is no secret!" Suli protested. "You either inherit it in the blood or you don't! I'm sorry, but there's nothing I can do to help you."

Magda's face grew red and her eyes glittered. "You will help me. Whether you like it or not." Her smile was a threat. She began to murmur softly, under her breath.

Magda was using the Voice. Suli knew she shouldn't listen, but her mind was caught, curious. The words were difficult to make out, and she strained to hear: "The geese will die unless you tell me everything, everything, and I will have the greatest magic, everyone will know—you will tell me, tell me, tell me now, young Miss, tell me about changing..." Suli raised her hands to cover her ears, but the Voice droned on, and she was listening. She had to stop her. Magda would kill the geese.

Closing her eyes to concentrate, Suli began to murmur, too. "The geese are safe, you don't want to hurt them, you can't hurt them. You'll forget everything we've said tonight. All you want is to sleep, to dream, to float, float on the waves of sleep, you don't want to hurt anyone, just sleep and dream..." She opened her eyes and saw Magda's eyes flutter. Soon she was swaying, almost asleep on her feet.

"Gently, gently, down to your room. Softly, softly, ease into bed." She took Magda's arm and guided her to her bedroom. "Floating, softly, gently, sleeping..." The door was open. Suli led her to the bed.

Magda faced her as she sat on the bed. She stared unseeing and began to repeat Suli's words, "Softly, softly, gently sleeping, ease into bed, floating, floating." She was murmuring still when Suli pushed her gently, and she fell back on the bed.

"Sleep now, sleep until morning. Sleep!" Suli commanded.

Magda's eyes closed, and her breathing became slow and even.

Suli closed the door to Magda's room and walked thoughtfully back to the kitchen. She ate two bowls of the onion stew with bread. When she was done, she stared at the empty bowl, thinking.

She'd just used the Voice to control someone, exactly like a witch. It wasn't a training exercise; it was the real thing. True, she was protecting herself and the geese from the witch, but was she just like Magda now? The food churned in her stomach. If Magda remembered she'd used the Voice... At least now Suli knew for certain the missing geese were here. Magda had threatened to kill them. The most important thing was to find them and help them escape before Magda made good on her threat.

A shuttered lantern hung by the door. Suli lit it and cracked the metal shutters so only a sliver of light showed. She closed the kitchen door softly and crossed the garden, bleached white in the moonlight, to where she'd marked the path into the forest.

A deeper darkness waited under the trees. She walked as quickly as she could, sometimes stumbling over a root or stopping to free her dress when it caught on something.

As she walked, she thought about what using the Voice felt like. Magda had been defenseless, as though she'd tied her up. Only it was worse, because Suli had bound her mind. She understood why animals didn't use the third kind of magic. It gave you too much power.

Her feet crunched on dead leaves, sending the dusty smell of autumn into the air, warning animals of her approach. She heard small rustlings near the path. After twenty minutes, she saw moonlight through the thinning trees and stepped into a clearing, hard-packed dirt beneath her feet. The clearing ended at a tall cliff, a finger of rock pointing at the sky.

Beneath the cliff's overhang was a round fence made of wood and brush tied together with vines. A herd of goats watched her silently, their golden eyes reflecting the beam of the lantern. Suli opened the doors to the lantern and swung it in a wide arc. A chicken coop lay a few feet away. But she saw no geese.

Then Suli heard the faint sound of honking, muffled. They were somewhere near. Her heart beat faster.

She held up the lantern. In the face of the cliff, a heavy door of oak was set into the rock with iron hinges. She pressed her ear to the door and heard, as though from far away, the sound of geese calling. She pulled on the door's iron ring, but it wouldn't budge. Then she saw the keyhole. What else did Magda keep in her pockets, besides flint and steel?

Suli pounded on the door with both fists and pressed her ear against the door once more. Silence.

She couldn't do more, not without a way to open the door. She called loudly, saying she was Tala's cousin, and she'd be back to free them. If they were just ordinary geese, they wouldn't care. But Magda wouldn't lock ordinary geese in a dungeon.

Dragging a dead branch behind her to erase her footprints, she retraced her steps. No creature bothered her on the way back, and when she reached the cottage she held her breath, listening. No light showed. She knew she shouldn't risk going back inside, but she couldn't face another cold night without a blanket. It would only take a moment to look for one.

Inside, the cottage was silent. The embers on the hearth glowed faintly, revealing the darker hallway. So far, she'd only seen the kitchen and Magda's bedroom. She'd take the lantern and search for a linen cupboard or another bedroom. If Magda caught her, she had a good excuse. Unless Magda remembered she'd used the Voice.

She walked slowly down the narrow hallway, passing Magda's closed door. The next open door was a bedroom. She held the lantern high, revealing an iron bedstead covered by a pile of clothes. She put the lantern on the shelf by the door and dug through the pile. She was soon rewarded with a musty-smelling yellow blanket. Pulling it free, she bundled it in her arms and turned to examine the room.

A jumble of jugs, bottles, and boxes sat on a shelf against the far wall. Bunches of dried herbs hung from the rafters, giving off a bitter smell. The skeletons of strange animals hung beside them, casting grotesque shadows. She was retracing her steps with the lantern raised high, when her eye caught a glint of gold.

It was a plain gold ring, with no stone or writing on it. Why keep a ring in a workroom, why not simply wear it? For a moment she was tempted to try it on, but she remembered Coalfeather's story about Prince Obsidian. Who knew what a ring belonging to a witch might do?

There was one more door, at the very end of the passage. Clutching the blanket and lantern with one hand, Suli opened it carefully. Firewood was stacked from the floor to the roof. She closed the door, fumbling at the latch. She turned and almost dropped the lantern.

Magda blocked her way. "Spying out my house, young Miss?"

Goosebumps rose on her neck and arms. "No, Cousin, I—I was looking for a blanket. It's cold in the storeroom." *Why didn't you stay asleep?*

"Then why are you opening doors? Isn't that a blanket you're holding?" Magda's voice was terrifyingly sweet.

"I—I wanted to see if there was another bedroom. I could use more than one blanket," Suli said defensively.

"Ha!" Magda said. "One spare blanket is all I've got, and you've found it. Your spying is done. I'm going to make sure you're locked in securely this time!" She grabbed the lantern and pushed Suli roughly to walk in front of her.

Suli heard a rattling sound. Over her shoulder, she saw the keys in Magda's hand. They'd been in her pocket all the time.

Magda showed no sign she remembered that Suli had used the Voice on her. She was suspicious, but she didn't remember. "Please," Suli said, turning.

"What?"

"May I keep the lantern?"

Magda smiled contemptuously. "Tala's apprentice is afraid of the dark! You haven't gotten very far in your training, have you?"

Suli hung her head. If Magda thought she was afraid of the dark, she wouldn't suspect she'd been in the forest.

They entered the kitchen, and Magda found a candle stub on a shelf and lit it. "There," she said. "You don't need more than that. Now, move! I'm locking you in again. Tomorrow, I'll find out how you escaped."

Suli obeyed. The geese had to be freed as soon as possible: As long as they were Magda's prisoners they were in danger. She needed those keys, but Magda was angry and suspicious now. She'd wait for a better time.

24

MAGDA'S MAGIC

THE NEXT MORNING, when Magda opened the storeroom door, she seemed friendly enough. She made no reference to finding Suli in her cottage the night before. It was as if the Voice had erased her memory of everything that had happened, just as Tala had said. It made Suli uneasy.

"It's time I taught you magic," Magda announced at breakfast. She sifted strange-smelling leaves into an old brown teapot and poured hot water over them. "I'll let this steep until tonight. It will help you." She sat down at the kitchen table and smiled.

Suli eyed the pot while she chopped vegetables. Was Magda going to drug her? "What kind of magic, Cousin?"

"Don't worry, it won't be too hard," Magda said, in a syrupy voice. "I could teach you some magic right now; does that interest you? Something simple, perhaps: how to scare away pests that eat food in the garden, or how to call a bird to land on your hand. Of course, there's stronger magic, too." Magda gave her an appraising look. "But I'm not sure you deserve it. I'll tell you more when you've proven yourself."

"What do you mean?" Suli asked, keeping her eyes on the knife in her hand while she sliced turnips.

"I can see you're still loyal to Tala. Loyalty is admirable, when it's deserved, but you should do what's best for *you*, and I can teach you more than she ever could." Magda continued in a singsong voice, "Consider your magical future. Don't you want all the powers of a wise woman? Tala hasn't taught you much."

She's using the Voice. Suli tried to block out everything but the knife in her hand.

"I can give you amazing powers. Make animals do your will; cause falcons to fall out of the sky and land on your arm; make mice walk into the mouth of cats—anything, you could make people or animals do anything. But only if I teach you how."

Suli tried not to listen.

"For example, I could lend you my magic ring. It makes you invisible."

Suli looked up. She needed to be invisible when she stole the keys from Magda.

Magda saw her interest and smiled. "I *could* teach you all of these things, but first you must prove your loyalty, young Miss."

The knife lay forgotten in Suli's hand. "I don't understand. How do I do that?"

"Well, first tell me the truth about what Tala has taught you."

Her hand on the knife was slippery with sweat. "I've told you the truth."

Magda shrugged. "I expected you to be stubborn. Tonight, you'll do something for me. The tea will help you scry. To persuade you, I'll give you a taste of what I offer." She waved her hand at the vegetables. "Leave that. Come outside."

Suli followed Magda out the door. She couldn't tell if the Voice controlled her. They stood in the yard, and Magda held out her hand. A golden ring lay in her palm.

"This is magic. Watch." Magda smiled slyly and slipped it on her finger. She disappeared.

It took a moment for Suli to remember to use her side-Seeing, but when she did, there was Magda, grinning in triumph. She was using the same spell she'd used that day by the lake. Coalfeather said side-Seeing couldn't see through the third kind of magic, so it wasn't the ring that had made her invisible. She remembered to gasp and look shocked. "Where are you, Cousin?"

Magda reappeared, holding the ring between her thumb and forefinger. "You see? This is just one of my treasures. I could teach you to use them all. What do you say?" She looked smug. She thought Suli couldn't refuse.

"What do you want me to do?"

"I want you to scry and see if I win against Tala. Do you agree?" Magda asked sharply. The smile was gone.

"Of course," Suli said, thinking quickly. "You don't have to give me anything; you only had to ask." She hoped that would keep Magda from forcing her to take the ring.

Magda narrowed her eyes. "Is that so? Well, let me warn you, young Miss: I can tell when you're lying, so don't try to fool me. I punish those who lie to me. Severely."

Suli nodded silently.

"Go work in the garden. And today I'd better see some progress, or I'll tell the snake to bite you! You got little enough done yesterday."

Suli walked into the garden, relieved to be away from the witch. She found the spade where she'd left it the day before and started digging around a clump of nettles, going in at an angle to avoid the stinging leaves. She'd been tempted by that ring. She was afraid to steal the keys without being invisible, and she wasn't sure she could do the spell Tala had taught her. If Magda hadn't pretended to use the ring, she might've believed her and lost her head. She wondered what the ring really did; it probably controlled the wearer, just as the cap did in Coalfeather's story. She shivered. Magda had nearly fooled her.

She tipped the nettle, roots and all, into the wheelbarrow and smiled. Luckily, she'd had Coalfeather for a teacher.

AT NOON, Magda called her to come and eat. Afterward, she ordered Suli back to the garden, while Magda went to her room for a nap. Suli guessed she'd have two hours before the witch woke up.

She followed the path into the forest, walking slowly; it was too hot to run. After half an hour of walking, she arrived at the clearing. She hid behind a sprawling juniper bush at the clearing's edge and waited, listening. If the geese were still locked up, she couldn't do anything, but Magda had said something was on guard, so they might be outside. She wanted to see the guard before it saw her.

She heard the sound of splashing in the distance. She darted from tree to tree, creeping closer.

Peering around the silvery bole of an ash tree, Suli saw white, grey, and brown geese splashing and diving in a fast-moving stream. A huddle of geese lay together without moving in the dappled light under the trees. Some had bald patches where their feathers had fallen out. She was about to step forward to speak to them when she noticed a dark shape nearby. She stepped back, her heart pounding. A wolf lay in the shadows beside the geese. He was chatting amiably with them. He doesn't look cruel, she thought. But how could she speak to them without attracting his attention?

Of course. She closed her eyes and changed. Head erect and wings folded, she walked with dignity to the stream bank and slid into the water. No one paid her any attention. The younger geese splashed each other and competed to see who could hold their breath the longest underwater. She examined the others, looking for someone sensible. A cluster of older geese floated together. She paddled over to them. "Good day, Aunties. I'm Suli —Tala's cousin. I'm going to help you escape tonight."

One of the geese started to hiss, frightened. Out of the corner of her eye, Suli saw the wolf sit up and turn to watch her. The geese stared at her, shocked. "Tala? Is Tala here? We wanted to warn her, but the witch keeps us locked up," one said sadly.

"No, Tala isn't here," said Suli. "I'm her apprentice, and I'm here to help you escape. But you have to help me. Is the wolf on guard all the time?"

"He really isn't so bad, you know," one of the older geese said. "He's quite polite to us now. He's as much a prisoner as we are. He knows we can't fly."

Suli stared at the speaker. Magda must have used the Voice to convince them they couldn't fly. She suspected the geese had forgotten they could change shape too.

"That's true! Ralph is sorry he was such a bad man. He was our jailer while the witch was away, but he's apologized. It's probably safe to turn him back," another old goose said wisely.

"Does he guard you all the time?" Suli repeated, more sharply this time.

"Oh no, the witch locks him up in the shed at night, poor thing. She wants him dependent on her for his food," said the more sensible one. "So you're Suli, eh? I've heard about you from the mice. I knew your father."

"Did you? We should talk, later. Tell me, does anyone guard you at night?" Suli asked, as she paddled closer.

"There's no need. We're locked in the cave. We can't get out."

Although she was afraid the question would upset them, Suli asked, "Do you remember how to change?"

The geese stared at her blankly.

"Change what? What are you talking about, child? We can't fly; we're guarded by day, and locked up at night. Change? The only change we know is death," one old goose said grimly.

So she was right. Magda had convinced them they were only geese, just as Tala said. That explained why none of them had tried to escape by running away.

"I'll get you out," she said. "Tonight. Be ready." She couldn't explain now that they could become human, it would just confuse them. She swam to the bank and climbed out, walking slowly until she could hide behind the trees again. She waited until she thought the wolf was looking the other way, and changed. She wasn't quick enough. The wolf padded silently around the tree to stand in front of her, barring her way. A long chain drooped from the metal collar around his neck.

"Who are you?" he snarled. A string of drool slobbered from his lips.

"Uh, hello, Master Wolf. My name is Suli," she said, uncertainly, in pidgin. It was difficult to remember vocabulary with a wolf staring at you with his amber eyes.

"What are you doing here? No one ever comes here. They're afraid of the witch," he said with a growl. Then he bent his head to scratch behind his ear with his hind leg, his eyes closing as he searched for the right spot. The chain rattled as the collar bounced up and down.

"I had to speak with the geese," Suli said, deciding not to lie. "Why are you here?"

The wolf tilted his head to one side and stared at her. "I noticed you changed into a human from being a goose. That's unusual, isn't it?" he asked. His tone had become friendly.

"Yes, I suppose it is. Is your name Ralph?" She could See he was just as curious about her as she was about him. He didn't seem to be interested in eating her, at least not immediately.

"That's right. I used to be the miller down in the village on the other side of the mountain. The witch said I was cheating people so badly I needed to be punished, and here I am. No one objected, I'm sorry to say."

"The witch turned you into a wolf?" Suli had begun to think Magda wasn't very good at magic, but if she could turn people into wolves, she'd underestimated her.

"She claims I was becoming one anyway, and she just helped it along, the way she did with the goats." He sniffed.

"The goats?" Suli repeated faintly.

"They used to be people, too. Tell me, are you here to rescue the geese, by any chance?" He was watching her intently, eyes gleaming. He crouched down as though about to spring.

Suli tried to swallow, but her mouth was dry. "Um, no, of course not. I only wanted to visit them. Aren't you supposed to guard them, so they can't escape?" She began to edge away from him slowly.

"Well, ye—es." The wolf stood and paced back and forth. He still blocked the way back to the path. It made her nervous, watching the powerful muscles slide and bunch beneath his fur. "But guarding the geese is why I'm chained, and I'm so tired of being a prisoner! I just thought—" suddenly he was inches from her face, smiling hugely, the long yellow canines dripping, "—if you're going to rescue them, why not rescue me, too? She locks me in the shed at night, you see. I'm quite miserable. And what she feeds me! So disgusting. Better not talk about it, or it will put you off."

"I—I see," Suli said, backing away again. "What would you do if I rescued you? You'd still be a wolf. I don't know how to change you back." He sounded sincere, but he was a wolf. She didn't trust him.

"Oh, that's all right," he said. He curled himself into ball, his head resting on his flank. "I like being a wolf. The animals in this forest are quite friendly, once you get to know them."

"But—wouldn't you have to eat them, once you're free?" Ralph was the oddest animal she'd ever spoken with.

"No, no, I've worked that out. I've decided to stick to fish mostly. Oh, maybe a vole or a rabbit now and then. I mean, you can't please everybody, can you? Anyway, if you could help me out, the key to the shed is on the witch's key ring, the one she keeps in her pocket. Think it over, will you?"

Suli tried to See him again, the way she did with people. He wasn't lying. But she didn't quite trust him. Maybe wolves could eat you without worrying about it ahead of time.

"I'll consider it," Suli said, "but I've got to hurry back now, or the witch will know I've been here. Please don't tell her."

"Of course not. That would spoil the plan," Ralph said, nodding. "Besides, she never talks to us—animals are beneath her! Nice meeting you, Suli! See you soon, I hope!" The wolf waved his paw, smiling hugely.

Still afraid, Suli turned her back on him to return to the path. If he wanted her to rescue him, he probably wouldn't leap on her from behind, but she turned once to check anyway. He'd gone back to chatting with the geese.

She hurried back to the house. The air was warm, and the resinous smell of pine needles and the drowsy buzz of insects made her sleepy. Wise women were supposed to help any animal that needed them; did that include a wolf who was once a man? Magda might turn him into something worse if the geese were free and she no longer needed a guard. Suli sighed again. Ralph probably was her responsibility. The geese were frightened by the idea of leaving their jail, but their guard had begged for freedom. She wasn't certain she could persuade the geese to leave, even if she had the keys.

25

IN THE FIRE

THE GARDEN WAS STILL in the heat of the day. There was no sign of Magda. Suli worked the handle of the pump until cool water gushed out. She stuck her face in the stream to gulp it down. Then she walked to a shady area and began to pull weeds, piling them in one large mound to impress Magda. Half an hour passed before she heard Magda's heavy boots clomping down the hallway in the cottage. It was time to test the invisibility spell. Once Suli knew she could do it, she would try to get the keys.

She lingered in the garden until the sun sank and it was time to cook the evening meal. Standing in plain sight among the beans and cabbages, she waited for Magda to call her. She held out her hand and saw it flicker a moment before it disappeared.

Magda stood in the doorway and called, "Suli! Come and help with dinner! Suli! Where are you?" Magda looked straight through her.

Suli smiled. *It worked!*

Magda slammed the door and came down the steps, walking right past her to wade into the cornfield. "Suli!" she called.

She released the spell and went to the pump to wash, the water gushing over her feet and hands as she pumped.

"There you are! Didn't you hear me call?" Magda said, emerging from the rows of corn.

"Did you? I didn't hear." Suli bent over, hiding a smile.

"Come inside," Magda said, "It's time to watch the fire."

Suli thought she meant she was cooking, but when she came inside Magda pointed to the cane chair by the hearth. "Sit there," she ordered. The fire burned fiercely, despite the heat of the day. "Drink this." Magda handed her a cup of foul-smelling tea from the brown pot. Reluctantly, Suli put it to her lips and tasted it, grimacing. It tasted as foul as it smelled. She only pretended to drink it, but Magda noticed and forced her head back, holding the cup against her lips. Suli swallowed it all.

"Now you'll stare into the flames and tell me what you see. If you do that well, I may decide to trust you. I might even let you wear my ring—the one that makes you invisible." Magda gave her a crafty smile.

She thinks I want the ring to escape, Suli thought, and that gave her confidence. Magda didn't suspect she planned to free the geese. "Yes, Cousin," she said meekly.

"Don't look so innocent. Mistress Parker heard someone say you're good at scrying. It'd better be true. I don't need an apprentice who can't do anything."

Suli gazed at her calmly. "I know how. What do you want me to see?" There was no point in denying it; she didn't have to tell Magda what she saw.

"Find out what happens to Tala. If you lie, I'll know." Magda's face was pale and sweaty with nervousness. She looked as though she both did and didn't want to know the answer.

Suli's mouth felt dry. The tea made her feel very far away from the fire and the room. Her fear was far away, too. She knew she'd be able to see what would happen to Tala. She wouldn't tell Magda anything that would help her, but would Magda know if she lied?

"I need quiet." Suli settled herself in the chair, hands in her lap, and waited.

Magda nodded and walked away, leaving Suli alone.

She stared into the fire, concentrating. The darkness in the center of the flames coalesced into shapes. She recognized herself. Suli-in-the-fire opened a door, and the geese flew across the sky. The geese would escape! Then she remembered that the imprisoned geese thought they couldn't fly. Whatever it meant, she wouldn't tell Magda.

She sat for a long time without moving or blinking, with the feeling of cool water behind her eyes. When she finally stirred, Magda came to stand over her. "Well? What did you see?" She crouched down by Suli's chair, staring intently at her. "Does Tala go to jail? Does she hang?" Magda sounded both thrilled and horrified at the idea.

Suli shook her head. "I didn't see that."

"Well, what *will* happen to her?"

Suli spoke slowly, uncertain whether she did the right thing. "I saw Tala, and I saw you. The two of you were arguing."

"Yes? Did one of us put a spell on the other? Who won?" Magda asked.

"Nobody won. You argued, then Tala said something and you made up. You were crying, and Tala put her arms around you."

Magda rose to her feet. "I see what you're trying to do, young Miss. You think you'll help Tala by persuading me to make up with her. It won't work. There's only one thing Tala could do to 'make up,' and she refuses. Besides, it's too late. Tala is in jail. The Outsider won't let her go!"

"I'm not trying to fool you," Suli said. "That's what I saw. If you can tell when I'm lying, you ought to know I'm telling the truth." If Magda could imagine being friends with her sister it might help. Suli couldn't tell her about the geese; she didn't understand it anyway. "I told you the truth," she said again.

"I don't think so. No ring for you, young Miss. No magic,

either. You can keep grubbing in the garden until you show sense. Set the table."

Suli stood slowly, her muscles stiff, and did as she was told.

While they were eating, Suli asked, "Why do you hate your sister so much?" The tea had taken away her fear—everything was still far away.

"I think you know," Magda replied. "I'm sure Tala told many lies about me."

Suli met her gaze. "Tala is sad that you're angry with her. "

Magda snorted. "Tala sad about me? I don't think so." She pushed her chair back and stood up.

"But what did she do?" Suli persisted. Underneath Magda's anger lay a huge sadness at the loss of her sister. She could See it.

"What did she *do*?" Magda repeated mockingly. Her face was red, and her wiry hair stood out around it. She loomed over Suli. "What did she do? She stole Dafyd away from me! They were always together, always flying somewhere, always leaving me behind. No one noticed, or cared, that I was alone. Who cared about Magda, the only one who couldn't change?"

She grabbed Suli's shoulders and shook her. "That's what she did, young Miss! My dearest friend and my only sister flew where I could never go, and they weren't even sorry about it. Well, I've made her sorry since, and she'll be sorrier yet! You'll see!"

Shaking her a final time, Magda lifted her out of the chair and pushed her to the door. "To bed with you! Now! Before I turn you into something! I'm sick of the sight of you—with your father's eyes!" Magda's own eyes were wild, her voice high and shrill.

"But the dishes..." Suli said, finally frightened.

"Never mind the dishes. Go! I'm locking you in, right now!" Magda pushed her.

Suli walked in front of Magda all the way to the storeroom, glancing back nervously every time Magda pushed her.

Magda shoved her through the door and turned the key in the lock. She stood in the darkness, listening to Magda stomp away, her angry mutterings punctuated by sobs.

"Are you all right, Suli?" a mouse squeaked in the darkness.

"I'm fine," Suli replied softly. "Can you get a message to Andragora? I need help. I can't wait to get the witch's keys by myself. If you can get the keys from her apron pocket—it had better be tonight. The witch is so angry, I don't know what she'll do."

"I'll tell her," the voice replied.

She heard rustling and then silence. She sat in the hammock and swung back and forth. By asking about Tala and making her angry, Suli might have lost her chance to save the geese. Magda might hurt them before Suli could get free.

26

ESCAPE

THE MICE BROUGHT SULI the keys, working in relays to carry them up inside the wall and then over on a crossbeam, where they pushed them over the edge. The ring of keys fell with a *thwack*, waking her.

She had to use both hands to turn the storeroom's key in the rusty lock before she headed for the dark and silent cottage, the mice following.

Just inside the door she stood still, listening. Magda seemed to be asleep. She found the lantern by the door and checked the oil: There was enough. She opened the lantern's shutters a crack and stepped outside, the keys in her pocket. Andragora and her band of mice were waiting. "You don't have to come, I know the way," Suli said.

"But we will. Every animal should be free of the tyrant." Andragora stood on her hind legs, feet planted wide.

Suli nodded. "Stay behind me, so I don't step on you."

They followed her to the path into the woods, the garden bathed in the pale light of the three quarter moon. Under the trees all was darkness.

Once the cottage was out of sight, Suli opened the lantern

doors wide, shining a broad beam on the path. Gleaming eyes appeared in the forest on either side of the path, but nothing else was visible in the darkness, and no animal interfered with their progress. They ran quickly, Suli breathing hard, the mice making no sound.

They ran until the trees began to thin and the cliff appeared, tall in the moonlight.

Suli waited for her breathing to slow before she crossed the clearing and stood before the door in the rock. She placed the lantern beside it and tried each key until one fitted and turned. She pulled hard on the iron ring, leaning back with all her weight, to drag open the heavy door. The rusty hinges squealed loudly.

Raising the lantern, Suli called softly, "Hello? Anyone there?"

The only answer was an echoing, whispering sound.

She walked slowly into the cave, holding the lantern in front of her. A gentle path sloped downward, and she heard the sound of water dripping into a pool somewhere below.

Words, spoken in goose, floated up amidst the whispering echoes. "Who's that?"

"Is it the witch?"

"Why's she here so late?"

Suli walked down the sloping path, raising the lantern high. The mice waited at the door. Below, water had scooped a round bowl in the rock, and on its floor the geese lay huddled together for warmth, their heads on each other's backs. Orange and pink spires of rock sprang from the floor, while frozen waterfalls of white and yellow dropped from the ceiling. Suli dragged her eyes from the colorful rock to the geese. Some looked ill, with pink skin where feathers should be.

"Hello, everyone," Suli called, her voice echoing. "I'm Suli, Tala's cousin. The door is open; you can escape! Come—it's time to leave!" She saw fear in their eyes; maybe they didn't understand human language anymore. She closed her eyes and changed.

The geese rose to their feet. A few shook their heads from side to side, as though trying to clear them. One asked, "Do you work for the witch? Are you her servant? What does she want?"

"No, you don't understand." Suli extended her wings and spoke loudly. "I'm here to help you. Come! We must hurry!" She tried to chivvy them toward the door with her wings.

"But we can't fly," argued a young female. "Do you know where the lake is? I don't know how to get there without flying."

"It's all right. I'll lead you to the lake; it isn't far. You'll be safe there. I'll explain more when we get there," Suli said.

"You want us to wander around the woods at night? What about the witch?" someone asked.

"The witch is asleep. If you'll all line up in an orderly way, I'll lead you to the lake. You'll be safe there. The Free Folk will explain what you must do to stay safe," Suli said loudly.

"It's no use," said a female sadly, "we can't fly. We can't escape."

"Nonsense!" said Suli brusquely. "You're not dead, are you? You can still walk?"

The geese stared at her, shocked.

"You must like living here," Suli said sarcastically. "You've gotten used to having someone else find your food and make your decisions for you, haven't you? All nice and cozy here, living happily with the witch?"

An older gander snarled at her, "You've no right to speak to us like that!"

"No? I went to a lot of trouble to open that door, and all you can do is moan about how you can't fly! Shall I lock you back in? I don't suppose I'll ever get the keys again." Suli folded her wings against her back and stared pityingly at them.

An old goose came forward. "This youngster is right. This is our chance. There may not be another one—we should take it, and thank her for helping us, instead of complaining. I, for one, am walking to the lake as fast as I can!" The old goose walked quickly to the door, without looking back to see if anyone followed her.

But they did. In twos and threes, and one by one, they followed the old goose to stand in a ragged line outside, blinking in the moonlight. Suli changed back into a human, and carefully locked the door.

"Right! Everybody ready?" Suli was about to lead the way when Andragora stepped in front of her.

"No, Suli. Go back before the witch finds you gone. If you put the keys back into her pocket, she won't know how they escaped. Even if she suspects you, there won't be any proof. My people will lead them to the lake."

Suli bit her lip, considering. What Andragora said made sense, but she had wanted to be there when the flock was reunited. "You're sure? There's still the danger the witch will discover you before you can get to the lake."

Andragora nodded toward the other mice. "Everyone has agreed. It will be our revenge against her. She's killed many of my people."

Suli turned to the geese. "The mice will lead you to the lake. Hurry now!"

She watched them slowly file under the trees, and noticed the goats watching silently from their pen. *Why not?* She opened the gate. They could decide for themselves whether to stay or go. Then she plunged into the darkness under the trees once more.

Her nervousness grew as she approached the cottage. She imagined an angry Magda waiting somewhere in the dark. Every snap of a twig startled her.

The moon hung low in the sky. Long blue shadows stretched from the rows of corn. She walked quietly to the padlocked shed. It was time to decide whether to free the wolf before returning the keys. She wanted to, but she was afraid.

She lifted the lock, rattling the chain. A rustling inside

revealed the wolf was awake. She was breathing fast, the sound loud in the silence.

Suli tried the keys until she found one that fit. The padlock fell open. Carefully, she slipped it from of the chain, dropped it to the ground, and slowly unwrapped the chain around the door handle, trying to muffle the sound. The chain fell and she pulled the door open.

The wolf leaped out silently, his teeth bared, coming right at her. Then he was on his hind legs, his paws on her shoulders. Suli stared into his face, trembling with fear.

The wolf licked her face and whispered, "Thank you, Suli!" Then Ralph bounded into the forest without a backward glance.

Hands shaking with relief, she carefully wound the chain back around the door handle. Her fingers fumbled with the padlock; every time she jangled the chain, she glanced over her shoulder. It was taking too long. The padlock closed with a click. She flitted across the yard to the kitchen door.

She opened it slowly, waiting for her eyes to adjust to the darkness. Moonlight spilled through the window.

Suli walked down the long hallway holding her breath. When she reached Magda's door, she gently turned the knob and pushed it open. The sound of Magda's even breathing filled the darkness. Suli closed her eyes and made herself invisible. The apron gleamed white in the moonlight across the foot of Magda's bed. Wrapping her fingers around the keys to silence them, she slipped them in the pocket and tiptoed out of the room, closing the door behind her. She hurried outside.

She wanted more than anything to fly to the lake to see if the geese had made it. But if Magda caught her in goose form...

Suli changed and glided up into the starry sky, breathing cold, clean air. She laughed. Free! She was free and flying under the moon and stars. Free of the witch, free of the ground, free of being locked up. She hadn't realized until that moment how much she'd missed flying. By air, the lake was only a few minutes away. She had to know whether the geese were safe before she returned to her prison.

The distant roar of the waterfall grew louder. And there was a louder sound: The geese were honking madly. Her wings beat faster.

The trees ended, and Suli shot over the water. Below her, the shapes of geese and ducks were dark silhouettes against a sheet of silver. The cries of geese were louder than the falls. On the near bank, a great flock of wild and Sigur's geese called out in celebration, wings flapping. The wild geese mixed with Sigur's folk, ducks and cormorants joined in, and all were singing. The geese had made it! She couldn't just fly back, not now. She circled lower and landed near the flock. Andragora and the mice stood together, watching the joyful reunion.

"Andragora! Did everyone make it? Did you have any trouble?" Suli called.

Andragora beamed. "Everyone's here. Some of the geese cried, afraid the witch would catch us, but they look happy now, though, don't they?" The little mouse gestured at them, her chest puffed with pride.

Suli smiled. "They do. Without your help, they couldn't have escaped! I'm in your debt."

Andragora bowed. "It was an honor to help. But we must go now—we still have to find food for our families."

Suli bowed in return and went to join the groups of geese.

They did look happy, crying and hugging their families. Lamisa stood with her neck entwined around another goose. Orion came over, smiling uncertainly.

"Isn't it wonderful—the geese are free!" Suli said to him.

Orion nodded. "But how are you? How did you get away from the witch?"

"The witch is asleep, or she was when I left her. Don't worry about me, I can handle her. I don't think she has as many powers as people think."

"Be careful," said Orion, "She may want you to think that. We wanted to help you, but Tala ordered us not to go near the witch; she said you have to take care of Magda yourself. I don't know if I should tell you that, but I've been miserable, leaving you alone. Is there something we can do?"

She was too surprised to reply for a moment. It hadn't occurred to her that Tala would tell Orion and Lamisa to stay away, but it made sense. She was the one Tala had been training for weeks to deal with Magda.

He looked so unhappy, any resentment at being left alone disappeared. "Don't worry. I've been able to stay one step ahead of her ever since I arrived." When she said the words, she knew they were true. "But I still don't know how to help Tala."

Orion nodded. "We haven't come up with a solution, either. I think Tala wants you to be alone with Magda so she'll trust you."

Lamisa came over. "Suli! Thank you for freeing my sister! I'm glad you're safe, but hadn't you better go back? You don't want the witch to know it was you. She'll be furious."

Orion laughed and stepped forward to lay his neck against Suli's, a goose hug. "I'm glad you know why we haven't been to see you. It's been awful, staying away."

Lamisa hugged her too. "Be careful!"

"Goodbye!" Suli called, leaping into the air. She was thoughtful. Orion had confirmed what she'd guessed. Tala wanted Magda to trust her.

The cottage was dark and silent when she landed. She changed and brushed away her goose tracks before she crept back to the storeroom. She wedged the door tightly from inside so it would appear locked in the morning and then lay back in the hammock. She was too excited to sleep immediately. Each day on the mountain, her confidence had grown. She was better at Seeing than Magda, she could scry and Magda couldn't, and she'd been able to fool her with the invisibility spell. She'd freed the geese and the wolf right under Magda's nose. But none of that helped Tala.

She went over everything she'd learned, but no answer came to her before she fell asleep. Now that the geese were no longer hostages, she was free to help Tala. She simply had no idea how.

27

MAGDA LEARNS THE TRUTH

THE NEXT MORNING, Magda opened the door to the storeroom without noticing it wasn't locked. Suli followed her to the kitchen, rubbing the sleep from her eyes. She started breakfast while Magda stomped off to feed the animals. Soon Magda would know the geese were missing. Suli stood in the doorway and waited, her stomach queasy.

The sound of Magda crashing through the forest, her boots stomping along the path came toward the cottage. In the distance, a crow called a warning, and Suli went back to the stove. A minute later, she heard a loud angry cry. When she looked out the door, Magda was staring into Ralph's empty shed. "What's wrong?" she called.

"Aaaargh!" Magda yelled and shook her fists at the sky. "Thieves! Villains! The wolf is free!"

Suli felt a stab of doubt. Had she done the right thing? The witch would suspect she'd stolen the keys. There was no one else who could have.

She went back to the stove, pretending to be busy with the pots.

The sound of Magda muttering curses approached. The door

banged open, and Magda stood in the doorway, pointing at Suli. "Did you hear anything last night?"

Suli kept her face blank. "No, I slept soundly."

"It must've been another wise woman. But why now? Because of Tala?" Magda asked herself. She fell into her chair with a thump. "Where's my breakfast?"

Suli placed a bowl of barley and oats before her and brought the teapot to the table. She sat down and began to eat, hoping Magda wouldn't notice her nervousness.

"Who knew?" Magda asked herself under her breath, her spoon suspended in the air.

"Cousin," Suli said. "What's the matter?"

"I think you did," said Magda, narrowing her eyes. "You live here. You've been spying out my secrets. You're the only one who could've known the geese were here!" She slammed her hand on the table. "Tell me," she said softly, "how did you charm the locks off the doors?"

"What are you talking about? The only charms I know are for the garden. You haven't taught me any others." Suli's voice was steady, but her hands were clammy.

Magda leaned over the table until her face was only inches from Suli's. "Did you set the geese free?"

Suli let her face go slack, hoping she looked stupid and afraid.

Magda straightened. "Tala sent you to spy on me. I should have realized that. It was a risk bringing you here. And what have I learned? Nothing!" She slammed her hand on the table again, and Suli jumped. "Now the geese are gone, my guard has run away, and I haven't the slightest idea how Tala changes. Do you? Well, do you?" Magda was breathing fast, and her eyes darted around the room.

"Yes," Suli said. Her heart was banging in her chest, but she was fed up with Magda's bullying. The geese were safe, and she was the only person Magda could hurt now. "I know how she changes. So do you, but you refuse to believe it."

"You do, eh? Well, you're going to teach me!" Magda grabbed her by the shoulders and lifted her off her chair so that Suli hung in the air, feet dangling.

Shocked by her strength, Suli yelled, "Put me down! Or I won't tell you anything!"

Magda smacked her, sending her sprawling to the floor. "You'll do whatever I say. Tell me how Tala changes! Now!"

Suli scrambled to her feet, backing away. "You already know. You have to inherit the ability." There were tears in her eyes and her face stung.

"Ha!" Magda barked. "So you still refuse to tell me! We'll see about that! If you aren't afraid of me yet, you will be!" She snarled the last words. "Right now, I want you out of my sight! Move!" She gestured toward the door.

"You know the truth about changing, Cousin. And you can't lock me up forever. The Investigator will ask where I am."

"Go!" Magda screamed. "Go to the storeroom!" She gave her a shove. "Move! Before I really hurt you!"

Suli moved toward the kitchen door, but Magda grabbed Suli's arm and twisted it behind her back. Then she pushed her out the door and marched her to the storeroom. After locking her in, Magda hit the door with her fist and left, muttering.

Shaken by Magda's anger, Suli stood by the door in the dim light, her mind racing. Freeing the geese had been the right thing to do; they were safe now, no matter what happened to her or Tala. But Magda could still do something terrible to her.

When Magda had slapped her, her mind had cleared. She thought she finally understood her. Only a few months ago, Suli had been like her: angry and lonely, proud of her magical ability. She, too, would have denounced a witch to the witch finder if she'd had the chance. Magda felt abandoned by her family. Suli knew what that felt like, too.

She crossed to the hammock and sat down, swinging back and forth. It did her no harm to be locked up; it was a welcome break from working all day in the garden. But that might not be all Magda would do.

Hours passed. She ate some of the dried apples. She watched thin bars of sunlight move across the floor.

Suli pulled the whistle from beneath her dress and looked at it. Magda had given it to her at least partly out of kindness. The only advantage she could gain by giving her a memento of her father was her goodwill. Magda could be kind, but she was so used to being angry that her anger had become a habit. Being angry at Tala gave her a purpose and she might not be able to live any other way. If Suli tried to change her mind, Magda could turn her into a goat, or something worse. And it wouldn't help Tala.

She blew the whistle. "Hello? Andragora? Are any mice about?"

A few minutes later, she heard rustling above her in the thatch and a tiny voice called, "Suli? Did you want us?"

"Hello. Do you know what Magda is doing? Did she go to the lake to look for the geese?"

"Yes. The crows brought news. They've been following her all day. She went to the lake as soon as she locked you up, but the geese stayed in the middle, and she couldn't get near them."

"Did she use the Voice?"

"Yes, but it didn't work. They're too far away," the voice squeaked triumphantly. Something small dropped from the rafters to a sack near her foot. Andragora smiled up at her. "She's furious. She mutters to herself that she's losing her powers. I've never seen her like this. You'd better be careful, Suli. She'll punish you, since she can't hurt the geese."

"That's what I wanted to ask you," Suli said. She looked down and plucked at the loose threads in her skirt. It was difficult to find the words. "Do you think I can persuade her to change her mind about Tala? I tried to explain about changing, but she got so angry…" Magda had scared her. It was easier for Suli to think of her as an enemy, but she was certain Magda still cared about her sister. There had to be a way to get her to help Tala.

Andragora sat back on her haunches, her forelegs folded on her chest. "If you want my opinion, the witch is evil. You either control her with a spell, or kill her. Like it or not, she's your family, and it's your responsibility to make her harmless. You have to stop her."

"You don't think she can change."

"Of course not," Andragora said. "She's a witch."

Suli shook her head. She didn't share Andragora's certainty. Of course the mice hated the witch, and she couldn't blame them. She had no intention of killing Magda, but Andragora was right; she had to stop her. Magda was family, and family was the reason Magda was so angry. But she was unhappy and sad, too. What kind of magic was there for that?

Suli's father abandoned Magda to spend all his time flying with Tala and the others who could change. If your best friend and your sister could fly, and you couldn't, what could you do? The witch wanted Suli to tell her the secret of changing. Maybe all she really wanted was to be able to fly. And she couldn't; you either had the ability or you didn't. Suli felt sorry for her. And Magda missed her sister. That was part of why she was so bitter.

She couldn't help Tala without helping Magda first.

"Andragora, if I convince Magda of the truth, that there's nothing she can do to become a shape-shifter, what do you think she'll do?"

The mouse nodded seriously. "She's afraid of you. She suspects your powers are greater than hers. She thinks you charmed the locks off the doors to free the wolf and the geese. She might do anything."

Suli bit her lip. She had to get Magda to drop her accusation against Tala. In spite of everything, she didn't believe Magda wanted her sister to die.

Since she'd come to live with Magda, she'd had time to think about everything she'd learned. She owed Tala a great deal. Tala had taught her exactly what she needed to know to protect herself from Magda, and from the Outsiders, too. Tala truly was a wise woman, and Suli understood better what it meant to be like her. The Investigator didn't care if Tala was innocent, and Suli was determined not to let him or Magda harm her. That meant doing whatever she had to. Even if that meant helping Magda. But first she had to know what other crimes Magda might have committed.

Suli suspected this was what Tala had intended all along. The Elders said, "Suli is the one who will stop the witch," and Tala hadn't disagreed. Tala didn't want Magda to die; she wanted her to stop being a witch.

Coalfeather said to use animal magic. Tala said it was better to use no magic at all. It was time to prove their training hadn't been wasted.

❦

THE SUN WAS SETTING when Magda let her out of the storeroom and ordered her to cook. They ate dinner in silence. Magda left the table to sit before the fire, staring into it as though scrying the past. She spoke few words, and her movements were slow, as though her earlier outburst had drained her.

"I'm sorry. I didn't mean to hurt you," Magda said quietly, when Suli joined her by the fire. "But my powers are waning. Soon I'll be powerless and at the mercy of all the creatures who hate me."

Suli looked at her in surprise. Perhaps Magda could no longer See and was afraid of everyone she'd harmed. "Cousin, why are you so angry at Tala?" She waited, expecting another outburst.

Magda frowned at the fire. "That's none of your business."

Suli spoke slowly, careful to keep her voice low and even so Magda would listen. "You've made it everyone's business. It's why you kidnapped the geese and were cruel to the other animals. If you won't say, then I'll tell you why." Magda didn't look at her.

"Tala said that when my father stopped spending time with you, you blamed her for it. Is that true? I think you should have blamed him. He doesn't sound like much of a friend."

Magda frowned. "Dafyd was the best friend I ever had. But I —I suppose it's true it was more his fault than hers. Everyone I cared about just left. They were having too much fun to worry about me. I thought they were mocking me, because I couldn't..." She glanced sharply at Suli. "You *do* know, don't you?"

"Know what?"

Magda gave her a shrewd look and said, "You know about the geese. Tala must've told you I was the only one who couldn't change. The one who was left out."

Suli nodded. "That must have been awful. But it wasn't Tala's fault you couldn't change—or my father's. You do understand the truth, don't you? Whether you inherit it or not—it's simply luck. Tala and my father were children. Children can be thoughtless and mean. But you're a grown woman now, a wise woman. Can't you forgive them?"

Magda's face flushed red. "Why should I? They didn't care that I cried myself to sleep every night. No one did. I was supposed to just accept I had no gift, and get on with my ordinary, normal life. But I paid them back: I refused to be ordinary. I refused to let them ignore me." She smiled bitterly.

"By becoming a witch," said Suli. She folded her arms across her chest. "Did that really make you feel better? Did it feel good to imprison the geese? Did it make you feel strong to steal crow fledglings? What happened to them?"

Magda inhaled sharply and her eyes darting around the room. "How do you know about that? Did Tala know?" Her eyes widened with understanding. "You set the geese free."

"Answer my question. What did you do with the crows'

babies? Tell me that!" Suli rose to her feet with her hands balled into fists.

Magda rose, too, and backed away from her. "You know too much to be an apprentice!"

Suli snorted. "Don't be silly! Any child of six would understand that you've behaved badly. The wise women are angry with you because you've misused magic and accused Tala; the animals hate and fear you because you kill them or steal their children. That's not wise; that's misusing the three kinds of magic! What did you do with the crows' babies?" she demanded again, moving closer.

"Nothing! I wanted them to be tame, to be my flock, but they flew away once they were old enough. They never came back," Magda said sadly.

It was Suli's turn to be surprised. Magda had wanted a flock of her own and had tried to create one by raising fledglings stolen from the nest. Only it hadn't worked; crows aren't easily tamed. The birds in the forest had probably warned them that Magda couldn't be trusted. If the witch hadn't had such a bad reputation, they might've stayed. Suli returned to her chair, shaking her head. "They were probably afraid of you—that's why they flew away. They knew you were a witch. How could they be sure you wouldn't hurt them?" Suli asked gently.

Tears spilled from Magda's eyes. "That's just it! I'm alone! No one cares about me. I don't want Tala to die, but it's too late now. I don't know how to help her." Magda sank into her chair, covering her face with her hands.

Suli shook her head at Magda's self-pity. At least she wanted to help Tala; that was something. She knelt beside her chair. "If you attack everyone, what do you expect?" she said softly. "But I'll help you. You're my family."

Magda looked up, tears running down her face. "Really? Why should you help me? I've threatened you and accused Tala. You're plotting against me, too."

"I'm not plotting against you. I think you should stop hurting Tala, but that's not the same thing. And you've done things for me," Suli said.

"Such as?"

"You gave me my father's whistle. You didn't have to do that. And you told me about my father. No one else will talk about him."

Magda wiped her eyes and took a deep breath. "Is that true?"

Suli nodded. "My grandmother won't talk about him, and Tala told me hardly anything about her life. I didn't even know you were her sister until just before the hearing."

Magda shook her head and stared into the fire. "I suppose all this is just the distant past to her."

"I doubt it. But no one was allowed to talk about my father in my grandmother's house. You're the first person to tell me what he was like, and I'm grateful."

"Well," Magda said. She leaned back in the chair, hugging herself. She looked worn out. "I don't know how to stop being what I am, Suli. I can't change; not back into a wise woman, not into a goose, not even into a woman who can talk to her sister. I'm stuck as I am."

Suli rose and stood before the fire. "I've an idea," she said. "If you're willing to try, I believe I know the magic that will help you to change."

28

SULI'S MAGIC

THE NEXT MORNING, Suli and Magda stood in the yard by the pump. Suli called the "I'm here!" call in Crow and then, "Kaark! Coalfeather! Magda wishes to speak with you! She'll tell you what happened to your fledglings!"

Curious mice appeared at the edge of the clearing, hiding beneath leaves, or climbing up inside the juniper bushes. Starlings and sparrows perched in the thickets nearby. Blue jays darted from branch to branch, and hawks hovered over the yard, listening. Suli wasn't certain the crows would come. They might think she'd been bewitched by the Voice. Finally, she heard a loud "Awk!" in the distance.

Then, "Caw! Caw!" The entire crow flock settled among the green leaves of a tall ash tree. Kaark looked down his beak haughtily at Magda and spoke. "We are here because Suli, our good friend, has asked us to come. What have you to say?" Suli translated his words.

Magda stepped forward and bowed. "Greetings, Crow people. I ask your forgiveness. I stole your children to raise them as my own. I did not wish them harm, and no harm came to them. I wanted them to be my flock, but they flew away when they were old enough to live by themselves, and I never saw them again. I'm very sorry. I know you must hate me for this. Please believe I'd never do such a thing again. I ask you to forgive me, if you can."

Suli translated Magda's words. Kaark stared intently at the witch. He turned to the flock, among them the parents whose children had been stolen. They spoke together in whispers. Finally, he spoke to Suli. She smiled as she translated. "We've heard your words. We're glad no harm came to our children, but no apology can heal the wound you gave us. However, we want peace in the forest, and an end to fear. We will forgive you, Magda the witch, if you help to free Tala and stop harming the creatures here. Will you swear to do that?"

For a moment, Suli thought Magda would change her mind. Magda closed her eyes and pressed her lips together as though she were in pain. When she opened her eyes, they were filled with tears. She looked at Suli, who nodded encouragingly.

Magda wiped her eyes, and looked up at Kaark. In a rough voice, she said, "I'll help free Tala, and no creature need fear me again! I swear it."

Suli swiftly repeated her words in Crow.

There was raucous cawing, and many different kinds of birds joined in the clamor. Squirrels chittered in the trees, and the mice squeaked from the forest floor. Kaark said in pidgin, loud enough for all to hear, "Then there is peace between us, Magda, and the crows will help you free Tala." Suli translated his words.

Magda bowed to Kaark, tears running down her face.

Suli glanced up nervously, wondering if he would laugh. He looked down his beak at her, as though he'd never laughed in his life. "Thank you for making this possible, Suli. It was worth all the time and trouble it took to teach you Crow."

She was about to reply when Magda said, "Thank you, Suli. Your magic just might work." She was smiling.

THE CROWS HAD FLOWN AWAY. Suli and Magda sat in the kitchen trying to think of a way to help Tala. Magda said she'd go to the hearing and tell the Investigator she'd lied and that Tala was innocent, but Suli thought they needed something more foolproof. She didn't trust the new Magda, not completely. She said she'd think about it, and would Magda mind if she moved some plants in the garden? She thought she could make the plants happier, and she didn't want to leave until she'd tried.

So that afternoon, Suli returned to the garden. She sat on a grain sack, legs in front of her, laying the weeds in a pile beside her. Magda had never noticed she'd moved the midden. It had been hard work, moving eight wheelbarrows of composted plants, but already the living plants looked happier.

A loud rustling announced someone coming through the rows of corn. Magda came into view and lowered herself to sit on the ground beside Suli.

"There's something else I need to tell you," Magda said, out of breath. She looked down at her hands in her lap. "I have to explain why I—about Tala."

Suli waited, wondering what else Magda had done.

"The Investigator knocked on my door two weeks ago," Magda continued, not meeting her eyes. "He stood on my doorstep and said he knew I was a witch. He said the villagers would testify against me." She took a deep breath. "He said I could save myself from hanging if I accused someone else. I didn't..." she looked up with a pleading expression. "I had no intention of mentioning Tala, but he volunteered her name himself. He said, 'Your sister, perhaps. Everyone knows you hate her.'" Magda swallowed. "It was a cowardly thing to do, but he convinced me she'd be safe enough. He said if Tala were innocent, she'd go free—and that by accusing her, I'd be safe, too. He convinced me we'd both be safe.

"At first I told him that just because I was angry at my sister didn't mean I would accuse her, and besides, she wasn't a witch.

Then he laughed and said, 'Oh yes, you will. It never fails. When I give old biddies a chance to save their miserable skins by accusing someone else, they usually take it. What makes you think you're any different?' Then he said unless I accused Tala, he'd take me into town with him, and they'd hang me within the week."

Suli stared at her, shocked. It had never occurred to her that Magda hadn't meant to accuse her sister; she thought it was simply one more thing done out of anger.

"I know it was cowardly to give in, but I couldn't think what else to do. And I never thought Tala would really be in danger. She's much better at magic than I am, and I thought—well, hoped really, she'd find a way to escape." Magda nodded and said to herself, "That was cowardly, too.

"But now," Magda continued in a frightened voice, "He'll probably accuse me as well! Why not? Why keep faith with someone you had to blackmail? He was just making certain there'd be more than one witch for his trial!" She looked down. "There must be a way to get Tala out of this, but all I can think of is to confess I was lying." She finally looked Suli in the eye. "But if I do, he'll hang me." Magda's face crumpled, and she began to cry silently.

Suli thought the Investigator would accuse Magda no matter what happened to Tala, but she held her tongue. "Don't worry, Magda, there has to be something we can do. Let me think." She thought of what Tala and Coalfeather had taught her, but nothing seemed helpful. Then she remembered the journey to Weatherstone, and the fear on the woman's face when they'd stopped to ask for directions.

"He said 'old biddies' always accuse each other when blackmailed. Perhaps that's how he 'finds' witches everywhere he goes." She saw the misery on Magda's face and didn't continue. Suli rose, dusting her skirt with her hands. "Don't worry, I have an idea. Perhaps the crows will help."

She called to a crow across the yard and asked to speak to Coalfeather, while Magda watched, mystified. "Leave this to me. We'll go to the hearing, and you'll accuse Tala of witchcraft, just as you did before." Magda regarded her with a strange expression, then nodded and pushed herself to her feet. For a moment, Suli thought how strange it was that Magda was asking for her help.

Faint stars had begun to appear in the sky of early evening when Coalfeather landed beside her. They walked together, hidden in the rows of corn, and Suli told him her idea.

THE NEXT MORNING, a messenger arrived with a letter from the Investigator. The man was from Weatherstone, and had obviously heard tales about Magda; he shifted nervously from foot to foot, glancing over his shoulder while he waited in the yard.

"The trial is tomorrow," said Magda, reading the letter in the kitchen. Suli stood by the window, watching the messenger. "Both of us are summoned; you have to testify, too. They want to know what Tala taught you. We don't have much time to decide what to do."

"What will you tell the messenger?" Suli asked.

"That we'll be there. We can't say anything else."

Suli nodded and stepped outside, ignoring the messenger. She walked until she was hidden in the corn and then called loudly and urgently in Crow.

29

THE TRIAL

FOG VEILED the sun in Weatherstone the next morning. Magda wore the shiny black dress, and Suli wore her blue one.

They walked past the Exchange to the Mayor's house. Behind it stood a shed of weathered wood that served as the town jail. They stood before the padlocked door, and Suli softly called Tala's name.

"Suli, is that you?" Tala's voice was a whisper.

"Yes, Cousin. And Magda's here; she wants to talk to you."

"Come inside, quickly!"

The door swung open, and Suli realized the padlock was locked only around the handle. She peered inside. Tala sat on a rough wooden plank that served as a bed. Dim light fell from a hole in the slanted roof.

They quickly stepped inside and pulled the door closed. Magda sat beside Tala on the makeshift bed while Suli remained by the door. There was nowhere else to sit.

"Well, Sister?" Tala turned to face Magda. She had dark shadows under her eyes, and looked as though she hadn't slept for days.

"Tala, I, I want to—to apologize," Magda said in a rush. "I'm sorry for all the trouble I've caused. I should never have let that murdering swine of an Investigator use me. There's no telling what he'll do if he sees one of us doing magic. I was wrong to involve Outsiders in our affairs."

"Quite right," said Tala. "It's extremely dangerous now—for all of us, not just me. But do you still blame me for Dafyd?"

Magda shook her head. "No. I know it's not your fault I can't change. I was angry for a long time, but it's no one's fault. No one wanted me to be left out; it just happened."

Tala nodded. "Good. I've wanted to talk to my sister for a long time." She held out her hand. Magda took it, and Tala held her sister's hand between both of hers.

"What are we going to do?" Suli prompted.

"I'll tell the Investigator I was wrong, and that Tala isn't a witch. He'll drop the charges," Magda said.

Tala shook her head. "It won't be that easy. The crows bring me news. The Investigator almost lost his job a few months ago because the Prime Minister said he wasn't doing enough to stamp out witchcraft. The Investigator told the Mayor that our village could be a treasure trove of witches—which would be good for him. Even if you admit you were lying, he may decide not to believe you. Finding a witch saves his career. We have to prove my innocence in a way that forces him to let me go."

Suli remained silent. She wanted to tell the sisters about her plan, but she wouldn't raise their hopes. Without Coalfeather's help, it wouldn't work, and he hadn't returned.

"It's simple," Magda said. "I'll continue to accuse you, then we prove I'm lying. If we show I'm biased and everyone sees it, the Investigator will have to dismiss the case. It's easier to prove I'm lying because I hate my sister than to explain why I'm suddenly telling the truth. The Investigator might say I'm dropping the charge because I'm afraid of you, or your magic," Magda said.

"Hmm," Tala said. "There's some sense in that. But how do we discredit you?"

Magda was silent a moment. "We tell the truth. I'll say I was jealous of you because when we were children you took all my friends. Enough people remember how angry I was then—they'll believe it. We don't have to mention it was about flying." She gave a rueful laugh. "I can be quite convincing when I'm angry."

Tala grimaced. "Yes. But will the Investigator believe it?"

"What about Mistress Parker?" Suli asked.

"Her story won't hold up," said Tala. "Not if the people of Weatherstone object. Everyone here knows Mistress Parker is lying. If her goat boy testifies, that should be obvious. The risk is that they'll be too afraid to speak against the Investigator. But all the villages have seen the Investigator in action this past year. They know if they let this continue, no one will be safe."

Suli nodded absently, but she didn't think proving that Magda and Mistress Parker had lied was enough. Even if the Investigator set Tala free, he'd simply accuse Magda instead. He'd still get his hanging, and his career would be safe. He was no better than a murderer; he knew he was accusing innocent women. Suli wanted him disgraced and thrown out of Weatherstone. Maybe that would make the Outsiders leave the wise women alone. And she wanted to prevent Magda from sacrificing herself. If only Coalfeather would return.

The sisters hurriedly embraced. Tala warned Suli and Magda to be careful. Then the two of them slipped out and closed the door.

The sun was burning through the tatters of mist, and villagers were already finding seats inside the Exchange, or gossiping before the door, eating pasties with their morning jollop.

Suli and Magda stood apart. Suli said she wanted to wait a moment. She scanned the trees, but there was no sign of Coalfeather. Magda twisted her hands nervously.

"Don't worry," Suli whispered. Magda watched everyone who approached warily. "Remember," Suli whispered, "You hate Tala

—she stole your best friend; you should scowl at her. It would help if you could accuse her of something outrageous, too."

Magda nodded, not taking her eyes off the crowd. When she saw Mistress Parker, she frowned. "I wish I didn't have to be friendly with this one," she said. Magda stepped forward and smiled, greeting Mistress Parker like a best friend, pulling Suli behind her. Suli hung back, forcing Magda to drag her to the seats in the front. Several people noticed, including the wise women of the villages, who sat together on the right side, the light falling on their colorful dresses. They nodded to Suli, but acted as though Magda were invisible.

Suli and Magda sat on the front bench, facing the Investigator's table. The bailiff entered, with Tala behind him. Tala sat down next to Suli, and Magda pointedly ignored her sister. Tala wore the same clothes she'd worn at the hearing: a brown homespun skirt, blue surcoat, and rope-soled sandals. In the dim light, Suli thought she looked sick.

The Mayor rapped his rock on the table, and everyone grew quiet. The Investigator spoke. "Welcome, people of Weatherstone, and neighbors," he nodded to the wise women, "to the proceedings against Mistress Tala Wing, accused of witchcraft." He turned to the bailiff. "Has the evidence been gathered?" he asked.

"Yes, sir," said the bailiff. "We've interviewed lots of folks, like you said."

"And those willing to testify are here?" he said, looking out over the crowd.

"They're here," said the bailiff.

"Then call the first witness."

The bailiff called Magda. She stood before the table, smiling a false smile, with her hands folded in front of her. She repeated her story, but this time added that Tala could turn herself into a tiny speck to spy on everyone. The wise women stared above her head, wrinkling their noses.

The Investigator thanked her, and Mistress Parker was called. She repeated the story that Tala had cursed her goats and could turn into a goat herself. Then her goat boy was called to the front. He was clearly simple-minded, and when asked his name he said, "I take care of the goats." When asked about Tala, his reply made no sense at all. He didn't make a good impression on the villagers, nor on the Mayor. The Investigator's face gave no sign of what he thought.

"Are there any others who will testify that Mistress Wing can change shape?" the Investigator asked.

"No, sir," the bailiff replied, "but there's lots who'll testify Magda has a grudge against her sister."

"Hmm," said the Investigator. "How about the girl, what did she say?"

"She's too young, Your Honor. We didn't interview her. That's what the law says," the bailiff replied.

"Are you saying that you know the law better than I do?" the Investigator asked quietly.

"No sir!" the bailiff replied. "But she's only an apprentice..."

"An apprentice to a possible witch. She may have seen something. Call her up."

The bailiff called her name, and Suli stood before the table, facing the villagers. She'd used her Seeing to examine the Investigator; his heart was cold. He would look for any excuse to declare Tala guilty. He was worse than a witch.

"So, Suli, you lived with Tala Wing for most of the summer, is that correct?" A smile was fixed on his face, but his eyes were hard black stones.

He'd hang me as a witch, too, if he could, she thought. She nodded, and the Investigator said sharply, "Speak up, girl, so everyone can hear you!"

Suli said more loudly, "Yes, I lived with my cousin, Tala, until a few days ago."

"And what has your foster mother taught you, hmm? To change into a goat?" the Investigator asked seriously.

Suli frowned at him. "Of course not. What sensible person would believe such a tale?" She faced the villagers. "Tala taught me to take care of the garden, to care for the goats and the geese, and to make butter. Also, she tried to teach me sewing, but I'm not very good." She hung her head.

Laughter rippled through the crowd. They'd liked the comment that no sensible person would believe in shape-shifting.

The Investigator narrowed his eyes and spoke with a hiss. "Did you see Mistress Wing go out at night and not return until morning?"

She shook her head.

"Speak up, child! How many times must I ask you?"

She faced the crowd and said, "How would I know if she goes out at night? I'd be asleep!"

The crowd laughed. The Investigator looked angry.

"My cousin takes good care of me. Leaving a child alone at night wouldn't be right," Suli added primly. She was lying, but she was dealing with a murderer who dealt in lies. He was willing to kill Tala simply to keep his job.

"And what about Mistress Magda Wing?" the bailiff asked— bravely, Suli thought, since it wasn't really his place. The Investigator frowned at him.

"She's all right," Suli said. "She feeds me. But she doesn't teach me anything, and she locks me in the storeroom to sleep." The crowd murmured at this. Seizing the moment Suli added, "Also, she hates her sister. She told me so, many times. Tala stole her best friend, when they were young. He was my father. That's why she offered to take care of me—she wanted Dafyd's daughter to be her apprentice."

The crowd was talking loudly now, excitement in their voices. Someone said, "I knew it!"

"You can tell Magda has a grudge," a young mother said, pulling her toddler closer.

The Investigator's face was red, and his eyes seemed to bulge. He scowled at Suli and then turned to the bailiff, his voice thick with rage. "Did you bribe this child to sabotage my trial?"

"Of course not, Sir. But there's plenty o' folk who'll testify that Magda and Tala haven't gotten on since childhood. Some knew the child's father, too. Perhaps we should call them?" the bailiff asked innocently.

Suli could See the bailiff hadn't liked the way the Investigator tried to bully his way to a conviction without evidence. That gave her hope. But the crowd's anger was focused on Magda now.

The Investigator sat back in his chair. His face was still red, but he said quietly, "Very well. I am willing to hear your witnesses; it may provide an interesting sidelight on Mistress Tala's case." He gave the bailiff an angry glance. "But don't forget this is *my* trial."

"Yes, sir." The bailiff bobbed his head respectfully.

Suli returned to the bench between Tala and Magda. Magda scowled at her and pinched her arm so hard she said, "Ow!" loudly in surprise. Those sitting behind her heard it. The tale soon spread through the crowd that Magda had punished Suli for speaking the truth.

The bailiff called three people from the village, a man and two women. Each testified they'd known Magda and Tala when they were children, and yes, Suli's father had been Magda's best friend in those days, until he ran off and joined a different group of children. Tala had been their leader. Magda's anger at her sister began then, they said.

"Very well," said the Investigator, rising once more. "It appears that the accusations against Mistress Tala Wing were motivated by a grudge. And yet," he said, his eyes on the crowd, "rumors of a witch in this village have reached even the towns on the coast. If Tala isn't the witch, who is?" His cold black eyes scanned the crowd for reactions. Suli saw a faint smile on his face as the villagers threw dark looks at Magda. He didn't care who he convicted, as long as he found a witch, and he'd known about Magda all along.

"Perhaps," he continued, "there was a reason that *Magda* Wing wished to cast suspicion on someone else, an even better reason than hatred of her sister?" He asked the question pleasantly, as if the idea had only just occurred to him. "Might it be that Mistress Magda, who lives all by herself on the mountain, where no man sees what she does, is the real witch?"

Suli watched Tala out of the corner of her eye. What should they do? There would be many who could testify against Magda.

A grey-haired woman, wrapped in a shawl of blue and purple, rose to her feet. Her voice carried to every corner of the hall. "In all the years I've lived in the mountain villages, I've never heard of a witch here. We would not allow it. Magda lives on the mountain because her bitterness prevents her from getting along with her neighbors. She's disagreeable, but that's all." She sat down, staring at the Investigator with an unforgiving expression.

"*You* may not think she's a witch," the Investigator replied in a condescending tone, "but that doesn't mean she isn't one. She could be clever at hiding her charms and spells."

The group of women sat in silence, their faces stony. Someone had said what needed to be said, and they would wait and see what the Outsider would do.

The Investigator shuffled his papers. "I propose we take a break while we discuss this," he said, nodding at the Mayor. "We will collect more evidence before we resume."

The bailiff called loudly, "Court is in recess!" He gestured for Tala to follow, and led her away.

Everyone in the room started talking at once. People headed for the doors.

"Come, Suli," Magda said, taking her hand. "Let's go outside while these fools decide what to do."

Mistress Parker walked past, flashing Magda a look of pure spite. "It isn't going to work out the way you planned, Magda, but I still want my gold," she hissed under her breath.

"You'll get everything you deserve," Magda said pleasantly. Mistress Parker flinched and hurried away.

That one will testify against Magda, too, Suli thought. Many people here know Magda is the real witch. But will they say so? Will they turn her over to the Investigator?

They had to wait for the crowd to slowly file out the door before they could push through. The villagers gave way before Magda, making the sign against witchcraft as she passed.

They crossed the square to the shade beneath the large oak. Suli brushed leaves and acorns away, and they sat down. They were far enough away from the crowd milling in front of the Exchange to speak without being overheard, but they would see when it was time to return. "We can't talk to Tala, or they'll know we're up to something," Magda said. She handed Suli bread and cheese from her bag.

They had started to eat when they were startled by a loud "Awk! Awk!" Coalfeather was perched on the branch above their heads.

Coalfeather leaned over and spoke to Suli. "I've found what you asked. I hope I'm in time. We had to fly to the other side of the mountain. But we found two wise women who will testify against him." He explained what they'd said. Magda watched them with a worried expression.

"What will happen to Tala?" he finally asked.

"I think Tala will be fine. Several people spoke in her defense, saying that Magda had always hated her. But now the Investigator wants to arrest Magda."

Coalfeather preened his feathers. "I'm not surprised. That's what they do, these men. They ride from village to village, looking for women to kill. Something is wrong with them."

"It may not work," Suli said. "He could still argue she's a witch."

"Use what I told you. At least the village will know the truth about the Investigator." Coalfeather bobbed his head and flew away.

The bailiff called loudly from the door of the Exchange; the trial was about to resume. Suli and Magda rose and brushed their skirts before returning to the dim coolness of the Exchange. But this time when they took their place on the front bench, Magda wasn't a witness; she'd become the accused.

The Mayor thumped the table with the rock, and the crowd quieted.

"We have enough evidence," the Investigator said. "Almost everything we need to make a decision. But if there's anyone who would like to add to the testimony we've heard today, let them come forward now."

Suli rose and walked to the table, turning to face the villagers. "I have one more thing to say."

The Investigator frowned, but covered his irritation by saying in a coaxing voice, "Perhaps you've seen Magda Wing use witch-craft while you lived with her?"

Suli turned to face the villagers, speaking in a loud, clear voice. "I did learn of evil deeds while I lived with Cousin Magda." She looked over where Magda sat, her face pale. She didn't know what Suli would say. The crowd was silent, straining to hear.

"When I was at Magda's house, she told me about someone who rides from town to town looking for difficult women: women who are old, or sick, or disagreeable. This man has made his repu-tation by accusing them of witchcraft and killing them. She told me that man there," she pointed to the Investigator, who looked at her with horror, "threatened to put her on trial if she didn't accuse her own sister. So Magda agreed, against her will. She hoped Tala would be safe, because everyone knows she's not a witch."

The Investigator's face had turned bright red, the veins in nose standing out. "Stop this girl! This isn't about the witch—she's lying! Bailiff—silence her!" He took a step toward Suli, but the bailiff blocked his way.

"That bad man," Suli continued, glancing at the Investigator, "kills women so he can feel important and powerful, not because he finds any real witches. There's evidence. He wrote letters to women in other villages, and some have kept them. In the letters, he threatens to hang them if they don't accuse someone else." The Investigator's face was no longer red; the blood had drained away, leaving it pale and shiny with sweat.

Suli faced the villagers. "You must stop him, good people of Weatherstone, or he will kill again. This Outsider, who looks down on *all* of us, will ride from village to village, killing our women. They do not understand our ways; they call what women do 'witchcraft.' This is what I had to say." She walked back to the bench and sat down.

There was scattered clapping, and then the stamping began. The crowd stamped their feet; it grew louder, as they found a rhythm. They chanted, "Su-li! Su-li!"

The Investigator found his voice. "It's a lie! It's a story made up by this girl! Surely you don't believe what a child says?" He pushed the bailiff out of his way, intent on reaching Suli.

Two men moved to stand in front of her, blocking his way. Then suddenly everyone spoke at once, a roar of sound, filling the Exchange. The villagers believed her. The anger that had been building all day was now aimed at the Investigator. Some of the villagers knew Magda was a witch, but that didn't mean they would let an Outsider kill her. That was not their way.

The bailiff pulled on the Investigator's arm, tugging him away. Tala and Magda stood with Suli, watching the crowd.

"I see it now, you and the girl are plotting together!" The Investigator shouted at the bailiff, but no one past the front row heard him. The bailiff pinned both of his arms behind his back and pushed him toward the door.

The Mayor banged his rock and shouted, "I declare this trial over. Magda and Tala Wing, you are free to go!"

The villagers talked loudly with their neighbors. Some shouted at the Mayor. Others shook their fist at the Investigator as the bailiff hustled him through the back door. Some called for tar and feathers. The wise women came over to congratulate Tala, and then they congratulated Magda, too. Suli was surprised, but Magda appeared stunned.

Tala smiled at Suli. "That was quite a surprise you gave us," she said. "Well done."

Suli took Tala's arm with one hand, and Magda's with the other, and steered both sisters through the crowd and out the door, into the sunlight. The sisters were free.

30

COMING HOME

Suli, Tala, and Magda made their way toward the oak tree where Kaark and Coalfeather waited for them. They moved slowly, pausing as the villagers stopped to congratulate Tala.

Suli ran ahead. "It worked! They're both free, and the Investigator is in disgrace!"

"Hush, Suli," Tala said, joining her beneath the tree. "This is neither the time nor the place to let the world know you talk to crows!" But she was smiling.

Kaark bobbed his head. "I knew they'd set you free, Mistress Tala." He aimed a bright eye at Magda. "We've done our best for you, witch, so let there be peace!" Suli translated.

Magda bowed her head and said, "There will be peace. I have said it."

Kaark made a rumbling sound and flew off. Coalfeather said to Suli in an undertone, "He's gone to tell everyone on the mountain what's happened. I have to go, too; the flock at the pond is waiting. I was on the window ledge and heard the whole thing. You did it perfectly. Congratulations!" He flew away.

Magda and Tala sat down beneath the oak, their heads together, whispering. Magda laughed, and Tala nodded her head. They grinned as though they were sharing secrets. "We should go home," Tala said in a normal voice. "There's so much to do!"

"It's not much time," Magda agreed. "How will you invite everyone?"

"Orion and Lamisa will take care of that. They've been waiting for a chance to help," Tala said.

"Good," Magda said. "Because I'm tired!"

"What are you talking about?" Suli asked.

"You'll see," said Tala, with a smug expression quite unlike her. "Don't worry, there'll be work for you, too. Let's go home. I want a bath!"

The three walked slowly through the village. The villagers greeted Tala with smiles, but they were wary of Magda. After years of being the witch on the mountain, that's only to be expected, Suli thought. A woman handed Tala a basket of vegetables. "We know you haven't been tending your garden," she said. Others handed Suli baskets of food. Soon she was heavily laden, the baskets growing heavier as she climbed the path to Tala's house.

Her arms and shoulders ached by the time they arrived at the pond. No one was there, and she felt a stab of worry. Where was the flock?

They climbed the final path to the house. At the top, Orion and Lamisa were hanging paper streamers between trees. Jars of flowers sat on small tables.

In an instant, the flock was there, descending from the air and deafening Suli with their honking and hooting. They landed together in the yard, crying welcome to Tala and Suli.

Then the geese saw Magda and fell silent.

Tala made no sign.

Magda stepped forward. "Greetings, Sigur's people," she said haltingly, "I know you've no cause to welcome me, but I— sincerely beg your forgiveness. I'm very sorry for the harm I've caused you. I hope I'll have time to make it up to you in the years I have left."

The geese looked at each other. Then Wilo, the eldest, whose two children had been kidnapped by the witch, spoke. Lamisa translated.

"Magda, you hurt us deeply, but now our missing people have returned. You helped Tala when she needed you. Since she welcomes you, we welcome you also. Let there be peace between us."

Some geese nodded their heads and honked softly, but others remained silent. They had no welcome for her. Magda bowed her head and said simply, "Thank you."

The geese began to chatter again, asking about the trial and what would happen next. Suli became absorbed in telling Orion and Lamisa all that had happened.

Tala said she couldn't wait another minute to take a bath, and asked Lamisa and Orion to start dinner. She changed and flew down to the pond, most of the flock flying with her. Orion, Lamisa, and Suli went into house. Magda followed, trailing behind.

"Tell us what happened at the witch's house while we work, Suli," Orion said, intent on adding vegetables to a pot. Lamisa tapped him on the shoulder and shook her head.

Suli glanced at Magda standing by the door. She looked ready to flee at any moment.

"No," Suli said firmly. "Cousin Magda, could you help me cover the tables?" She handed Magda a basket full of tablecloths. Suli took another full of napkins and went through the door.

Magda followed her outside. They worked together, Magda throwing the tablecloths over the tables and Suli placing the napkins at each place.

"Cousin, I've been wondering," Suli said, as they worked, "When we were in the shed with Tala, why didn't you tell Tala you were blackmailed into accusing her?"

Magda sighed, moving a jar of flowers onto another table. "Does it really make a difference? I accused her. I was a coward."

"You only accused her because he threatened you." Suli said. She had dropped a napkin. She picked it up and brushed it off.

Magda smiled. "I'm glad you exposed him in court. Maybe now the villagers won't hate me quite as much."

Suli bit her lip. Magda was right; not all the geese would forgive her immediately. Some never would, she thought.

🦢

THE NEXT DAY was bright and clear. Suli woke in her own bed, watching the leafy shadows dance on the wall. Birds chattered somewhere nearby. For a moment, she floated in absolute contentment. She was safe in Tala's house, Tala was safe from the Investigator, and everyone was safe from the witch.

In the kitchen, Suli found Magda cooking porridge. "Where is everyone?"

Lamisa and Orion came in, banging the door. "I see lazybones is finally up," said Orion.

"Good morning, Suli," Lamisa said.

"Morning," she replied, smiling. She'd missed them.

"It's about time you got up. You can finally start helping us instead of lazing about," said Orion. He fell into a chair.

She made a face. "I deserve a rest after the last few days!"

Orion grimaced. "Sitting on your behind in the nice cool Exchange, while we've been working in the hot sun? I don't see it."

Magda and Lamisa laughed, exchanging looks.

"Let her eat, and then she can help us," Lamisa said.

"No," Tala said as she entered. "Suli will help me in the house. You two can finish the decorations. Where are the flowers?" She dropped a bundle of linens on the table, and bent to look in a cupboard.

Orion was about to object, but Lamisa shot him a look. "Yes, Tala," he muttered.

"Once you've finished eating, Suli, come help me in the spare bedroom." Tala picked up the bundle and headed down the hall.

Together they made the spare bedroom ready for guests. Tala wouldn't say who was coming, only that it was a surprise. Orion brought a vase of hollyhocks and placed it on the bedside table. Behind Tala's back, he mouthed, "I know who it is!" before he left with a smug expression.

When all the tasks were done, Tala announced she needed time alone with Magda, and that Suli and Orion could spend time with the flock. They were out the door as soon as she finished speaking. "Orion!" Lamisa called, "be back before dinner!"

"Tell me what's going on," Suli demanded as they raced down the hill.

"I can't!" Orion said, laughing. "Tala would skin me. But you'll find out soon enough."

At the pond, she saw the rescued geese weren't there. "Are the geese afraid of Magda?" Suli asked Orion softly, so the other geese wouldn't hear.

"Maybe. They're at the lake. They want to be where they feel safe—from people, as well as witches."

She looked at the geese swimming in the pond. "Do you think the flock will be able to forgive Magda truly?"

"No idea," Orion said. "I'm going swimming. Are you coming?" He changed and dived into the pond. Suli still had to close her eyes and think about changing, but she dived after him, and soon they were splashing and diving happily in the warm sun.

❦

SULI GLANCED at Orion flying across from her. She was third

down from the leader, on the right leg of the V formation. Orion flew on the left flank. Their wings beat in the same rhythm, bodies pointing almost straight up, riding the current of warm air that lifted them up the side of the mountain. They were heading toward the lake. The geese sang a song of gratitude: for the sun, for the sparkling air, and for the currents that lifted them skyward. Suli felt the joy, but remained silent—she wanted to concentrate on the sensation of flying, of floating on the wind, bathed in the warmth of the sun. She was happy.

Beneath her, the trees were tiny twigs. Cloud shadows shifted the colors of the trees, grass, and bare rock. Near the summit, the sound of the waterfall vibrated on the air. Then the forest ended, and they were over the lake and they began to descend, each one precisely in formation, dropping gracefully to the water. They braked, wings flapping and feet pushing the water, before gently folding their wings and coming to rest on the glittering surface. The geese already there sent up a greeting, and the Free Folk, in their usual place by the waterfall, swam towards them. A few of the rescued geese were sleeping in the sun on the bank.

Suli floated, the sun's warmth comforting on her back, watching the geese gossip with each other. It was strange how connected she felt to the rest of the flock. She'd never want to return to being only human again. Never would she give up flying, or the solace of being a part of the flock. It would be worth staying a goose forever, just for that.

Magda would have seen everyone else settling into this new web of belonging and felt excluded. How lonely she must've been, losing not only her best friend but her family, too. Everywhere she looked, there were those who could fly, and she was alone.

Suli understood her father's choice. The freedom of flying was intoxicating, a joy no human could understand unless they, too, could change. Of course her father wanted to spend all his time in the air. She didn't blame him.

The sun was starting to set, gilding the slopes of the mountain, when Suli and Orion flew back down the mountain together. She tried again to find out who was coming to stay and what the party was for, but Orion just laughed. "I like knowing something you don't for a change."

31

LEAVING DAY

THEY LANDED at the pond and changed. Orion said that if she came with him to the gate at the bottom of the path, she might see something interesting. The two of them were waiting there when a hay cart slowly rumbled into view. Someone was perched on top of it. Suli's brother Eb walked beside it.

"Grandmother!" she shouted, running down the path. The tiny figure climbed down with Eb's help and Suli threw herself into Grandmother's arms. "What a wonderful surprise! Why didn't anyone tell me you were coming?"

"No time. Tala said to come at once," Eb explained. "Grandmother won't tell me why, only that we had to be here by tonight. I guess Tala didn't starve you to death after all." He grinned, and she hugged him, too. She introduced them both to Orion and led them up the hill, introducing them to everyone they met in the yard. Then Eb and Orion started talking about fishing and the last she saw of them, they were heading toward the pond.

"Why are you here, Grandmother?" Suli asked suspiciously as she settled her things in the guest room. "Something's going on, but no one will explain."

Grandmother, her hair still black as a crow's wing despite her age, just smiled, her eyes crinkling. "You don't want me to spoil the surprise, do you?"

"Yes," Suli said.

Grandmother shook her head, smiling.

"But why? Why won't anyone tell me?"

"Because that's how Tala wants it," Grandmother said. "Try to enjoy the suspense. Tell me about your training. Do you still want to be a wise woman?"

How could she possibly explain? "Yes. I finally understand what they do. And being a wise woman doesn't make you safe. My crow teacher, Coalfeather, taught me that."

"A crow teacher?" her grandmother repeated faintly. "He must be a wise old bird."

"But Grandmother, why didn't you tell me I could change? Flying is the most amazing..." She groped for words. "I love it."

Her grandmother smiled sadly. "Just like your father. I didn't tell you because I wasn't sure. I needed Tala to find out for certain. Changing hasn't been good luck for our family. Perhaps I hoped you couldn't."

"You mean because of what happened between father and Magda. Well, I won't let it change Eb and me," Suli said fiercely.

To her surprise, Grandmother laughed. "I don't think you have to worry. Eb is nothing like Magda. And he's quite happy with his own plans, as I'm sure he'll tell you." Her expression changed. "What happened when you lived with Magda? Did she hurt you?"

Suli shook her head. "Not really. She was angry at Tala, not me. And she gave me a whistle father made. At her house I met mice, and a snake, and a wolf..."

"A wolf?" Her grandmother looked startled.

"The wolf was a much better person than the witch Investigator."

A smile twitched at the corner of Grandmother's mouth. "I

think you're going to be a good wise woman, Suli. So does Tala: She said so."

Suli blinked in surprise and felt her face go hot. It was just like Tala to praise her to her grandmother, but not tell her. "I'll be glad when things are normal again and I can continue my training." She noticed Grandmother's change of expression. "What? You will let me continue my training, won't you?"

"We'll see."

She was about to ask what she meant when Eb came into the room and threw his bag on the floor. "Orion says you know advanced magic now. Does that mean you can order the pots and pans to make dinner, while you sit back and eat cream?"

She couldn't tell if he was serious or not. "It doesn't work like that."

He grinned. "Did Grandmother tell you I'm to be a carpenter? Master Planer has already drawn up the contract, and my friend Jabe says…"

A knock on the door interrupted Eb's news. Tala stuck her head in and told Suli to change into her blue dress.

❧

THE SUN SLID down the side of the mountain and waited a moment before dropping below the horizon. Long shadows fell across the yard. Colors faded, and the shadows beneath the trees thickened. Lamisa and Orion lit candles and arranged food on the long table.

Eb and Suli were speaking quietly under the trees when the cries of the wild geese drew nearer and then the wild flock flew over the house. Suli and Eb ran to the path in time to see them land in the pond. She was about to start down the path when Lamisa stopped her. "Wait, Suli. More people are coming."

Lamisa pointed. A long procession of women, men, and children snaked up the path. Suli recognized some of them from the trial; the wise women of the villages had come with their families. They carried dishes of food, pies, and jugs of drink. Lamisa and Orion showed them where to put the food and when Suli tried to help, they waved her away. She stood to the side, feeling awkward, not knowing what to do.

"Caw! Caw!" Kaark's entire flock arrived, settling in the fir tree next to the house. Suli ran to greet them, pulling Eb along with her. She introduced them. He stared from his sister to the crows with an open mouth.

"Hello, Suli," Coalfeather said. "Everyone has come for your party. We're letting the yearlings stay up late."

"My party?" said Suli. "What do you mean?"

Kaark laughed. "You'll see, Mistress."

Suli blinked and smiled uncertainly.

More people arrived. Birds and animals appeared from the woods. Three more wild geese landed in the yard. Mice jumped nimbly from their backs.

"Andragora!" Suli cried. "How wonderful to see you."

"Congratulations, Suli," Andragora said, but before she could say more, a loud honking drowned out all other sound and all the geese landed in the yard.

Magda, Lamisa, and Orion stood at the bottom of the kitchen steps. Tala, dressed in white, came out the kitchen door and stood on the top step. She raised her hands and when everyone quieted, she spoke. "Dear friends, thank you all for coming. Welcome to my home and to the celebration of Suli Wing's Leaving Day, the day she leaves childhood behind."

Suli exhaled sharply and tried to stand taller as everyone turned to look at her. It was just like Tala not to tell her! And Magda had known too, she could see. Grandmother was beaming.

Tala continued, "Welcome to the mice of Blue Mountain, who not only helped Suli free the imprisoned geese, but helped me to escape as well." Everyone clapped and cheered. Andragora and her people marched in a line to stand in front of Tala. They bowed in unison. Magda studied her boots.

"Welcome to the Free Folk," Tala said, "who found me and helped me escape from the witch."

Suli saw Timber and Tilfrost step forward and bow their necks. She clapped and smiled at Timber. Everyone clapped and cheered and honked their approval.

"I must also thank Orion, who taught Suli to change and to speak Crow!"

More loud clapping and honking.

Tala said, "And last, in the place of honor, I thank Kaark and his flock, who helped Suli when I was not here. My greatest thanks go to Coalfeather, who shared his wisdom on the proper use of magic."

Kaark called, "You're welcome!" loudly from a branch near the tables, and Coalfeather bobbed his head. Everyone clapped, and Orion whistled loudly through his teeth. Suli clapped so hard her hands hurt.

"The wise women of the villages," Tala continued, "pass on our cherished traditions to our daughters. That is what we are here to do tonight.

"Let me tell you about Suli. When she first came to me, she was suspicious; she thought the magic she saw around her was witchcraft. The people of her village didn't trust her, and she found it difficult to trust in return. But Suli has learned the most important lesson: that the mark of a wise woman is not magic or power, it's being ready to help others. She has demonstrated this time and time again. As foster mother to Suli, I declare her worthy to be called a wise woman among our people. In normal times, her training would continue for at least another year, and I recommend that she stay here for at least that time. But these are not normal times: Outsiders threaten our villages. I won't always be here, and Suli is ready *now* to be welcomed to our circle. Let us hear whether her other teachers agree. First, Coalfeather."

Coalfeather flew to the top step. He waited until all eyes were on him, and then croaked loudly in Crow. Orion stepped forward and translated.

"At first, Suli was like many humans, impatient and looking for simple answers to questions that are not simple. But she has good sense and a good heart. Suli offered to protect us from the witch with the Voice, even before she was certain she could. She helped animals when they needed her, when they were sick or in danger. And most important of all, she risked being called a witch by agreeing to live with Magda."

Tears stung Suli's eyes. She hadn't realized that Coalfeather had known she was afraid to do that. He winked.

"Suli convinced the witch to apologize for her evil deeds and to stop harming others." Coalfeather fluffed his feathers, puffing out his chest, "And she learned that you don't need magic to help others. I agree with Tala: Suli is ready to be a wise woman!"

The crows cawed loudly, flapping their wings in approval. Everyone else clapped, honked, squeaked, or shouted.

Tala spoke again. "The crows have declared Suli ready for her new responsibilities. But to make sure I'm not making a mistake," Tala paused dramatically, "I call on her second foster mother to tell us whether she agrees."

The sound of scattered clapping died away as Magda climbed the step. She cleared her throat. "While living with me, Suli demonstrated wisdom, bravery, and compassion. I tempted her with a magic ring, but she wasn't fooled, showing wisdom. She risked being eaten by a wolf in order to set him free, demonstrating great bravery. She rescued the members of Sigur's flock, demonstrating her loyal and compassionate heart." Magda cleared her throat again. "She risked her own safety to free the geese and the wolf, yet raised no hand against me. She didn't harm me, even when that might've been safer. She's the reason..." Her voice grew hoarse and she coughed. "She showed me I could reconcile with my sister. She saved both of us from the witch

Investigator, and took care of her community, even when that meant taking care of a witch." Magda looked at Tala. "I agree that Suli is a wise woman."

There was silence.

Tala nodded and looked out over the assembled animals and humans. "Then as Suli's foster mother and teacher, I say to you all, family, friends, and allies, that Suli Wing has left childhood behind. She is now a wise woman. Please welcome *Mistress* Suli Wing!"

The roar of clapping, cheering, honking, cawing, and squeaking threatened to deafen Suli. Tala motioned for her to join her on the steps.

When Suli stood on the top step, Tala and Magda stepped down to join everyone in the yard, turning to applaud her. Suli was too surprised to speak.

Kaark called, "Speech! Speech!" and others joined in, calling, "Speech!"

Suli had no idea what to say. Eb was grinning, her grandmother had tears in her eyes, Timber nodded, and Coalfeather bobbed his head. Orion raised an eyebrow as if to say, *Well?* Then she knew what to say.

"Dear Grandmother, cousins, and friends: I've learned so much since I came here. Tala taught me to observe carefully, to think for myself, and to trust my abilities. Sigur's people accepted me as part of their family. Orion taught me to change, to fly, and to speak Crow." She smiled at him. "I will never forget that.

"From Coalfeather, I learned the wisdom of the Crow people and the dangers of using the third kind of magic." The crows called loudly in approval.

"Lastly, from Magda I learned that magic and power are not enough; you have to take responsibility for your actions. You need the wisdom to know when you're wrong and the courage to admit it."

Everyone clapped and cheered for Magda and she smiled, shaking her head.

"So you see, everything I've done was because someone helped me, or taught me, or simply welcomed me. Without the generosity of my teachers and my new community, I wouldn't know how to be a wise woman. So to all of you, dear teachers and friends, thank you." Then Suli bowed, and there was a tremendous roar of approval. Kaark laughed.

Tala raised her hands above her head, and cried, "Let's eat!"

Then the party began. They ate, they sang songs, and they played games. Kaark told jokes, which Suli translated, but no one understood except the crows. The Free Folk taught Sigur's people a special dance, and the mice and crows played tag (Kaark cheated, hopping with his wings open, laughing madly) with a great deal of squeaking and flapping of wings.

The small children played ball with the mice; then the crows offered to fly defense for two teams, swooping in and out. Suli wandered over to watch, when suddenly she was surrounded, and everyone spoke at once.

"Did I tell you? I'm to have my own room in the woodshop," Eb said proudly, "and Melissa says we can start courting once I'm a second-year apprentice..."

Timber said, "You must fly with us, cousin Suli, to understand what flying means. You cannot know the pull of the stars or feel the pull of far places across the ocean until you journey with us to our winter home."

"I told Lamisa this would happen," Orion said, "and she didn't believe me. I'm glad you're staying, Suli."

Andragora tugged the hem of her dress. "My people will teach you also. The crows are not the only ones with wisdom."

"The Elders were right," Lamisa said serenely. "They knew you'd stop the witch."

Out of the corner of her eye, Suli saw Tala, Magda, and her

Grandmother whispering and laughing together. Every now then they'd glance around them to make sure no one overheard.

"Congratulations, witch Suli!" Kaark called from the fir tree. "The Council says you must come to our next meeting."

"Ignore him," Coalfeather called, landing beside him with two younger crows perched next to him. "He's proud of you, too. Let me introduce my yearlings: This is my daughter Jet, and my son Bluewing." Two young crows stared at her with goggling eyes, clearly impressed that their father knew her. "Goodnight, Suli, we're off home," he called as he lifted into the air, the two youngsters falling in behind.

"Goodnight," she called.

32

THE WISE WOMAN

TWO MONTHS LATER, Weatherstone dozed peacefully in the late autumn sunlight. It was just after noon, and most folk were either eating their meal or sleeping after it. A lone figure walked through town, a girl dressed in blue with a bag over her shoulder. She knocked on an unpainted door. A small child opened it and she stepped inside.

A woman lay on a pallet by the fire, her face covered in sweat.

"I brought more of the cooling tea, Mistress," Suli said, setting down her bag." She took a jar from her bag and asked the child to fetch a kettle of water.

SULI THREW the bag of medicines in a chair, and sat at the kitchen table, too weary to start dinner. She lived alone in Tala's house now. Tala and Magda had been gone for two months, traveling from town to town on the coast to learn the Outsiders' ways. Lamisa and Orion had come by for dinner once or twice, but Lamisa spent most of her time studying with the Elders and

Orion stayed with the Free Folk at the lake. She hadn't seen either of them in weeks.

The weather had turned cold and unsettled, the wind gusting from every direction. Walking back to the house after penning the goats and chickens for the night, Suli saw the wild geese passing over the house in a giant "V." They cried farewell to her and to the geese in the pond, saying they were leaving for their winter home. Their haunting cries faded into the distance, and Suli felt a pang of loneliness.

Dark had fallen early. She lit the lamp, leaning against the kitchen table. With Tala away, she was the village wise woman and people and animals could ask for help at any time, day or night. She was always tired.

She carried the lamp to her room and pulled a box from beneath the bed. She took the corncob dolls from the wrapping paper and brought them back to the kitchen table.

The fire sent shadows dancing around the room but all was warm and cozy in the pool of golden light around the lamp. It felt as though years had passed since she'd played with dolls. Now she was supposed to be grown up, and a wise woman too. She picked up the doll dressed in faded blue. "Princess Fig, it's nice to be needed, but I need a break now and then. You probably wouldn't understand, since a Princess doesn't have to work all the time."

A loud "Caw!" came from the open window. Coalfeather perched on the sill. "You sound sad, Suli. How are you?"

"Coalfeather! It's good to see you. I was just thinking I have no one to talk to, and here you are. Like magic." Suli grinned.

Coalfeather cocked his head and made a rumbling sound. "You only have to call me, Suli, and I will come. I would have come before, but I've been teaching the younger crows. Have you been busy?"

"Yes, by the Sisters! Everyone needs something all the time. If it's not sick babies, it's cows with infected udders."

He smiled. "Being a wise woman isn't what you'd thought it would be?"

"Well," she said, "I suppose I imagined I'd use magic all the time, but mostly it's just work. I like helping people, but I wouldn't mind sleeping, too."

Coalfeather's smile grew broader. "So your training is complete."

"I don't know about that," she said darkly. "There are several things Tala should have explained before she went away. But I'm learning."

"Good." The crow bobbed his head. "A wise woman never stops learning." He strutted across the sill.

"Coalfeather still lecturing you?" Orion was leaning on the windowsill.

The startled crow jumped into the air and landed on the table. He made a rumbling sound and glared at Orion, ruffling his feathers.

"I thought you left with the Free Folk," Suli said to Orion.

"Not me. This is my home. Why should I leave?" He disappeared from the window. The door opened, and Orion sat down across the table. Coalfeather hopped away, watching him warily.

"Why are you here, Coalfeather?" Orion asked.

The crow looked down his beak. "Suli is my student, and part of my flock. Just because she's a wise woman now does not end my responsibility to her, or hers to us."

Suli felt warmth spreading through her at his words.

Orion frowned. "Actually, she's part of *my* flock."

"I'm proud to be part of both flocks," she said quietly. "I belong to the animal and human communities too. That's the best part of being a wise woman. I belong to everyone."

"I'm glad to see you, Orion. I was just telling Coalfeather it's been lonely here lately. I only ever see folk when they want something."

"Oh?" Orion leaned back, tipping his chair off the floor. "What do they usually want?"

"Tonight it was a sick cow. I gave the farmer a decoction. Then Andragora's people brought a mouse with a broken leg, and I set that; he'll be fine if he stays off it for a week or two." She smiled ruefully. "I shouldn't complain. It's been simple stuff, mostly." She walked over to lift the teapot from the shelf. "Tea, Orion? Coalfeather, would you like some nuts?" She opened a tin by the stove and looked inside.

Orion nodded. "Sounds like you know what you're doing. But what about all that fancy magic you learned?"

Coalfeather snorted, and strutted over to face Orion. "Suli is a wise woman, and wise women know better than to use magic all the time. Only those who lack imagination or common sense think magic solves their problems. Suli has both. Tala and I have taught her well." He spread his wings and hopped to emphasize the point.

Orion held up his hands. "I'm just asking. So you help, with or without magic."

"Yes," Suli said. She poured hot water into the teapot. "Before I came here, I thought I'd fight witches and perform powerful magic. But it's mostly healing, and I like that. I suppose," she said thoughtfully, "it's just helping folk when they need it. I don't need magic for that."

Suli turned to face Orion, hands on hips. "So if you're checking up on me, you can report to Lamisa that I've learned that lesson." She put the teapot on the table with a dish of nuts beside it. Coalfeather hopped to the dish, delicately grasped a peanut, and flew to windowsill, cocking his head to listen.

"Me? I don't report to anybody, but I'm glad to hear it," Orion said, dropping his feet and to the floor. "Will you ever go home?"

She narrowed her eyes. "What do you mean? This *is* my home."

He smiled faintly. "That's how I feel, too. Now: How about inviting us to dinner?"

Coalfeather flew back to the table and selected another nut. "Good idea. Then we can talk about the kinds of magic Suli hasn't learned yet..."

"No!" Suli and Orion said together, laughing.

"You're both invited for dinner, but if only you promise not to talk about magic," Suli said.

Orion rose to help. "I promise."

Coalfeather made a rumbling sound. "Then so do I." He flew back to the table, selected another nut, and bobbed his head.

ABOUT THE AUTHOR

Elizabeth Forest writes speculative and historical fiction for all ages. Find Elizabeth on the web at:

https://www.elizabethsforest.com
twitter.com/elizasforest

If you liked this book, please leave a review at your favorite bookseller!

ALSO BY ELIZABETH FOREST

Suli's adventures continue in *The Cursed Amulet* available from your favorite bookseller.

When Suli is invited to fly with the wild geese on their annual journey to the arctic, she jumps at the chance.

But she cuts her journey short to rescue a young girl with strange powers. Together they stumble across plots and secrets that threaten the very foundation of wise women's magic.

https://www.elizabethsforest.com/books/cursed-amulet/

Made in the USA
Middletown, DE
04 May 2021